"I should like to congratulate you upon winning the curricle race, Mr. Redmayne," said Elyza. "I think it was famous!"

She looked up expectantly into his face, but Redmayne only smiled and said he had quite enough of that race, and what he really wanted to do was thank her for coming to his rescue with her yellow riband.

"Oh, *that!*" said Elyza, blushing deeply. "Anyone would have done *that!*"

"The point is that *anyone* didn't; *you* did," said Redmayne. "And I'm deuced sorry if it got you into trouble — as I expect it did."

"Oh, yes, but let's forget all about it," Elyza said, wondering if anyone had ever been happier than she was at that moment, with Redmayne thanking her for rescuing him as he had once rescued her, and looking down at her out of his blue eyes in a way that he had never looked at her before . . .

WIVES, LIES AND DOUBLE LIVES

MISTRESSES   ($4.50, 17-109)
By Trevor Meldal-Johnsen
Kept women. Pampered females who have everything: designer clothes, jewels, furs, lavish homes. They are the beautiful mistresses of powerful, wealthy men. A mistress is a man's escape from the real world, always at his beck and call. There is only one cardinal rule: *do not fall in love.* Meet three mistresses who live in the fast lane of passion and money, and who know that one wrong move can cost them everything.

ROYAL POINCIANA   ($4.50, 17-179)
By Thea Coy Douglass
By day she was Mrs. Madeline Memory, head housekeeper at the fabulous Royal Poinciana. Dressed in black, she was a respectable widow and the picture of virtue. By night she the French speaking "Madame Memphis", dressed in silks and sipping champagne with con man Harrison St. John Loring. She never intended the game to turn into true love . . .

WIVES AND MISTRESSES   ($4.95, 17-120)
By Suzanne Morris
Four extraordinary women are locked within the bitterness of a century old rivalry between two prominent Texas families. These heroines struggle against lies and deceptions to unlock the mysteries of the past and free themselves from the dark secrets that threaten to destroy both families.

Available wherever paperbacks are sold, or order direct from the Publisher. Send cover price plus 50¢ per copy for mailing and handling to Pinnacle Books, Dept. 17-465, 475 Park Avenue South, New York, N.Y. 10016. Residents of New York, New Jersey and Pennsylvania must include sales tax. DO NOT SEND CASH.

Eliza

CLARE DARCY

PINNACLE BOOKS
WINDSOR PUBLISHING CORP.

PINNACLE BOOKS

are published by

Windsor Publishing Corp.
475 Park Avenue South
New York, NY 10016

First Pinnacle Books Printing: January, 1991

Printed in the United States of America

Chapter One

The slim youth in the bottle-green coat was in a sad predicament. In one hand he held the reckoning for a night's lodging, supper, and breakfast; with the other, beneath the landlord's frowning gaze, he sought desperately in his pockets for a purse that quite evidently was not to be found.

The coffee-room of the inn in which he stood was a very pleasant and comfortable one, with an agreeable view from its casement windows, showing a splendid June morning sun preparing the world for a fine summer day; but the youth in the bottle-green coat was not, apparently, in a mood to appreciate the amenities of the prospect about him. His girlishly smooth face — he was a very young youth — was pale with dismay, and his hands trembled slightly as he laid the landlord's bill upon the table beside him and began hastily to turn out his pockets one by one.

"I — I must have been robbed!" he exclaimed at last, looking up with an appearance of some trepidation into the landlord's unencouraging face.

The landlord, a large man, managed to look skeptical, disdainful, and also a little threatening at one and the same time.

"In-deed, sir! In *this* house, sir?" he said, in a tone suitable for suggesting that aspersions had been cast upon the Royal occupants of Windsor Castle.

The slim youth, still desperately searching his pockets, said in a perturbed voice that he expected that must have been the case.

"It was the little man in the moleskin waistcoat who ran against me as I was coming into the coffee-room, I expect," he said. "But he has gone off in the London coach. I saw him from the window."

The landlord, regarding an inexpertly tied bundle of awkward size reposing on the floor beside the youth, suggested that the missing purse might be in that. His glance had now transformed itself into the self-reproachful one of a man who has admitted into a hostelry used to catering exclusively for ladies and gentlemen, all travelling in the first style and accompanied by their own servants and proper luggage, a lowly coach-passenger with a bundle, and who has lived to regret his act.

The youth, not to be outdone in chameleonlike changes of countenance, looked rebellious and said it wasn't in the bundle.

"Ho!" said the landlord, rapidly descending from his Olympian pedestal at this hint of mutiny in the ranks and becoming any honest publican bilked of his fair dues. "Ho! *Ain't* it, young master! Well, we'll see that!"

With one long arm he picked up the bundle from the floor. The slim youth immediately flew at him and attempted to wrest it from his grasp.

"Ho!" said the landlord again. "You would, would

you, you young varmint!"

His free hand flung the youth back against the table. He was just about to untie the bundle when a bored, equable voice drawled behind him, "What seems to be the trouble?"

The landlord, dropping the bundle, swung around. In the doorway stood a fair-haired, deeply bronzed young man, his dandy russet coat fitting his broad shoulders so exquisitely that it would have gained the approval even of Mr. Brummell, that Beau of Beaux, his snowy cravat tied with equally fashionable elegance, his buckskins shaped to his muscular thighs without a wrinkle, his top-boots dazzling the eye with their mirrorlike polish.

"Oh, it's you, Mr. Redmayne!" said the landlord, doing another chameleon-change and now exuding obsequiousness and eagerness to please. "Nothing at all, your honour—that is, nothing that need concern *you,* sir! A young chub as can't—or *won't,*" he said, looking menacingly at the slim youth, "pay his shot."

The lazy flicker of Mr. Redmayne's glance took in the slim youth and returned without haste to the landlord.

"Why not?" he enquired.

"Why not?" repeated the landlord, looking rather blank. "Well, he *says,* sir," indicating by his tone the unreasonableness of the slim youth's contention, "that he was robbed. In *this* house, your honour!"

His gaze appealed to Mr. Redmayne's impassive one to consider the absurdity of such a statement. Mr. Redmayne, however, remained enigmatic.

"How much?" he enquired.

"How much, sir?" The landlord again looked bewildered.

"The young gentleman's shot." Mr. Redmayne turned to a small, uneventful-looking middle-aged man who had materialised behind him like a genie out of a bottle. "Quigg will attend to it," he said. "Just tell him the amount," and he walked on into the coffee-room.

The landlord, after standing paralysed for a moment, swallowed and asked urgently, "Are you—do you wish to have breakfast here, your honour? Not upstairs—? That is to say, in your own private parlour—?"

Mr. Redmayne sat down at the table. "No," he said. "Frankly, I don't much care for the view up there."

The landlord, appearing to feel that he was expected to change it, looked guilty, but Mr. Redmayne, gazing from the window at the pleasant English country scene of sundappled meadow and hedgerow to be seen from it, was not observing him.

"Quigg will tell you what I require," he said, in a tone of obvious dismissal.

Quigg and the landlord went out, and the slim youth, who had been standing as if petrified ever since the stranger had so munificently rescued him from his dilemma, now stepped forward and addressed him.

"Sir—sir—" he stammered. "I should like to thank you—"

"Think nothing of it," said Mr. Redmayne. He dismissed his generosity with a slight wave of the hand, his gaze fixed upon the hedgerows showing their summer tangle of hawthorn and canterbury bell, clouds of lady-smocks and campion, pinky wild geraniums. "I

8

haven't been in England for a long while," he said suddenly. "It's like—" He seemed about to say something more, but broke off and after a moment enquired rather absently, "Would you care to breakfast with me?"

The slim youth, looking regretful, said that he had already breakfasted.

"Have some more," suggested Mr. Redmayne. "I travel with a retinue of servants, but that isn't the same as good company, is it?" His eyes, which looked startlingly blue in his very bronzed face, for the first time surveyed the slim youth with some attention. "Eton?" he asked abruptly.

"N-no, sir." The slim youth then appeared to be alarmed by his own denial, and added rapidly, "Harrow!"

"Well, it's much the same, isn't it?" said Mr. Redmayne. "Unfortunately, for family reasons, I myself was educated chiefly in India."

The slim youth, seeming to take courage, said that for his part he detested Harrow, which brought a smile to Mr. Redmayne's face. It was a smile that appeared suddenly, showed an almost boyish willingness to please and to be pleased entirely at variance with his usual reserved impassivity, and at once disappeared, leaving the observer warmed and dazzled.

"No, you don't," he said. "Or at least if you do, you oughtn't to. If a man wishes to move in Good Society, he needs a proper education." The slim youth, looking somewhat surprised to hear these sententious sentiments from the elegant and for some reason slightly dangerous-looking young dandy, blinked, and Redmayne went on, with a relapse into his normal manner, "Sit down, Mr. — ?"

He looked interrogatively at the slim youth, who said rapidly and with a rather suspicious emphasis, "Smith!"

"Mr. Smith," said Redmayne, giving him a searching glance that brought the colour into his cheeks. "Perhaps," he continued calmly, "if you are on your way to Bath you would care to have a seat in my travelling-chaise. There's plenty of room. The servants and Quigg go in the second chaise, or in the chariot for the luggage—"

Young Mr. Smith, looking dazzled all over again, sat down obediently, as if mesmerised. *Three* carriages!" he said approvingly. "Well! I *do* call that travelling in style!"

Redmayne, accepting this tribute without visible signs of gratification, glanced up as a retinue of waiters came hurrying into the room, one bearing a large York ham, another a sirloin, another hot toast and buttered eggs under a cover, and so on to the very limits of the facilities offered by the Beckhampton Inn, for it was this great posting-house on the Bath Road that he had honoured with his custom. Young Mr. Smith, who admitted to having earlier breakfasted rather frugally on coffee and rolls, was induced without difficulty to accept a generous helping of ham, some buttered toast, and a dish of raspberries, and to confess as well that he was indeed going to Bath and would like nothing better, in view of his present penniless circumstances, than to accept the kind offer of a seat in Mr. Redmayne's travelling-chaise.

"The thing is, sir," he confided, the fright and dismay occasioned by the confrontation with the landlord evaporating under the genial influence of excellent food and Redmayne's sympathetic if slightly aloof presence, "that I shouldn't have come here in the first place. I mean, I hadn't much money, and I was travelling by the Accommodation coach, only I had no notion that it wouldn't stop for meals, and we'd left London at nine in the morning, and except for a very nice fat woman who gave me an apple and a bit of sausage from her basket I'd had nothing to eat all day. And at seven o'clock thought I *couldn't* go on to Bath without having some dinner, and besides I hadn't had much sleep the night before, so I made up my mind to stop here and have a good meal and rest and then go on again in the morning. It was a rather close-run thing as far as the money was concerned, but whatever that beast of a landlord may tell you, I *did* have enough to pay my reckoning, if my purse hadn't been filched."

Redmayne asked rather idly what the reason was for his journey to Bath. Young Mr. Smith immediately coloured up furiously.

"I — I —" he stammered. "You see — That is —"

Redmayne's voice interrupted him. "That's all right," he said. "No need to explain. No business of mine to ask personal questions."

"B-but — I don't mind, *really!*" protested young Mr. Smith, looking alarmed lest he be thought ungrateful to his benefactor. "As a matter of fact, I — I am going to Bath to visit my aunt. My great-aunt, actually," he corrected himself scrupulously. "She is — she is a very old lady —"

"I see," said Redmayne noncommittally.

Mr. Smith, casting a quick glance from under his

11

very long lashes at him, seemed somewhat perturbed by what he saw, although there was no change of expression in the blue eyes regarding him; and bent his head over his dish of raspberries, thus affording his companion an excellent view of his cropped dark curls, which were undeniably rather raggedly cut for a young gentleman professing to be a Harrovian. The bottle-green coat, too, though carefully brushed, was far from being in the latest mode, while the dun-coloured smalls, now invisible beneath the table, had undoubtedly, Redmayne recalled, exhibited darns in the knees. He sat in thoughtful silence, regarding young Mr. Smith.

His regard seemed to make Mr. Smith more than a little nervous. Having finished the raspberries, he drank a glass of water, appearing rather to avoid his companion's gaze, and ran a finger under his inexpertly tied cravat, as if he suddenly found it constricting his breathing. Presently the dark eyes under the long lashes flew up to Redmayne's face for a moment and then jerked away.

"I—I think," said Mr. Smith in a rather breathless voice, "if you don't mind, sir, that—that perhaps I shan't be able to accept your very kind offer to take me to Bath. You see, I—I—"

Redmayne continued to regard him with perfect tranquillity. "That, Mr. Smith," he said, "is entirely up to you. No business of mine, of course. Only it isn't *Mr. Smith*—is it?"

The slim youth's eyes again went imploringly and miserably to his face.

"Nor even—*Miss* Smith?" Redmayne continued imperturbably.

12

His eyes were resting on the piquant, delicate features beneath the ragged dark curls, on the unmanly curves faintly revealing themselves to an enquiring eye beneath the heavy cloth of the coat. The slim youth—or, it might be more accurate to state, the slim and very unsuitably attired young lady—caught her underlip between her teeth in dismay.

"Never mind," said Redmayne encouragingly. "I won't cry rope on you. No affair of mine. Only are you quite sure you don't want to go back to wherever it was you came from now? I'll give—lend you the money, if you like, for the journey."

He paused, seeing tears welling up suddenly in the young lady's enormous dark eyes.

"No. No, I can't! I won't!" she said, shaking her head violently, as if to emphasise the words.

"*Can't* and *won't*," Redmayne pointed out, noting with obvious relief that the tears were already being resolutely winked away, "are two different things, you know. Which is it, Miss—?"

"Leigh," said the young lady grudgingly. "Elyza Leigh. And it's both. I *can't* go back because if I did they would make me marry Sir Edward. So I *won't*."

She looked defiantly at Redmayne, who looked amused, but not in a superior sort of way, rather as if he found a certain agreeable absurdity in the situation and was inviting her to share his appreciation of it. It was all a part, Miss Elyza Leigh felt, of a kind of charm that, in spite of his entirely matter-of-fact manner, he seemed to be unable not to exert; no one could have accused him of doing it consciously, but it was nonetheless undoubtedly there.

13

"Dust-up with your people?" he enquired sympathetically.

"No," said Miss Leigh. "Because I haven't any people. Except for Great-aunt Sephestia, that is, who is in Bath, and Papa, who is in Morocco. He is Sir Robert Leigh, the diplomatist," she explained, "and before he went to Morocco he decided it was time for me to make my come-out. That is, of course, it was Great-aunt Sephestia who told him that it was, for I was only fifteen the last time he saw me and I don't believe he *quite* thinks of me as being grown-up yet. And so he brought me to London two months ago," she went on, talking faster and faster as if, now that she had found someone to tell her troubles to, she could not stop, "and said I was to live with a lady named Mrs. Winlock, who was recommended to him by one of his friends because she brought out a very plain girl two Seasons ago and saw her married to a quite eligible gentleman, although she was Nobody at All in Society—like me."

Redmayne, seeing the half-defiant, half-doleful glance she cast him at this point, said reasonably that he did not see the comparison, as she was neither plain nor, as Sir Robert Leigh's daughter, Nobody at All in Society.

Elyza looked doubtful. "Well," she said, "I don't know about that—I mean about not being plain, because Mrs. Winlock is forever saying what a pity it is that I am not tall, which is the mode, you know, and have not got classical features. And she is quite right, at any rate, in saying that I have not *taken* this Season. Sir Edward Mottram is the only man who has made up to me in the least, and that is only because his

14

mama and Mrs. Winlock have decided he was to do so, because I am to have thirty thousand pounds when I marry and the Mottrams are quite dreadfully badly off. But perhaps," Elyza went on, plumbing the depths of self-abnegation, "it is as Mrs. Winlock says, and it is not so much because I am not tall and classical that I have not *taken* this Season, but because I am the Product of a Misalliance and my manners are atrocious and I tell lies—"

"*Do* you tell lies?" asked Redmayne, looking interested.

"Yes!" said Elyza without hesitation. "I told Mrs. Winlock I had the toothache so she would have to take me home from the Kennets' ball, and I told Sir Edward I had been engaged four times to put him off from the idea of wanting to marry me."

"And had you?"

"Of course not!" said Elyza with scorn. "I had scarcely ever *seen* an eligible man before I came to London, because Aunt Phoebe—she was Papa's sister, who brought me up, in Devonshire—cared a great deal more about birds than she did about people. She was very learned, you see, and had known Dr. Johnson, and was the authoress of several books about owls. And when she died last year and I came to live with Great-aunt Sephestia in Bath it was almost as bad, for *she* is nearly ninety and never goes *anywhere,* or let me do so either, because she said I was far too young, though she *did* allow me to have a dancing-master, and to accompany her companion, Miss Cranborne, to concerts of an improving nature. Of course, if enough gentlemen had asked me to do so, I *might* have become engaged several times during the

Season, as I have heard some really *fast* girls do; but they didn't. I have learned, you see," said Elyza, with a certain amount of self-satisfaction, "a *great* deal since I came to London, because, even though I have not *taken*, one can always look on."

But at this point the landlord re-entered the coffee-room to see if anything more was wanted, and this interesting conversation perforce came to an abrupt end.

Chapter Two

The landlord was followed by the indeterminate-looking Mr. Quigg, and, to Elyza's great fascination, by a very tall, dark, magnificently bearded gentleman in full Indian dress and turban, who, bowing to Redmayne, addressed him in some unknown tongue. Redmayne answered him in an equally incomprehensible manner, upon which the magnificent apparition bowed once more and left the room.

"Ready to start now," Redmayne said cheerfully. He nodded to Quigg, who at once engaged the landlord in businesslike conversation. Redmayne looked down rather quizzically at Elyza. "Well, Mr. Smith?" he enquired. "Is it Bath or London for you?"

"If you please," said Elyza, casting a rather worried look at the landlord, as if suspecting that he, too, might be about to penetrate her disguise, "I should like to go on to Bath. Only if you don't wish to take me now, I shall *quite* understand. I — I daresay I shall manage somehow."

The slight quaver apparent in the last words, and the determined tilt of her firm little chin above her very amateurishly tied cravat, seemed to lay to rest any qualms Redmayne might have felt over living up to the offer he had made.

"Right," he said, nodding decisively. "You come along with me, Mr. Smith, and I'll deposit you on your great aunt's doorstep, as safe as a church, before the last stroke of noon sounds today."

"Oh, *thank* you!" said Elyza, jumping up with a radiant face. "I promise you, you won't regret it!" — which seemed to make Redmayne wonder for a moment if he would, for he was apparently eight or nine years older than Elyza and obviously more experienced by the equivalent of at least a few centuries of time.

But optimism on this occasion carried the day against experience, and he walked out of the coffee-room with Elyza hurrying in his wake. Upon the inn doorstep outside she paused, transfixed, at the sight of a splendid travelling chaise, its silver-mounted harness glittering blindingly in the morning sunlight, its polished bodywork picked out with gold and crimson, a glimpse of elegant pale-blue velvet squabs visible through its shining windows. Behind it stood a second, only slightly more sober chaise, which in turn was followed by a huge travelling-chariot, piled so high with luggage that it seemed in imminent danger of overturning.

"Oh!" gasped Elyza, overcome. "Are they all *yours*, Mr. Redmayne? Goodness! Are you transporting all your worldly goods to Bath?"

Redmayne said in a negligent way that he rather expected to be staying only for a short time in Bath, but that he liked to be comfortable when he travelled.

18

"Comfortable!" said Elyza. She remembered just in time that she must not expect, in her coat and breeches, to be handed up into the chaise like a young lady, and stood aside with a proper air of respectful courtesy to allow Redmayne to mount into the carriage before her. "I should think you must be!" she went on, as she jumped in briskly behind him. Looking from the window, she watched as a small procession of servants — the magnificent, turbaned Indian, an impeccably superior gentleman's gentleman, a retinue of liveried retainers in claret-and-black, their coats splendidly laced not only at throat and wrist but even at the seams, their cocked hats bordered with broad fringes of gold — filed out of the inn and took their places in the second chaise and the chariot. "Goodness! How many of them there are!" she exclaimed. She turned to Redmayne. "Do you bring your own sheets with you?" she enquired. "I once met a duchess who said she did — silk ones, with a monogram and a crest, I expect."

Redmayne, looking interested, said he hadn't thought of that, but he would mention it to Quigg, who would attend to it on the next occasion that he travelled.

"I'm not yet entirely accustomed to English manners, you see," he explained, "having lived out of the country for so long."

"Yes, but it's not at all necessary — I mean, after all, *you* are not a duke!" Elyza blurted out; and then, self-convicted of rudeness, or, even worse, of lèse-majesté, for it seemed quite possible, she thought, by the splendour of his entourage, that Mr. Redmayne, in spite of his fair hair, might be a young rajah travelling incognito, blushed to the roots of her hair.

Redmayne, however, appeared quite undisturbed by her frankness, and said no, he was not, but he sometimes thought a baronetcy might be rather agreeable.

"To start with," he remarked casually, and so dazzled was Elyza by the matter-of-fact manner in which he said this and by the obvious magnificence of his presence that she half expected to hear him go on to say, "Quigg will attend to it," and it would forthwith be done.

Instead, as the postillions in their striking claret-and-black livery sprang on their horses and the chaise drew out of the inn-yard to resume its journey towards Bath, he began a conversation that appeared to center chiefly about a desire to learn anything Miss Elyza Leigh was disposed to impart to him about the Season she had just left so abruptly in London.

Had she, he enquired, made a considerable acquaintance in London?

"Oh, yes!" said Elyza, who was perfectly willing to tell all she knew, and indeed felt it her duty to do so, since it offered her her only available opportunity to repay her companion for his generosity towards her. "That is, I *met* everyone, of course, because Mrs. Winlock is very well-connected and is asked everywhere. But I shouldn't think," she continued frankly, "that half of them remembered who I was an hour after they'd met me. Oh, they always bowed to me in the Park and at the balls and evening-parties Mrs. Winlock took me to, but I'm quite sure most of them didn't recall my name."

"Why not?" asked Redmayne.

"Why not?" Elyza looked at him, a little startled.

20

"Yes," he repeated. "Why not? You're not at all a badlooking chit, you know—that is, you wouldn't be if you hadn't got your hair cut in that odd fashion and were wearing the proper clothes. And by the way, why *are* you wearing those clothes?" he broke off to enquire, looking with disfavour at the bottle-green coat and the darned Inexpressibles.

Elyza said with some spirit that if he knew Mrs. Winlock he wouldn't ask, because if she, Elyza, had gone to the coach-office in her usual apparel Mrs. Winlock, who would very probably have guessed that she had Bath as her destination, would have been able to confirm that fact by describing her to the clerks at the various coach-offices and then have despatched the Bow Street Runners after her.

"Whereas she will never think of looking for a boy," she concluded, gazing with some complacency at her breeches and boots. "These are the hall-boy's Sunday best; James, who is one of Mrs. Winlock's footmen and a great friend of mine, got them for me. He is the only person who has been *really* kind to me since I came to London, and I *don't* think he will tell Mrs. Winlock about the clothes."

Redmayne said that was all very well, but in the first place it was highly improbable that Mrs. Winlock would call in the Bow Street Runners to search for her, and in the second place her great-aunt might be too shocked to let her into the house in those clothes, so if she had a dress in her bundle she had best change into it before she went there.

Elyza, who was obviously enjoying her breeches, looked rebellious.

"Don't be a nodcock, Mr. Smith," said Redmayne.

"I may not know much about English Society, but I *do* know that if any of those duchesses and countesses who can't remember your name saw you in these clothes, you'd have so little reputation left that even thirty thousand pounds wouldn't get you a husband. They'd remember who you were *then,* right enough."

Elyza, lifting her chin, said that she didn't want a husband.

"Oh yes, you do," said Redmayne calmly. "You probably have one all picked out already"—upon which Elyza coloured up so pink that her companion grinned and asked who the lucky man was.

"Nobody!" said Elyza, still very pink. "He—he doesn't know I *exist!* How could he, when there is Corinna Mayfield—"

"When there is *who?*"

The words were spoken so sharply that Elyza stared. For the first time since she had met him she saw signs of agitation upon Redmayne's face, and his hand reached out and gripped her arm with an intensity that made her wince.

He released her immediately, however, and, leaning back against the blue velvet squabs again with a fair imitation of his usual imperturbable manner, asked in a noncommittal voice if she was acquainted with Miss Mayfield.

Elyza, looking puzzled, said, "Yes. Are you?"

"Well, actually—no," said Redmayne. "That is, I have seen her, but I have never been presented to her." He seemed to find it difficult to continue, looked at Elyza as if for assistance, and went on after a moment, still in that elaborately noncommittal voice, "She's a—a very attractive young lady."

"Yes, she is," agreed Elyza cordially. "I think she is the most beautiful person I have ever seen in all my life. So do heaps of other people; in fact, she's the Beauty of the Season. But where did *you* see her? I thought you said it was a long while since you had been in England."

Redmayne said something not very distinguishable about having made a brief visit to England on business two years before, and then asked abruptly, "Do you know her well?"

"Corinna? Oh, no! That is, I've been to dozens of balls and parties, of course, that she attended, too, and she *does* seem to be able to remember my name when we meet, which is more than most of the other really popular girls do. But we're not in the least intimate."

"But you *do* know her?" Redmayne was frowning slightly, still with a certain intensity in his blue eyes. "I mean to say, if you meet her in Bath—I suppose that old aunt of yours doesn't keep you so close that you don't go to the Pump Room or the Assemblies, does she?"

"But I shan't meet Corinna in Bath," Elyza objected. "I couldn't, even if Great-aunt Sephestia agrees to help me and doesn't send me back to Mrs. Winlock. She is not in Bath."

"No," said Redmayne. "But she will be. Arrives there tomorrow." A faint flush mounted in his bronzed cheeks. "I've made enquiries," he explained.

"Well, you made them of the wrong person, then," Elyza said decidedly. "The Mayfields *were* to have gone to Bath, before they went to Brighton for the summer, to visit Corinna's grandmama, who lives there and is excessively rich and very disagreeable. But she sent word to them at the last moment that she does not wish to see them now because she is not at all in plump currant, and so they are going directly to Brighton instead. They are leaving London tomorrow. I know because I overheard Corinna say so at the ball I attended at Almack's the night before I ran away," she concluded positively.

She noted with surprise that Redmayne was looking rather nonplussed by this information.

"To Brighton!" he said after a moment. "Well, see here, Miss Leigh, I am afraid I shall have to change my plans. I'm not going to Bath, after all. I'll take you on to the next posting-house and pay the charges for a post-chaise to carry you there —"

Elyza's dark eyes, expressive of the liveliest astonishment, regarded him interestedly.

"Do you mean," she asked, "that you are not going to Bath because Corinna will not be there? Goodness! I expect that means you are in love with her!"

Redmayne regarded her repressively.

"Well, there is no need for you to look at me like that," Elyza said. "*Dozens* of men are in love with her, so it will not be at all odd if you are, too."

"Does she — ?" Redmayne began, and stopped.

"Does she favour any one of them in particular, do you mean?" Elyza enquired helpfully. "I don't *think* so — though, perhaps," she went on, suddenly adopting an air as *dégagé* as Redmayne's and almost as unconvincing, "she seems to find Mr. Everet's attentions more agreeable than those of any other gentleman."

"Mr. Everet?"

"The Honourable Mr. Jack Everet. The famous Corinthian," Elyza explained, looking straight before her with an air of intense interest, though there was little to be seen there but the claret-and-black-clad backs of the postillions bobbing rhythmically up and down. "I daresay he is the most famous man in London, outside of Mr. Brummell," she added, as if compelled to make this statement by a stern adherence to pure fact.

Redmayne frowned. "Handsome — is he?" he enquired, after a moment.

"Excessively," said Elyza, still in the interest of purest truth.

"Dresses well?"

"Exceedingly!"

"An excellent whip? First-rate shot? Bruising rider to hounds?"

"I myself," said Elyza scrupulously, "have had no occasion to observe him in those activities, except when he drives his curricle with great dash and style in the Park. But I understand that he is noted for excelling in all of them."

Redmayne said something under his breath that sounded like, "Damn, blast, and hell!" — no doubt led on to this freedom by the misleading sight of a pair of breeches and boots beside him, but then, recalling Elyza's maidenly condition, coloured slightly and said, "I beg your pardon."

"Not at all," said Elyza, still absorbed in the postillions.

Redmayne asked suddenly, "Is he rich?"

"Rich?" Elyza turned doubtful eyes upon him, as one who had never considered the matter. "Well, I don't suppose he is really *rich*," she said, after a moment, "because he is a younger son, but he *seems* quite well-off. He is very lucky at play, I have heard people say. But of course Corinna need not consider fortune particularly when she marries, you know, for she has a very comfortable one of her own. And if she wishes to marry a *rich* husband," she added, again as if compelled by duty to state the facts of the matter, "there is Lord Belfort, who is a marquis, and seems very much taken with her. *He* is very rich, I believe."

Redmayne looked gloomy, and then, abruptly, quite positive and determined.

"Well, I can see I'd best lose no time in getting down to Brighton," he said. "I'll have Quigg get me a house — that's the thing to do there, isn't it? Not a hotel. I couldn't entertain properly at a hotel."

Elyza, looking dazzled again, said she understood from Mrs. Winlock that it was quite impossible to obtain a house in Brighton, even a not very desirable one, at this late date, and was not at all surprised when Redmayne said automatically, "Oh, that's all right. Quigg will attend to it."

"Who *is* Quigg?" Elyza asked, unable to restrain her curiosity any longer.

Redmayne came out of the abstraction into which he had fallen.

"Oh — Quigg," he said. "He's a very useful fellow. Spent a good deal of time on the Continent, I believe, managing the household of a Royal Duke. I found I needed someone of the sort when I came to England. Put him in charge of my own household and now everything runs like clockwork."

Elyza, impressed, said that as far as she was able to see it did indeed, and then wondered if Quigg had produced the retinue of claret-and-black-clad servants,

26

the fantastically elegant travelling-chaises and chariot, and the huge pile of luggage burdening the latter by a mere wave of his hand and a mysterious incantation.

"If you've only just come to England, he must have done it all in a *very* short time," she said.

"Less than a week," said Redmayne matter-of-factly. "I couldn't spare the time for details myself, you see. All this business with tailors—nothing I brought with me from India was quite *à la mode*, I found." He glanced down at the impeccable sleeve of his russet coat. "Weston, in Old Bond Street, made this coat for me," he said, "but because of the shortness of the time I let Schweitzer and Davidson do my evening clothes. Both make for the Regent, I am creditably informed."

Elyza knowledgeably agreed that she knew this to be true, because she had heard Colonel Hanley, a military gentleman who always gallanted Mrs. Winlock about and was acknowledged to be something of an authority on such matters, say as much. She added with an air of slight regret that she herself had never met the Regent, but might have done so had she gone to Brighton with Mrs. Winlock for the summer as she would have done had it not been for the affair of Sir Edward, since she understood the Prince always entertained lavishly at the Pavilion while he was in residence there.

"Who is this Sir Edward?" Redmayne asked suddenly, putting his own preoccupations momentarily aside and taking up her problems with the brisk air of one prepared to deal with them in a satisfactory manner before returning to weightier matters. "And why must you marry him if you go back? A girl can always say *no*—can't she?"

"No," said Elyza baldly. "She can't. Not when there isn't the least prospect that anyone else will ever wish to marry you, and you are obliged to live with a *horrid* person like Mrs. Winlock until someone does. She is a dreadful woman; she hasn't any heart at all. She cares for nothing except to marry me off as soon as possible, so that Papa will be grateful to her and write another very large cheque for her on Hoare's Bank, as he did before he left to go to Morocco. I *do* wish I weren't such a coward as to *need* to run away from her, but you can have no idea how—how *wormlike* she made me feel, always criticising what I did and how I looked, as if I were the stupidest, plainest girl in all of London! And that made me do all the things she disliked more than ever, like having no conversation when she introduced me to someone, and hiding behind the potted palms at Almack's so she couldn't find me and oblige me to dance with some spotty boy or fat old man she'd dragooned into asking me to stand up with them." She looked vengefully at her breeches and boots. "I wish I *was* a boy, really," she said. "Then it wouldn't matter so much that my mama was an innkeeper's daughter, and I shouldn't have to marry anyone—*ever!*"

Redmayne looked interested. "Was your mother an innkeeper's daughter?" he asked.

"Yes! She died when I was two and I don't remember her, but Papa has a miniature of her and she was truly lovely! When I hear one of those old dragons gossiping about her behind my back, I should like to scratch their eyes out!" And she gave a very creditable imitation of a dowager thrice her age whispering with relish behind her fan: "My dear, her mother was an innkeeper's daughter! Yes, really! Of course young men *will* sow their wild oats, but Sir Robert—too, too eccentric of him!—actually married the creature!"

She broke off, swallowing hard, her eyes suspiciously bright behind their very long lashes.

"Look here," said Redmayne decisively. "This won't do. The trouble with you is, you're letting these people bullock you. No sense in that."

"*You* can say so, because you're a man," Elyza pointed out. "If *I* were a man, I shouldn't let anyone bullock *me,* either. Or," she added, "if I even had someone like you to—to help me—"

"Well, of course I should help you if you were in Brighton, instead of going haring off to that old aunt of yours in Bath," Redmayne said magnanimously. He added abruptly, as if struck by a sudden idea, "Now that I think of it, *you* might help *me* as well. I mean to say—you are well acquainted now in the *ton,* aren't you? Know all the ropes, that sort of thing—"

Elyza, looking a little brighter, said did he mean she might introduce him to people, because she would be very pleased to if she were in Brighton, only of course she wouldn't be.

"Gammon!" said Redmayne. "The more I think of it, the more it seems to me that you will be a clothhead to carry out this scheme of yours of going to Bath. Ten to one your great-aunt will be quite as anxious to see you married to this Sir Edward as Mrs. Winlock and your father are—By the way, how can you know whether your father wishes you to marry the fellow or not, since he is in Morocco?" he broke off to demand.

Elyza looked depressed. "Well, it is no good thinking he won't," she said, "for the Mottrams are a very old family, and Sir Edward is a horridly *sensible* young man, exactly the sort of husband Mrs. Winlock said he told her he thought I should have, because of my being so volatile myself." She regarded Redmayne dismally. "Papa hardly *knows* me, you see, she said, "because of always being in Lisbon or Vienna or St. Petersburg while I was with Aunt Phoebe in Devonshire or with Great-aunt Sephestia in Bath. And when he does see me, he—he *roars* at me—"

"Well, even if he roars, he can't make you marry Mottram," Redmayne pointed out. "The worst he can do, it seems to me, is to send you off to live with your great-aunt in Bath, and if you go there yourself you'll only save him the trouble. You don't *like* living with her, do you?" he enquired.

"Oh, no!" said Elyza fervently. "Only when Mrs. Winlock told me that Sir Edward was coming to wait upon me the next morning to make me an offer, I couldn't think of *anything* but getting away before it happened, so that I couldn't say *yes* no matter how much they all urged me. And the only place I could think of to go was to Great-aunt Sephestia." She looked at Redmayne doubtfully. "I suppose you don't think that was a very good idea?"

"No, I don't," said Redmayne decidedly. "It never pays to run away from trouble. Much better to stay and face it out. I'll tell you what—you go back to London and then down to Brighton with your Mrs. Winlock and I give you my word you won't have to marry anyone you don't like."

"Won't I?" said Elyza, already looking half convinced by his certainty. "Truly?"

"Truly. Good God, it seems to me you have been

going about things in the worst possible way, allowing that old brimstone to frighten you into fits, so that I daresay you've brought people to the point of thinking you a regular knock-in-the-cradle. And as for your mother having been an innkeeper's daughter"—he snapped his fingers—"you may take it from me that that needn't signify. Do you know Lady Lade? I'm told she had an intimate connexion with a highwayman before she married Sir John, and Sir John is one of the Regent's closest friends."

Elyza, who had had the notorious Letty Lade pointed out to her in the Park, was rather doubtful that she could ever emulate that extremely dashing female's disregard of the obvious deficiencies of her background; but such was the effect upon her of Redmayne's own confidence that she began to look much brighter and said perhaps it *would* be better if she went back to London instead of carrying out her scheme of going to Bath.

"Of course it would," said Redmayne decisively.

"Only she will be so *very* angry with me for running away—" Elyza ventured, apprehension again creeping into her voice at the thought of the scene she would be obliged to face if she returned to Mrs. Winlock's no doubt welcoming but certainly militant arms.

"That's all right. Give her as good as you get," said Redmayne. "She can't eat you. And leave the rest of it to me. Once I've been properly introduced into Polite Circles in Brighton, I'll make a point of it to see that matters take a new turn as far as your social life is concerned. I'll be entertaining a good deal, you know. It makes it easier that it will be Brighton instead of Bath. Things are much gayer there, I understand."

.He appeared to lose himself momentarily in visions of an elaborate series of Venetian breakfasts and evening-parties at which, Elyza was quite sure, Corinna Mayfield was to figure as the chief ornament. More practically, her own mind turned to their present situation.

"But," she suggested, "if I am not to go to Bath, and you are not going there, either, shouldn't we be turning back instead of going on? I mean, we *are* both going in the wrong direction now."

She looked out the window of the chaise, which showed her the long bare line of the downs stretching away beside the road, with the huge trotting White Horse carved in the chalk of one swelling shoulder by the eccentric Dr. Allsop of Calne some thirty years earlier becoming clearly visible as the chaise turned the flank of a hill. Having exclaimed suitably at this wonder, to the extent of interrupting completely the response that Redmayne had begun to make to her suggestion, her attention was then further distracted by the sight of a number of booths that had been erected in a field beside the road a little farther on, near the spot where the roofs of what was evidently a small village appeared, half-hidden by the summer fulness of its embowering trees. A considerable throng was congregated about the booths; a colourfully decorated gypsy wagon, drawn up nearby, had spilled out its freight of bright-shawled women with their ragged barefoot children, who scattered through the crowd in search of palms to be read for a piece of silver, while three of their male companions were already engaging in an acrobatic exhibition, and farther off a rope-dancer was supervising the preparation of his act.

"Oh!" exclaimed Elyza giving a little jump upon the seat in her excitement. "It is a fair, Mr. Redmayne! *Could* we stop—just for a *very* little while? I have never been allowed to visit a fair in my life!"

Chapter Three

To her great satisfaction, Redmayne displayed no marked reluctance to allow himself to be persuaded into acquiescing to this scheme. There was, he remarked, little use in his hurrying on to Brighton, since according to Elyza's information the Mayfields would not be leaving London until the following day, and as for Elyza's own situation, a delay of an hour or two in her return to London could certainly do little to intensify Mrs. Winlock's disapproval of her action in running away.

To say the truth, it crossed Elyza's mind as she and Redmayne descended from the chaise that her companion, in spite of his negligent manner, was almost as pleased as was she to visit the fair—a fact that was confirmed, as they walked across the much-trodden greensward towards the booths, by his remarking that it had been almost twenty years, by Jupiter, since he had seen an English fair, and then, owing to unfortunate circumstances, he had been unable to spend more than a few minutes enjoying it.

"What *were* the unfortunate circumstances?" enquired Elyza, who felt by this time that, because of the intimate nature of the confidences they had exchanged, there was now nothing sacred in the past history of either.

But to her surprise Redmayne first looked slightly non plussed and then answered her rather shortly.

"Matters having to do with my position," he said simply, after a moment.

"Oh! I see!" Elyza looked up at him, feeling rebuffed and respectful. "I—I daresay when one's people are very important, there *are* a great many restrictions placed on where one is permitted to *mingle*," she said, anxious to show that she appreciated the finer points in the code of polite social behaviour.

Redmayne, however, merely looked noncommittal, and as her attention was distracted at that moment by a booth displaying a large and hideously coloured placard, which depicted a dancing bear, a dwarf, and an enormously stout female in a spangled dress and announced that all these wonders were to be seen inside, conversation on the subject lapsed while they debated the merits of buying tickets for this attraction at once or going on to explore the remainder of the fair.

They decided upon the latter course, and for the ensuing half hour wandered through the hurly-burly of the fair under a hot blue midsummer sky. First they inspected a number of other booths, some offering opportunities for engaging in games of chance and others displaying for sale an extensive variety of articles ranging from ballad sheets to gingerbread rocks; then they witnessed a blindfold wheel-barrow race and a wrestling match between two stout rustics, with the winner bearing off a cheese as prize; and finally they

35

had their palms read by a gypsy woman in a scarlet head scarf and golden earrings, who obligingly predicted long life and good fortune for Redmayne and told Elyza she would marry a fair stranger from a foreign land.

Elyza cast a droll, conspiratorial glance at Redmayne. "Oh!" she said. "Will—will *s-she* be very beautiful?"

The gypsy gave her a quick, sidelong look out of penetrating black eyes, muttered enigmatically that handsome was as handsome did and deceivers were sometimes themselves deceived, and melted away into the crowd.

"Oh, dear!" said Elyza, slightly dismayed. "Do you think she knew I am not *really* a boy?"

"I daresay," said Redmayne equably. "Not much those people miss. Plenty of that mumbo-jumbo in India. Ram will tell you a splendid fortune if you like."

"Is he the Indian I saw at the inn? *Oh!* There he is now!" she exclaimed, feeling suddenly impelled to glance around by a peculiar feeling that someone was watching her and observing the giant turbaned figure standing impassively a few feet behind them. "Does he always follow you about like this?"

"Well—yes," Redmayne said rather apologetically. "I'm afraid he's rather got in the habit of it. Not much need for it here, I expect, but there *have* been occasions in India—"

He said no more, but a certain grimness about his usually pleasant mouth made Elyza think suddenly of the horrid stories of hold-ups and even murders with which her fellow passengers in the Accommodation coach had frightened one another as the stage had lumbered across Hounslow Heath, that sinister stretch of barren waste, the habitation of snipe and frogs and the haunt of lurking highwaymen. Perhaps, she thought, life in India was so dangerous, even for persons as highly placed as Redmayne, that a sort of bodyguard was necessary.

At any rate, it was most useful, she found, to have the obliging Ram present to take in charge the extravagant number of sweetmeats, baubles, ribands, and fairings of all kinds that Redmayne, with a fine disregard for her male attire, insisted upon purchasing for her from the vendors who accosted them. Several small boys, it was true, apparently considering the tall Indian as something in the nature of a gorgeous and frightening exhibit from one of the booths, who had unaccountably escaped from confinement and was on view without the necessity of paying out a penny for the privilege, had taken to following him about, obviously in the hopeful expectation that he would at any moment produce a scimitar and slice off someone's head; but as neither Ram himself nor Redmayne appeared to object to this admiring retinue, Elyza decided that it was superfluous for her to do so. The sun was shining brightly; she was enjoying herself immensely; and she quite forgot for the moment that she was a runaway from an eligible marriage, with her affairs still in a most tangled and perilous state.

A placard announcing that the performance of a theatrical piece invitingly entitled *Murder and Madness, or The Rival Brothers,* and offering its audience not only the services of Mr. Montague Downing, the celebrated London Thespian, but also a panorama of the Swiss Alps, complete with an avalanche, was shortly to take place in the largest of the booths presently engaged their attention. Redmayne paid two shillings for a box and they went inside, where a slender young man in a modestly dandified blue coat and high shirt-points, who was occupying the adjacent box in solitary splendour, looked at them with an air of interest and appeared not only ready but eager to enter into conversation with them. A glance cast by Redmayne in his direction appeared to decide him.

"I say, sir!" he said. "You're the one with the Indian, aren't you? I saw you outside. Are you—? Is he—? I mean—"

Redmayne, observing a young man whose well-cut blue coat, Marseilles waistcoat, and unexceptionable top-boots bespoke his gentle status, whose age bespoke Oxford, or Oxford certainly in the recent past, and whose manner bespoke an engaging mixture of diffidence and good breeding, smiled his extraordinary smile and said he had just returned to England from India.

"Then he's genuine," the young man said with a satisfied air. "I knew it. *Not* part of the fair." He looked at Redmayne and Elyza rather shyly. "My name is Crawfurd," he said. "Nicholas Crawfurd. I live near here; our place is just past Corsham Regis—Crawfurd Court, it's called. But I'm on my way to Brighton now. That is, I was until I stopped off to have a look-in at the fair."

He then fell silent, blushing, and apparently self-convicted of having put himself forward in an unbecoming way. But Redmayne looked at him quite kindly and said his name was Cleve Redmayne and his friend was Mr. Smith.

"How do you do?" said Elyza companionably, for away from London Society and the repressing effect of Mrs. Winlock she had quickly reverted to what that lady had characterised as her entirely unseemly habit of conversing with strangers as if she had known them all her life. "I noticed you, too; you were in the booth watching the man washing his hands in boiling oil at the same time that we were."

Mr. Crawfurd, encouraged by her cordial manner, said knowingly that that was all a hum and he could explain how it was done. Redmayne, listening with his usual tolerant aloofness to the conversation, did not see fit to put an end to it, and even enquired politely of Mr. Crawfurd, as the curtain was about to go up, whether he had a large acquaintance in Brighton.

"Oh, no! In point of fact, it will be my first visit," Mr. Crawfurd confessed. "That is, I daresay I shall find a few friends there when I arrive—"

"Oxford friends?" suggested Redmayne, adding automatically, in almost the same words he had used earlier to Elyza, "Unfortunately, for family reasons I myself was educated privately in India."

Young Mr. Crawfurd, who, like Elyza, seemed already sufficiently bedazzled by what he had seen of Redmayne and the magnificent Ram to have accepted without surprise the information that his new acquaintance had been reared by she-wolves in the American wilderness, said yes, Oxford friends, as if slightly ashamed of having nothing more exotic to offer upon his own account. And then the curtain went up—or, rather, was pulled aside by two men wearing what might, by some stretch of the imagination, be called Swiss costume, who later reappeared upon the scene as a pair of villainous conspirators seeking the life of Mr. Montague Downing, playing the hero.

By the conclusion of the play, which was not a very long opera but contained a highly satisfactory number of headless spectres, blood-curdling shrieks, and cataclysms of nature, culminating in the letting down of a backdrop depicting a snowy mountainside from which several human arms, legs, and heads emerged at improbable angles (the avalanche), the friendship between the two adjacent boxes had ripened to the extent that Redmayne, observing that he fancied Quigg would have made arrangements about some sort of nuncheon by this time, invited Mr. Crawfurd to share potluck with them.

To this Mr. Crawfurd gave an immediate assent, while Elyza confided to him *sotto voce* that from what she had seen of Quigg, which wasn't much, as she had only met him that morning, what he would actually have produced would be a banquet, complete with golden plates and probably silver goblets.

Mr. Crawfurd looked at her in slight surprise. "Oh!" he said after a moment. "Aren't you —? I mean, isn't he —?"

"Oh, no!" said Elyza sunnily. "I never saw Mr. Redmayne in my life until this morning, if that is what you mean. I was robbed of my purse at the inn where I stayed last night, you see, and he very kindly came to my rescue. And as we had both the intention of going to Bath, he offered me a seat in his travelling-chaise. Only now I have decided to return to London, after all, and *he* is going on to Brighton."

Mr. Crawfurd looked somewhat confused by this

explanation, but apparently considering that he might be guilty of rudeness if he asked any further questions, emerged beside Elyza in silence from the stuffy dimness of the booth into the noisy brilliance of the fair, which seemed to have become, if possible, even louder and more boisterous than it had been when they had left it. Here they found Ram awaiting them in the midst of a gaggle of small boys whom he was superbly disregarding. Redmayne sent him on ahead to prepare Quigg for the presence of another guest at their picnic nuncheon, while he, Elyza, and Mr. Crawfurd remained to cast a critical eye upon the performance of a conjurer in a very greasy green coat and skin-tight nankeen pantaloons, who was making rabbits appear and disappear and taking silver sixpences out of the ears of unsuspecting rustics.

"I daresay it must seem very small beer to *you*, sir, after India," Mr. Crawfurd said apologetically, as if, as a native of this part of the country, he was responsible for the quality of the entertainment it provided. "I mean to say, one hears all sorts of stories of the marvels those fakirs of theirs get off—walking on live coals and climbing ropes that simply disappear into the sky—"

"And diamonds as big as pigeon's eggs lying on the ground, all ready to be picked up," Elyza continued hopefully, upon which Redmayne smiled and, to the respectful awe of his young companions, withdrew from his breastpocket a small chamois bag, which he opened to reveal a diamond of such extraordinary size and coruscating brilliance that they could only blink at it, dazzled.

"It's intended for a small gift to a young lady," Redmayne said casually. "After I have it set, of course. I thought I'd find out first if she'd prefer a brooch or a ring."

It was on the tip of Elyza's well-instructed tongue to inform him that no young lady—and particularly Corinna Mayfield, who had been very properly brought up—would think of accepting such an expensive present from a gentleman. But she had reached the point by this time where it was easier to believe that Redmayne, like Royalty, was not bound by the ordinary rules of polite behaviour and might, and probably would, do as he liked; so she said nothing. Redmayne replaced the diamond in its bag.

"Isn't it," Mr. Crawfurd suggested a trifle nervously, "a—a bit dangerous to carry it about like that? I mean to say, a place like this is bound to be swarming with pickpockets. There was an old gentleman roaring away only a short while back about having had his snuff-box prigged."

Redmayne, having safely bestowed the chamois bag in his pocket once more, said calmly that that was Ram's affair.

"No need to worry while he's about, old boy," he said. "He's a very good man. A Sikh. Great warriors, all of them. I was able to do him a trifling favour once and he's devoted to me."

Mr. Crawfurd looked as if he didn't doubt it, being well on the way himself, it seemed, towards a case of hero-worship that might soon place him in Ram's category; and then the little party moved on to where Redmayne's improbably elegant travelling-chaise was drawn up along the side of the road in the shade of some conveniently heavy-leaved elms.

As Elyza had predicted, Quigg, with his usual magical efficiency, had managed to produce an excellent pic-nic nuncheon, featuring pigeons in jelly, pork pies and Stilton cheese, some sweet wood-strawberries dished up in dock leaves, and a vintage champagne. All this was spread upon snowy damask; the cutlery was the finest silver; and the wine was served in crystal of the approved shape and size. Mr. Crawfurd, accepting this magnificence with the same rather dazed approval that Elyza had felt upon her own introduction to it, sat down between her and Redmayne upon the grass and fell to with a hearty appetite, drinking the champagne glass for glass with Redmayne as if he were quite accustomed to it, which he obviously was not. He then artlessly proceeded to relate the story of his life, a very short one, consisting chiefly of Eton and Oxford and a never-to-be-forgotten holiday at Melton when he had met Assheton Smith and gone out with the Quorn.

Not to be outdone, Elyza matched this with an equally brief account of her own life as the fictitious Mr. Smith, endowing herself lavishly with a father, mother, and several sisters, a country home in Devonshire, and a career at Harrow. But, though both young people then looked expectantly at Redmayne, no revelations of a personal nature were forthcoming from their host. He was quite willing to respond to their questions about India, and to hint briefly at ti-ger-hunts and clashes with Mahratta horsemen; but it appeared that only in the most oblique fashion would he refer to his own part in these adventures.

"I expect," said Mr. Crawfurd reverentially to Elyza, when Redmayne presently left them to themselves while he had a brief colloquy with Quigg, "he is aw-fully modest. Don't care to talk about himself. I say, what a piece of luck, our falling in with him!"

"Yes—isn't it!" said Elyza enthusiastically. "It has made all the difference in *my* life already. I cannot tell you in what way *precisely,* but he has quite made me realise that I need not allow people to oblige me to ruin every prospect for future happiness by doing something I don't in the least wish to do."

But at this point their conversation was cut short by the return of Redmayne, who said he was obliged to concern himself for a short time with arrangements he was making for Mr. Smith's forthcoming journey to London, and suggested that the two young people go back to the fair to amuse themselves there until he had concluded them.

Chapter Four

It was a suggestion, it soon developed, that had far better not have been made. The sad truth was that young Mr. Crawfurd was not accustomed to taking a rather large amount of champagne in the middle of the day, and though he had every appearance of holding his wine like a gentleman, he was more than a little up in the world and therefore quite capable of performing actions that in more sober moments would have brought dismay, if not positive horror, to his mind.

In such a mood it was unfortunate that the first object to attract his and Elyza's attention when they had parted from Redmayne was an improvised ring in which a professional bruiser was despatching with skill and obvious relish a sturdy young rustic who had allowed himself to be enticed into a pugilistic encounter with him.

"It's Jem Cotgreaves!" exclaimed Mr. Crawfurd, pushing his way forward through the crowd gathered about the ring, the better to view the rather gory proceedings. "He is one of my father's tenants and the best of good fellows! But he's badly overmatched—outclassed completely! That fellow has plenty of science—knows exactly what he is doing!"

Elyza winced as what appeared to her a particularly vicious attack by the very large and disagreeable-looking pugilist sent young Jem staggering back in their direction, blood streaming freely from a badly cut lip.

"Had we—had we not better go away?" she enquired rather faintly.

"Go away! Certainly not!" said Mr. Crawfurd indignantly. *"I want to see the end of this!"*

To Elyza's great relief, the end was not long in coming. Young Jem, struggling back to the attack, was at once floored by what Mr. Crawfurd enthusiastically denominated a very wisty castor, and lay upon the greensward in peaceful unconsciousness until a bucket of water sluiced over him by his seconds made him sit up, gasping.

Meanwhile, his erstwhile opponent was parading triumphantly around the ring, bellowing a challenge to any member of the respectfully unobliging crowd who wished to step up and have *his* cork drawn.

"Dash it all, I believe I shall have a go at it myself!" young Mr. Crawfurd, flown with champagne, suddenly declared.

And to Elyza's horror he stripped off his coat and, responding to her impassioned pleas not to do it with a soothing statement that she was not to put herself about, since he had done a bit of boxing at Oxford, stepped a trifle uncertainly into the ring.

It is extremely doubtful that Mr. Crawfurd at his best would have been able to cope with such a large and professionally efficient opponent. After a hearty luncheon and several glasses of champagne it was sheer madness, as even Elyza knew, for him to attempt it. She stayed at the ringside only long enough to see Mr. Crawfurd, having positioned himself for combat in a pose that might have drawn the approval of Champion Tom Cribb himself, unfortunately remain in that classic attitude for one second too long and consequently receive the full force of a flush hit from his opponent's mighty left upon his slightly glassy-eyed countenance; then she turned and fled in the direction of Redmayne's chaise.

To her immense relief she ran upon Redmayne himself, coming in search of his two young companions, before she had gone fifty yards.

"Oh, Mr. Redmayne, do come quickly—*quickly!*" she gasped, pulling him by the sleeve in her urgency. "Mr. Crawfurd has gone into the ring to fight a horrid, large man, and he will be killed if you do not stop him! Oh, *do* come, pray! He is—he is a trifle foxed, you know!"

"The devil he is—silly young gudgeon!" Redmayne said, but with a grin that made Elyza reflect rather indignantly that he did not appear properly to grasp the seriousness of the situation.

He quickened his stride, however, so that Elyza had almost to run to keep up with him, and shortly arrived at the improvised ring, where roars of laughter and disapproving murmurs from the less bloodthirsty of the crowd gathered about it proclaimed that Elyza's fears were, at least to a certain extent, being realised. The bruiser, finding himself with a real swell as his opponent, and one who was slightly bosky as well, was amusing himself and the less particular part of his audience by playing with his prey, whom he could have floored with a single blow of his hamlike fist, as a cat plays with a mouse. Poor Mr. Crawfurd, one eye quite closed and a ghastly trickle of blood running from a corner of his mouth, went staggering about the ring, prodded and taunted by his opponent, like the blind-folded victim in a children's game of Blind Man's Buff.

"Nice work, I *don't* think," said an honest-looking countryman, turning away disgustedly as Redmayne, closely followed by an anxious Elyza, clove a way through the crowd. "Whatever made Mr. Nicholas think he could stand up to a brute like that — and him more than a little disguised to start with, by the look of him? We'd ought to put a stop to it before real harm comes to the poor lad!"

As he was clearly in the minority in this opinion, however, he found no takers for this proposal, and the dazed and miserable Mr. Crawfurd, still doggedly re-maining upon his feet with considerable assistance from the roaring crowd, willing members of which pushed him back into the ring with gusto each time he fell helplessly against the ropes, might have continued for some time to provide amusement for the rougher element among the fair-goers had not Redmayne abruptly pushed his way forward, vaulted the ropes, and, thrusting Mr. Crawfurd behind him, calmly con-fronted the bruiser.

"Very well, you've had your fun. Now let the lad go," he proposed in his entirely matter-of-fact way.

Mr. Crawfurd, suddenly finding himself *hors de com-bat,* sat down very hard upon the greensward and was horridly sick. The crowd, its occupation gone, hooted loudly, and the bruiser glowered at Redmayne.

"Oh, yer would, would yer?" he growled menacingly, casting a quick glance over the dandy coat, the superfluity of fobs and seals, and the crisp, fair locks exquisitely brushed into the elegant disorder of the *coup de vent* style. "And how about takin' yer coat off to me yerself, me bucko, so we can see what *you're* made of? Silk drawers and satin waistcoats, if I know yer style!"

"By all means," said Redmayne, without the slightest indication that he had heard this piece of gross impertinence, and forthwith removed his coat.

Elyza shut her eyes very tight together and prayed.

A few moments of excruciating silence ensued; then there was a sudden swift scuffle of feet on turf, the thud of what sounded like bone on bone, and pandemonium from the crowd. Elyza, feeling almost as sick as Mr. Crawfurd, peeped anxiously through her long lashes, and then her eyes flew open wide in delighted amazement. The bruiser was sitting upon the greensward, shaking his head with a dazed expression upon his face, and Redmayne was standing over him, his fists negligently at the ready.

"Had enough?" his bored, pleasant voice enquired.

The bruiser swore and, struggling to his feet, put up his own fists. He was at once neatly floored again with a left to the jaw that seemed to travel with such extraordinary speed and accuracy that Elyza, blinking, felt rather as if she had just witnessed a prestidigitator's trick rather than a pugilistic exhibition. This time the bruiser showed no signs of reviving, and Redmayne, shrugging himself back into his coat to the enthusiastic plaudits of the crowd, assisted Mr. Crawfurd to arise and began to lead him away.

"I'm — sorry! Made — dashed gudgeon — of myself!" Mr. Crawfurd was lamenting disjointedly.

"Not at all!" Redmayne said politely. "Entirely *my* fault, old boy. I shouldn't have allowed you to drink all that champagne. Mr. Smith," he added, looking round for Elyza, "if you are quite ready, we shall retire."

But Elyza was not looking at him. With an expression of the liveliest dismay upon her face she was regarding a tall, rather portly gentleman in a splendidly fitting blue coat and magnificent top-boots, who was also regarding her fixedly from the edge of the crowd.

"I think," she said, suddenly finding her voice and speaking very fast, "I think that I *should* like to leave now. At once, if you please. Could you — could you possibly hurry just a *little?*"

She had moved rapidly to place her two companions between herself and the portly gentleman, but to her dismay Redmayne, instead of doing as she had urged, halted and glanced down at her.

"What is it?" he enquired.

"It is Colonel Hanley — the man I was telling you of — Mrs. Winlock's friend — and he has *seen* me," Elyza hissed urgently. "But I don't think he *quite* recognises me — *Oh!*" The exclamation was caused by the sight of Colonel Hanley, glimpsed as she peered round Redmayne's shoulder, approaching purposefully. "What *am* I to do now? Here he comes!"

Mr. Crawfurd, dimly conscious of an emergency, pulled his handkerchief from his pocket, held it to his cut lip, and made a truly valiant attempt to look respectable. Redmayne looked noncommittal, and Elyza attempted to look as if she were not there at all.

Colonel Hanley came up to them. He was a man

who looked as if he would have been red-faced even in his calmer moments, and at present his countenance was quite purple.

"Miss—Leigh!" he ejaculated. *"Miss—Leigh!* I shouldn't have credited it—upon my soul I shouldn't! In male attire—well, one expected that, in view of your abigail's finding the hair you had cut off and the hall-boy's statement about his clothes. But when that landlord fellow told me you'd gone off with a—a—"

"A gentleman?" Redmayne suggested.

Colonel Hanley snorted. He glared at Redmayne.

"I suppose, sir," he said, "you will attempt to persuade me that you are unaware that this—this *boy* is a female?"

"Not at all," said Redmayne politely. "I am quite aware of it. May I suggest, however, that as a friend of Miss Leigh's you must be equally aware that this is scarcely the place to discuss her affairs? Perhaps we might repair to my chaise—?"

The Colonel looked at him as if he had said something profoundly shocking.

"Miss Leigh and I," he said, "will go nowhere with you, sir. We shall dispense with your company from this moment, sir. Miss Leigh is returning to her proper guardian—"

"Quite right, old boy. So she is. No need to fly up into the boughs over it," Redmayne agreed. He looked at Mr. Crawfurd. "May I present my friend Mr. Crawfurd?" Mr. Crawfurd managed a bewildered and somewhat ghastly smile and a very creditable bow. "The son of—" Redmayne continued, casting an enquiring glance at Mr. Crawfurd.

"Sir Ralph Crawfurd," said Mr. Crawfurd helpfully.

"Sir Ralph Crawfurd, of Crawfurd Court," Redmayne said. "My own name is Redmayne. I have only recently arrived in England from India, but you may be acquainted with some prominent Yorkshire relations of mine, the Kerslakes."

Colonel Hanley grudgingly admitted to knowledge of the Kerslakes. "Thought they was all dead, though," he said suspiciously. "The title's extinct now."

"So it is," said Redmayne. "As a matter of fact, I am connected on the female side. The last, unfortunately, of the blood."

"Indeed!" Colonel Hanley blew out his large sandy military moustaches. "Well, well, that is neither here nor there, sir," he said severely. "The fact that you come of a respectable family merely adds to the infamy of your behaviour in enticing this young lady—"

"He *didn't* entice me," Elyza, finding her tongue at last, said rebelliously. "I was robbed of my purse and he helped me. It was *very* kind of him."

The Colonel gave a short, unpleasant laugh. Mr. Crawfurd, game as a pebble in spite of his disreputable condition and his utter bewilderment at the turn events were taking, clenched his fists and took a step forward, but Redmayne placed a restraining hand upon his arm.

"Not just now, Mr. Crawfurd," he said soothingly. "We can't blame the Colonel for being suspicious. Looks deuced havey-cavey, you must admit."

"*Looks* havey-cavey!" the Colonel ejaculated. "By God, sir, it *is* havey-cavey!" He blew out his moustaches again. "Gal disappears from her home—"

"It is *not* my home," Elyza muttered, in emphatic parentheses.

"—frightens poor Mrs. Winlock into the vapours, what?" continued the Colonel, unheeding. "Sends me after her—don't want a scandal; that goes without saying—and what do I find? Greasy scoundrel of a landlord at Beckhampton tells me she's gone off with a young buck in a travelling-chaise you couldn't miss by the description of it, and I come on it drawn up at a fair and *you*"—he glared accusingly at Elyza—"looking on at a *prize-fight!*"

"She wasn't looking on, old boy," Redmayne said. "She'd come to fetch me. Bit of an emergency, you see. And no harm done, after all. I suggest you forget the prize-fight."

The Colonel said huffily and with some emphasis that he would make a complete report—"a *complete* report," he repeated—to Mrs. Winlock of the circumstances in which he had found Miss Leigh when he returned the young lady to her.

"Oh, I shouldn't do that," Redmayne said.

All three of his auditors looked at him. He was smiling faintly, Elyza saw, but there was something in those blue eyes, fixed unwaveringly now upon Colonel Hanley's face, that, curiously enough, gave her a feeling of danger. The Colonel quite evidently felt the same. He looked as if he were remembering that moment when the bruiser had gone down before a blow so swift and punishing that it had made the mind boggle and the flesh wince in sympathy, and his face grew purple once more.

To Elyza's surprise, however, Redmayne suddenly reached out and touched him lightly upon the shoulder.

"Much better to say you found her at a respectable

53

inn, under the care of a lady she'd confided in, who was on the point of taking her back to London," he remarked simply. "I can make it worth your while, old boy."

Colonel Hanley was looking at him as if he were mesmerised. "A—a lady—?" he gabbled. "But—"

"I'll provide the lady, old boy," said Redmayne. "No need to trouble yourself over *that* part of the matter. In point of fact, my man Quigg is attending to it at this very moment. The program runs like this. Quigg goes on to Chippenham, stops at the best inn, and asks the landlady for the name of a respectable elderly gentle-woman—retired schoolmistress or something of the kind—living in the neighbourhood. Always a nice old tabby of that sort in small English towns. We follow with Miss Leigh; she nips upstairs to a bedchamber and changes her clothes, comes down again and gets into a post-chaise with the tabby, and they drive off together to London. You see how simple it all is?"

"Yes, but—but—" sputtered Colonel Hanley, whose rather foolish blue eyes were now almost starting out of his head, "who's to say this female of yours will agree to go to London with Miss Leigh? It's preposter-ous!"

"Not at all. I'll make it worth *her* while, too, old boy."

Elyza looked at Colonel Hanley's bewildered face, wondering if he was seeing in his mind's eye, as she was in hers, Redmayne taking a small chamois bag from his pocket and pouring diamonds from it into an old lady's mittened hand until she agreed to do as he wished; but then recollected that the Colonel had not seen, as she had, the diamond intended for Miss May-field, so that this was rather unlikely. All the same, however, he seemed to have succumbed, just as she and Mr. Crawfurd had done before him, to a conviction of Redmayne's power to cause events to occur quite beyond the ordinary mortal's ability to produce. After a moment he remarked grudgingly that he dared say something of the sort could be arranged.

"Of course it can," said Redmayne encouragingly. "Much better than having her driving to London alone with you. I daresay your Mrs. Winlock was in such high fidgets over Miss Leigh's disappearance that she didn't think of that. You are no relation of Miss Leigh's, I gather?"

Colonel Hanley said rather stiffly that he was not, but that as a very old friend of Mrs. Winlock's—

"Should have come herself," Redmayne said decisively. He began to walk on and, as it were, wafted the Colonel, Mr. Crawfurd, and Elyza on in his wake. "Much the better plan. Very inadvisable, as I understand English mores, to have a young lady involved in a scandal. As a matter of fact, I've an idea it would be better if you kept mum about this whole affair—report back to Mrs. Winlock that you couldn't find any trace of Miss Leigh and let her turn up of her own accord with the tabby. Mr. Crawfurd, I am sure," he added, glancing at that young gentleman, "will not speak of the matter to anyone."

Mr. Crawfurd, his young, pleasant face growing quite distressed at the idea that anyone could believe he would be so ungentlemanly as to reveal the extraordinary story of which he had come—quite imperfectly as yet, it was true—to have knowledge, began at once to confound himself in assurances.

"That's all right then," said Redmayne. He turned

his attention again to Colonel Hanley and asked him if he had driven himself from London or had hired a post-chaise and would like to pay it off and come with them to Chippenham.

The Colonel said huffily that he was driving his phaeton and, with emphasis, that he would take Miss Leigh up with him now.

"Oh no, you won't," said Redmayne equably. "Much better for her not to be seen driving into the inn-yard in an open carriage. She's been fortunate enough up to this time not to meet any of her acquaintances, but it never answers to take unnecessary risks. Quigg will have made all the arrangements at the inn. We'll have her whisked upstairs in the twinkling of a bedpost."

The Colonel appeared to be about to utter some protest, but suddenly looked up to see Ram at his elbow and was struck dumb.

"And you, Mr. Crawfurd—?" Redmayne enquired. "Can we take *you* up?"

Mr. Crawfurd stammered that he was driving his gig, but looked so incapable at the moment of managing even a donkey-cart without landing it and himself in a ditch that Redmayne kindly told him he had best let one of his grooms drive it and come into the travelling-chaise himself.

"You'll feel better when you've had a bit of a wash-up at the inn," he said, to which Elyza irrepressibly added, "And look better, too!"

She was, in fact, so elated by the turn events had taken that she was able to face with equanimity even the prospect of her forthcoming meeting with Mrs. Winlock. After all, as Redmayne had said, that formidable female, no matter how formidable she was,

56

could not eat her, and with the example she had just had of the way in which her new friend had handled the Colonel, she was able to repose every confidence in his handling Mrs. Winlock quite as successfully, once they had all arrived in Brighton.

The great thing, she told herself, was simply to say *no* to everyone—to Mrs. Winlock, to Sir Edward, and to Sir Edward's rather terrifyingly lachrymose mama—until they went down to Brighton, and as she was aware that Mrs. Winlock's plans called for their doing so almost immediately, that meant that unsupported recalcitrance would be called for during only a very few days.

She gave a confiding twitch to Redmayne's sleeve. "How very glad I am that I met you!" she said to him. "And you *will* see to things in Brighton, won't you?"

Redmayne looked down at her, faintly surprised. "Certainly!" he said. "Haven't I told you as much?"

Colonel Hanley glanced round at them suspiciously, but it was a suspicion which, although Elyza did not know it, was tempered by meditation. The Colonel's situation in life was somewhat precarious; he had only eight hundred a year and expensive tastes, and he was therefore prepared to be properly grateful for small favours, such as a good dinner or a tip on a sure winner at Newmarket.

For larger favours he would, if necessary, have been prepared to forget his own name, and when he looked at Redmayne and his magnificent entourage he saw golden possibilities of such favours. Colonel Hanley nodded a little, self-importantly, to himself. He would forget, he decided, as Redmayne had suggested, the entire scene that had just passed, and report back to

Agatha Winlock that he had been unable to discover any trace of the missing Elyza — which, as Elyza would by that time have arrived in London herself, would appear quite normal to that lady and no doubt prevent her from visiting upon him one of the scolds that he had never got over dreading, though through long usage he had become inured to them as the price one had to pay for some of the more enjoyable pleasures in life.

Chapter Five

To Elyza the four-and-twenty hours that followed, even though they included her highly disagreeable reunion with Mrs. Winlock in London, were almost an anticlimax to this exciting morning. Redmayne's plan — as she had an idea all his plans did — succeeded to perfection. By the time they reached Chippenham, Quigg, with his usual efficiency, was already prepared to produce a nervous little elderly female in a black bombazine gown and a rusty bonnet, much fluttered by the tale he had confided to her of a runaway young lady who had been a fellow passenger of his from London, and who was at that moment dissolved in penitent tears in one of the inn's private parlours and much in need of female companionship and counsel.

Miss Timbury, a retired governess, had had long experience with young ladies who had done what they ought not to do and then regretted it. Introduced presently into the parlour where Elyza, having made a rapid change from Mr. Smith's bottle-green coat and darned Inexpressibles to the sprig muslin frock she had brought with her in her bundle, was to be seen sniffling very realistically into a handkerchief inspirationally dampened in the water pitcher of the bedchamber where she had changed her clothes, she at once reverted to type, said "Tsck, tsck," in a reproving but consolatory way, and remarked that things were never as bad as they seemed.

She then enquired what the matter was. Elyza, throwing herself with enthusiasm into her role, gave her a somewhat highly coloured version of her situation in regard to Sir Edward Mottram and Mrs. Winlock.

"But I realise now that I have been very foolish indeed to run away," she ended virtuously, "and I do *so* wish to go back, only" — with a very convincing sob — "I am *afraid* to—"

Miss Timbury said soothingly not to be a silly girl, upon which Elyza, who had received precise instructions upon this point from Redmayne, as well as the wherewithal to substantiate her statement, said it wasn't perhaps polite to mention it, but she was an heiress and had a good deal of money with her, and if dear Miss Timbury would only accompany her back to London and help her to face Mrs. Winlock, she would pay all the post-charges for her, going and coming, besides giving her a handsome present.

Miss Timbury, to whom a journey to London was a rare treat, particularly in a post-chaise, looked flustered and said, "Dear, dear!"

"Does that mean you will?" asked Elyza. "*Do* say it does! You see, I am so very frightened of travelling alone!"

Miss Timbury said of course she was, and it went without saying, at any rate, that it was most improper for a young lady of quality to be jauntering about the country without the companionship of an older female, like any hurly-burly girl of no background whatever. Sir Robert Leigh's name dropped into the conversation then clinched the matter, for it transpired that he had once, in his salad days, visited a country house where Miss Timbury, then a very green young governess, had been in charge of the young ladies, and she had never, she said fervently, forgotten his exquisite manners.

"So much the gentleman!" she exclaimed. "Such perfect address! Young men nowadays are so sadly lacking in the finer graces! I am sure my young ladies quite broke their hearts over Sir Robert, though of course it all came to nothing in the end, for none of them was older than fourteen."

Elyza who, like all young people, was quite stunned to learn that her father had ever been her own age and capable of inspiring romance, would rather have liked to pursue this subject, but, recollecting that Redmayne and his entire entourage, to say nothing of Colonel Hanley and Mr. Crawfurd, were waiting to see her launched safely on her way to London, confined herself strictly to the matter at hand, with such success that she was presently able to emerge from the inn with Miss Timbury at her side, mount into a post-chaise, and, after a brief halt at Miss Timbury's lodgings to collect a few necessaries for the journey, set off on the road to London.

Since Miss Timbury was timid of travelling at night, and especially of passing after dark through Maidenhead Thicket, which still had an unenviable reputation because of the many highway robberies committed there, she and Elyza broke their journey at the neat and pretty Seven Stars Inn, near Kith Green. As a result, Elyza's meeting with Mrs. Winlock on the following morning had the advantage of taking that fashionable female completely by surprise at an hour when she had not yet left her bedchamber and so was not armoured with her usual elegant complexion and costume. Hilliard, her dresser, flying upstairs to announce that a post-chaise had just halted before the house, from which Miss Elyza and an unknown female were alighting, had only just had time to array her mistress in a sea-green dressing-gown with a treble pleating of lace falling off round the neck when Elyza herself tapped at the door and, putting in her head, asked if she might come in.

It might have occurred to Mrs. Winlock, even in those initial few moments of shock, relief, and towering bad temper, that something had occurred to her ward during the brief period of her absence to work a remarkable change in her character. The Elyza who trod into her bedchamber this morning had the look of a young lady who had every intention of exhibiting a proper repentance for the heinous crime of running away, but she did not, Mrs. Winlock decided, really look repentant. Neither did she look apprehensive, or wooden, or desperate and mulish, which were all expressions with which Mrs. Winlock had become exasperatedly familiar during her two months' acquaintance with her ward. She looked, on the contrary, as if she had been having a very good time and expected to go on having it.

This, to a woman of Mrs. Winlock's experience and cynical knowledge of the world, was ample cause for suspicion, but the appearance of Miss Timbury, respectability incarnate, to vouch for her having discovered poor Miss Leigh in tears at the best inn in Chippenham, where she had got off the Bath and Bristol Accommodation coach, being unable, because of True Repentance, to go on any longer with her really very naughty scheme of running away, effectively scotched any notion that Elyza had spent the period of her absence in unlawful dalliance with some unknown member of the male sex.

"I am sure, my dear Mrs. Winlock," Miss Timbury fluttered, "you will forgive me if I beg you not to scold the poor child, for I found her in *such* a state—so anxious to return, but so apprehensive of the reception she might receive! I assured her that True Repentance always carries its own reward, and that in this case I was certain you would be so happy to see her return to the bosom of her family—in a manner of speaking, of course, for I understand that you are not actually related—"

Mrs. Winlock said, "Yes, yes," with some impatience, feeling how much more satisfactory everything would be if Miss Timbury would go away and leave her to deal with Elyza alone. But even after Miss Timbury, revived with a refreshing cup of tea and announcing at great length her intention of paying a wee visit, before returning to Chippenham, to a married cousin in Hans Town, had departed, with a sum handsomely exceeding the return post-charges pressed upon her by Elyza, Mrs. Winlock found that "dealing with" Elyza was not the same matter that it had been before. Taxed with her iniquity in running away, Elyza said that she was very sorry and wouldn't do it again, but added firmly that Mrs. Winlock really ought to understand that she, Elyza, would not and could not marry Sir Edward Mottram.

This statement, to Mrs. Winlock, came in the nature not only of a challenge but of a positive affront. A handsome woman of exceedingly fashionable connexions and uncertain means, she was accustomed to managing (for a large and discreetly arranged price) the social careers of unfortunate Elyzas, and she had had every intention of presenting Sir Robert Leigh, upon the conclusion of the present Season, with a most satisfactory *fait accompli* in the form of a betrothal arranged between his daughter and a very dull but impeccably respectable young baronet whose situation required him to wed an heiress.

In this instance her task had been complicated, it was true, by the extreme reluctance of both the young people to commit themselves to the fatal step, for Sir Edward Mottram, her prospective victim, was a serious, pompous young man who took little interest in the fair sex and none at all in Elyza, and who was motivated only by his terror of his mama to offer himself as a sacrifice upon the matrimonial altar.

But all, to Mrs. Winlock's way of thinking, had been brought to a satisfactory conclusion on the occasion of the past Wednesday's subscription ball at Almack's, when she and the Dowager Lady Mottram, seated together on a pair of rout chairs at the side of the ballroom, had watched Elyza and Sir Edward performing the steps of a country dance together in mute and miserable partnership.

"Dear Augusta," she had said to Lady Mottram, a tall and lachrymose female in a purple-bloom satin

64

gown and turban, "*do* see what a charming picture they make together! It must be so comforting to you to think that, if your Edward has at last formed a decided preference for a young lady — he is seven-and-twenty, is he not? — he has done so with his usual prudence! I believe you cannot be *quite* thoroughly acquainted with the extent of Sir Robert Leigh's fortune, but I can assure you — in the strictest confidence, of course — that the figure he mentioned to me, in reference to Elyza's dowry, was —"

She bent forward to whisper in Lady Mottram's garnet-decked ear. Lady Mottram's head had continued to droop in the fashion she felt most becoming to express her widow hood, but a gleam, instantly repressed, had stolen into her eyes.

"Really?" she said. "How splendid for the dear child! Of course, *I* know nothing of such matters; since my poor Henry passed away I have left such matters entirely in the hands of my solicitors, Messrs. Titchener, Titchener, and Golesworthy," she had added pensively, her eyes meeting Mrs. Winlock's and at once dropping again.

Mrs. Winlock said that she understood Messrs. Titchener, Titchener, and Golesworthy were eminently capable persons and would be able to deal splendidly with Sir Robert's solicitors, at which point, if the two ladies had been gentlemen, they would no doubt have shaken hands together and called for a bumper to celebrate the bargain.

But, being ladies, they had merely smiled at each other in a very delicate way and had begun to gossip about the unfortunate predilection Corinna Mayfield appeared to be forming for Mr. Everet, who had very little fortune and a dreadful reputation — alas, only too well deserved! — with women, when everyone knew that if she chose she might have Belfort and a marchioness's coronet for the asking.

And then, thought Mrs. Winlock, regarding her returned charge with no friendly eye, that graceless little monkey, informed on the way home from Almack's that evening that she was to prepare herself to receive Sir Edward's addresses on the following morning, had all but ruined everything by running away. Now one could only hope that her present return denoted a change of heart in spite of her defiant words; but at any rate, with her again beneath one's roof, one need not despair in spite of this latest outrageous escapade, which, if it were to become known, would certainly destroy all her chances. Mrs. Winlock looked with disfavour at her ward's raggedly cropped hair and slim little figure, wondering for the dozenth time why she should be burdened with a small girl in a Season when tall Beauties were the mode, and a small girl who, moreover, compounded her smallness by possessing a highly unclassical, tiptilted little nose and a pair of eyes so enormous as to eclipse utterly the effect of her other features.

"I was obliged, of course," she said to her acidly, "to make some excuse to Sir Edward when he called here on Thursday, expecting to see you, so you will not be surprised to learn that I told him you were in bed with a putrid sore throat. He will no doubt call again today to enquire after your health, but it will naturally be quite impossible for you to see him until we have done something about your hair. I shall tell him you are recruiting your strength for our remove to Brighton on

Monday, and then, when we are settled there, you may receive him. One can only hope," she continued, "that he never learns the truth about this disgraceful escapade, for he has, as you must be aware, the very nicest sense of the proprieties—"

"Which is exactly why he and I will not suit, ma'am," Elyza said hopefully; but Mrs. Winlock only gave her rather cruel, tinkling little laugh.

"My dear child, beggars cannot be choosers," she said. "I believe you will find that you and Sir Edward will suit very well, once you have brought yourself to face the obvious fact that no other gentleman is at all likely to wish to marry you. And if you repeat at Brighton the very *gauche* performance to which you treated us in London—which of course you will, for my best efforts have obviously been of no avail in attempting to give you some semblance of *manner*—I can assure you that your chances of bringing any other young man up to scratch are quite nonexistent. I have already written to Sir Robert," she added meaningly, "informing him of my expectations concerning you and Sir Edward; he will no doubt be delighted, so I would counsel you to behave with proper complaisance to Sir Edward when he calls, under pain of incurring your papa's severe displeasure."

Elyza said nothing in reply to this veiled threat, and was pleased to find that Mrs. Winlock's barbs lost much of their usual sting when one was able to hear them merely as unwelcome intrusions into the delightful anticipation of seeing Redmayne and young Mr. Crawfurd once more and resuming the adventure that had been begun on the road to Bath.

So she only remarked politely that if they were going to Brighton on Monday she really had a great number of things to attend to and walked out of the room, leaving Mrs. Winlock to array herself in a dashing half-dress of figured silk and go downstairs in a very bad humour, where she was able to vent her spleen upon Colonel Hanley, who had the ill fortune to arrive at the house at that moment with his mendacious tale of a total lack of success in discovering any trace of the missing Elyza.

Chapter Six

Elyza and Mrs. Winlock, setting out from London on the Monday morning, arrived in Brighton shortly before the dinner hour that same day. Elyza, who had been bred entirely inland — for Aunt Phoebe had detested anything so frivolous as a seaside resort and Great-aunt Sephestia never stirred from Bath — was so much excited by her first sight of the sea, even the very sedately sparkling expanse of it seen from Brighton's Marine Parade, that she quite forgot all Mrs. Winlock's precepts and behaved, as that lady coldly remarked, in as uninhibited a manner as any City mushroom's daughter on a summer holiday. She exclaimed in delight over the fantastic domes and minarets of the Prince Regent's Marine Pavilion, announced her intention of instantly trying the unknown joys proffered by the row of bathing-machines drawn up on the beach, and declared the house on the Marine Parade that Sir Robert's agent had hired for them to be the most delightfully situated one in the town, providing as it did an excellent view of the sea from its bow-fronted drawing-room windows.

As it was dinnertime when they arrived, any plans she might have wished to make for exploring the town had to be postponed until the morrow, and even then Mrs. Winlock firmly vetoed her desire to have herself dipped into the sea before breakfast by the bathing-women who were awaiting their morning customers at the row of boxlike contrivances on wheels visible across the Parade on the beach. Mrs. Winlock, always a high stickler for the proprieties, said coldly that as Brighton bathing-machines, unlike those at Ramsgate and Scarborough, had no awnings, it was one of the principal amusements of the more rakish gentlemen visiting Brighton to provide themselves with telescopes and spy upon ladies about to enter the sea, and she had no desire to see her ward among the objects of their curiosity.

Elyza looked rebellious at this dictum but, having been promised in compensation a walk along the sea-front and into the town, during which she would be able to see all the available sights, from the Royal Pavilion to Promenade Grove and Donaldson's Library, sat down with a good grace to her breakfast.

As it fell out, her docility was rewarded, even before she and Mrs. Winlock had arisen from the breakfast table, by the arrival of a visitor whom she would have been exceedingly sorry to miss.

"A Mr. Crawfurd has called, madam," said Satterlee, the butler, entering the breakfast parlour with an expression upon his face designed to indicate his opinion of young gentlemen who made morning calls at such an early hour. "To see Miss Elyza, madam," he added, as he saw a slight frown of nonrecognition crease Mrs. Winlock's brow.

"To see Miss Elyza?" Mrs. Winlock turned to Elyza in some surprise. "Do you know a Mr. Crawfurd, Elyza?" she enquired. "I am quite sure you were never introduced to anyone of that name in London."

"No, I—I did not meet him in London," Elyza said a little breathlessly, wondering rather wildly what story Mr. Crawfurd might have concocted to account for his claiming acquaintance with her and prudently determining not to commit herself to any statement that might run counter to it. She jumped up from the table. "He is a—a most *well-conducted* young man, ma'am; I am sure you will like him excessively," she said rapidly. "His father is Sir Ralph Crawfurd. Where have you put him, Satterlee?" she demanded of that disapproving functionary, who looked somewhat less disapproving, however, upon hearing a title mentioned.

Satterlee replied that the young gentleman was in the drawing room, whereupon Elyza made a dash for the stairs, but was restrained by Mrs. Winlock, who said she must know by this time that it was quite improper for her to see young men alone.

They accordingly went upstairs together, where they found Mr. Crawfurd looking very shy among the satinwood sofas and ormolu tables. Even Mrs. Winlock, however, Elyza saw with pride, could find nothing to criticise in his manner as he made a very creditable bow and apologised for calling upon them at such an early hour.

"The truth is, ma'am," he said to Mrs. Winlock, "that I learned last evening that Miss Leigh was arrived in Brighton, and as we are *such very old friends,*" he said with great emphasis, looking at Elyza, "I thought

I would just look in and see if it was your intention to attend the ball at the Castle Inn this evening. In which case," he added, "I shall be beforehand in soliciting Miss Leigh's hand for as many dances as she can spare me."

"Dear me!" said Mrs. Winlock, motioning their visitor to a chair and seating herself, with a somewhat ironical expression upon her face. "I had no idea Elyza was concealing such an ardent admirer from her past! I take it you are from Devonshire, Mr. Crawfurd? Or is it from Bath that this *very old* acquaintance dates?"

Elyza opened her mouth to say Bath, but fortunately shut it again as Mr. Crawfurd said Devonshire.

"I don't live there myself," he explained a trifle nervously. "Our place is in Wiltshire. But I have an uncle who lives in Devonshire. I was used to visit him quite frequently."

He then appeared to have shot his bolt, conversationally speaking, and fell silent, looking at Elyza in anguished appeal. Elyza, realising that her own inventive powers were far superior to Mr. Crawfurd's, at once sprang into the breach, and regaled Mrs. Winlock with a series of rather incoherent reminiscences of her own and Mr. Crawfurd's joint past to which that young gentleman listened with anxious attention, as if impressing every detail upon his mind against the possibility of his being catechised concerning it in the future.

To his obvious relief, however, Mrs. Winlock had no opportunity to do so at the present moment, for Satterlee appeared just then to announce her great friend, Miss Piercebridge, who had presumed, she said, as she entered the room on Satterlee's heels, upon old friendship to look in so early in the morning and see if there was anything she could do to help them in settling in.

Miss Piercebridge was Mrs. Winlock's most intimate friend, which distinction she owed to the fact that she was an Honourable, took as keen and virulent an interest in scandal as did Mrs. Winlock, and had an even smaller income, so that it was impossible for her ever to eclipse her friend by appearing in public with her in a more fashionable gown or bonnet. She was a tall, thin woman with very black hair and a very pale complexion, and she presented a rather *outré* appearance just now as she trod into the drawing room, wearing a French green chip hat suitable for a young lady half her age, which was tied with long ribands under her chin, and a Zephyr cloak, far too short for her, made of lace, with a sash round the waist and a series of lavender tassels finishing its hem.

These garments, as Mrs. Winlock was well aware, had been presented to her by a relation who had more money than taste, and whose fashion of dressing was so remarkable that there was no possibility whatever of everyone's not recognising her garments when they descended to Miss Piercebridge. Miss Piercebridge took her revenge for this by spreading any titbits of scandal, true or untrue, concerning her charitable relation industriously throughout the *ton,* and also by criticising the garments bestowed upon her with a detachment that seemed entirely unaffected by the fact that she was wearing them.

"Good morning, Elyza. I am happy to see you are quite recovered," she said, bending such a penetrating gaze upon her as she spoke that Elyza, who had been about to say, recovered from what, suddenly remembered her guilty secret, blushed, and said hastily that she felt quite well now.

The penetrating gaze then fell upon Mr. Crawfurd with equally dire results, so that he looked even shyer than ever when he was presented to its owner.

"Crawfurd," pronounced Miss Piercebridge, looking at him with what seemed an almost sybilline prescience as his name was uttered by Mrs. Winlock. "Crawfurd. With a *u?*"

Mr. Crawfurd rather nervously admitted to the u.

"Of course," said Miss Piercebridge, and nodded. "I knew your dear mama. She is now deceased."

Mr. Crawfurd said, "Yes, ma'am, I know," quite absurdly, and then looked as if he wished he were, too.

"She was a great flirt," Miss Piercebridge continued, with a censorious lift of her eyebrows. "I always thought she would marry Lord Portwood but of course it turned out for the best, since her sister Mildred did in the end."

Mr. Crawfurd, looking slightly surprised, said something unintelligible. Miss Piercebridge regarded him enquiringly and severely.

"I said, she hadn't got a sister Mildred," Mr. Crawfurd repeated rather desperately.

"Nonsense!" said Miss Piercebridge. "She is your aunt. Lady Portwood."

Mr. Crawfurd, now looking like someone who had entered the house under false pretences to steal the spoons, said obstinately that he didn't know any Lady Portwood.

"Then you are not," said Miss Piercebridge definitely, "one of the Buckinghamshire Crawfurds."

74

And leaving him this humiliating fact to ponder upon, she turned her attention to Mrs. Winlock, to whom she began to recite a list of all those persons of importance who had now arrived in Brighton.

Elyza, seizing her opportunity, retired to the window embrasure and unobtrusively beckoned Mr. Crawfurd to her side.

"I never said I was one of the Buckinghamshire Crawfurds," he began the conversation rather hotly, apparently feeling called upon to justify himself to someone. "Dash it, I—"

"No, of course you didn't," Elyza said impatiently. "Goodness, what does it matter? What I really want you to tell me is, why did you come here this morning and pretend you had known me forever? I was so surprised I almost said something stupid."

Mr. Crawfurd, looking harassed, said it was Cleve's idea.

"Mr. Redmayne's, that is," he explained. "He said I might call him that."

"Oh, is he here in Brighton, too?" Elyza looked puzzled. "But why didn't he come with you, then?"

"Well, he rather thought it wouldn't do," Mr. Crawfurd said. "I mean, both of us claiming to know you and all that. So he said I should come along first and establish the ground, and then later when we are together and meet you, I can introduce him. He'll be at the Castle Inn tonight; that's why I said that about the ball."

Elyza considered. "Well, I expect Mrs. Winlock will take me there," she said after a moment, "but actually I can't be *sure*, because she hasn't said anything about it yet. But we *are* going for a walk this morning, and she says we shall stop at Donaldson's Library to take out a subscription there, so I daresay we may very easily contrive to meet you and Mr. Redmayne if you will loiter about at some likely spot."

Mr. Crawfurd said he thought that a splendid idea and he would tell Cleve, and then their conversation was interrupted by Mrs. Winlock, and they had no further opportunity for private colloquy.

Shortly afterwards Mr. Crawfurd rose to take his leave, apparently considering with some relief that he had fulfilled the purpose of his visit, and as Miss Piercebridge also soon departed Elyza and Mrs. Winlock were free to carry out their plan to go for a morning promenade.

Brighton had now been for some years, owing chiefly to the Prince Regent's predilection for it, the most fashionable resort in England, and, as the season was at its height, Elyza had her first view of it at its gay, indolent, faintly raffish best. The Marine Parade, when they left the house that morning, was already thronged with fashionable ladies in the diaphanous, clinging, high-waisted gowns — primrose, blossom, sea-green, fawn, or cerulean blue — that were in the mode at the moment. They were accompanied by their equally elegant escorts in long-tailed, wasp-waisted blue coats and inordinately high shirt-points, their brilliantly polished Hessians sporting dancing tassels, their quizzing glasses at the ready to survey each charming passing face. All, like Elyza and Mrs. Winlock, were enjoying a splendid June morning, with that feeling of particular high anticipation that only a fine sea breeze, tangy with salt, a clear blue sky whipped with a few white clouds, and the dazzle of a crinkled, sparkling sea can inspire.

But Elyza's anticipation was the highest of all. Something extraordinary and delightful, she was quite certain, was about to happen to her here, and she viewed the bow-fronted houses of the Marine Parade, with their Corinthian columns and entablatures, the bright gardens laid out in geometrical designs that bordered the glazed red-brick pavement of the Steyne, and the Royal Pavilion itself, with its fantastic pile of domes and pinnacles gleaming in the morning sunlight, with the approval of an impresario inspecting the brilliant stage backdrop for an exciting drama, starring Miss Elyza Leigh, that was shortly to unfold.

She and Mrs. Winlock met several of their acquaintances as they walked up the Steyne, so that their progress towards Donaldson's Circulating Library was necessarily slow. Donaldson's, Mrs. Winlock informed Elyza as they walked, was one of the most fashionable gathering-places in the town. Here one might not only meet one's friends, who had come to change a book in the elegantly appointed rooms or merely to display a new frock or coat, but might also attend the card-assemblies and concerts that were presented every evening during the season, supplementing the balls held on alternate nights at the Assembly-rooms of the Old Ship and Castle Inns.

"It is quite probable as well," she was continuing, as they approached the library, "that we shall be invited to attend one of the informal receptions or concerts that the Prince is fond of giving during the season," when a squeak from Elyza suddenly interrupted her.

"Oh!" said Elyza. "It can't be—but it *is*—Mr. Crawfurd again." And, with the knowledge that she had now made her entrance upon this sparkling, sun-flooded Brighton stage and must utter the lines allotted to her, she added, "How very diverting, ma'am! *Do* let us stop for a moment and speak to him."

As Mr. Crawfurd was at that moment purposefully bearing down upon them, with Redmayne, who had been standing beside him, lingering slightly behind him, and the magnificently turbaned and bearded Ram hovering in the background, it was manifestly impossible for them to do anything else. Mr. Crawfurd pulled off his curly-brimmed beaver, bowed, blushed, and said, "Good morning," to them.

"How very nice to see you again so soon!" Elyza said, addressing Mr. Crawfurd but unable to prevent herself from looking at Redmayne. And at that moment, as her eyes fell upon that elegant and for some reason always faintly dangerous-looking figure, on the bronzed, slightly remote face with its intensely blue eyes, a strange thing happened to her. All the high anticipation, all the hope and expectancy of the past few days, suddenly burst inside her like the opening of a marvellous flower, its bright bud unfolding into a great, magical bloom that seemed to enclose in itself the sea, the sunlight, the blue sky, and the morning breeze; and her heart gave a leap of pure happiness.

Mr. Crawfurd, seeming to speak from somewhere very far away, said it was splendid to see her, too, and asked if he might present his friend, Mr. Redmayne.

"Mrs. Winlock—Miss Leigh," he said punctiliously.

Redmayne bowed and said he was delighted. He then looked at Mr. Crawfurd, who, as if recollecting himself, said hurriedly that Mr. Redmayne had just returned to England from India and had taken the

78

Duke of Bellairs' house on the Steyne for the season.

"The Duke of Bellairs' house!" Mrs. Winlock's eyes widened incredulously. "But how is that possible? The Duke himself—"

"I rather think," Redmayne explained, in his matter-of-fact way, "that he decided Worthing would be more beneficial to the Duchess's health this season."

Mrs. Winlock's incredulity appeared to deepen. "But, my dear man," she said, "that house must certainly require no fewer than forty servants!"

"Forty indoors, I believe," Redmayne corrected her apologetically. "Of course there are the gardeners and grooms and so on, and it is possible, I believe, that I may have to bring in additional help when I entertain. In point of fact," he added, "I expect to be giving a small *soirée* later this week. I hope I may send cards to you and Miss Leigh, ma'am?"

Mrs. Winlock still looking rather stunned, said by all means. Redmayne then enquired if they would be at the ball at the Castle Inn that evening, and, upon Mrs. Winlock's stating their intention of attending it, said in that case he would ask Miss Leigh if she would allow him the privilege of standing up with her for a set of country dances.

Elyza, finding her voice for the first time, said fervently, and with a dazzled smile, "Oh, yes. Yes!"

"That's all right then," Redmayne said, impressing her with equal admiration and terror by looking at her with the polite, interested gaze of a gentleman who has just been introduced to a young lady and finds her charming, so that for a moment she almost wondered if she had dreamed the episode of her meeting with him at the Beckhampton Inn and their visit to the fair.

79

A group of ladies then came up and greeted Mrs. Winlock, and Redmayne and young Mr. Crawfurd made their adieux.

"What an extraordinary young man!" Mrs. Winlock said a few minutes later, as she and Elyza entered the library together. "He must be rich enough to buy an Abbey if he can afford to hire the Duke's house; it is almost as large as the Royal Pavilion! I must certainly find out who he is. He seemed quite taken with you, by the bye, Elyza—which I must say is as extraordinary as all the rest of it, although I will admit you *are* in looks this morning. I do believe having your hair curled in front and cropped behind quite suits you, although personally I have never cared for that extreme sort of style. But at any rate it is an improvement upon the way it looked when you arrived back in London from that disgraceful excursion—exactly as if you had been dragged backwards through a bush."

Elyza said nothing. They had entered Donaldson's Library, and the first person her eyes fell upon, standing in the centre of the room surrounded by an eager throng of gentlemen, was Corinna Mayfield, dressed in jonquil muslin, a broad-brimmed Villager hat crowning her shining fair curls.

Quite suddenly, all the light went out of the day.

Chapter Seven

As she dressed for the ball at the Castle Inn that evening Elyza told herself that if there was anything in the world she detested it was the mawkish sort of girl who was forever fancying herself in love with the latest handsome young man she had clapped eyes upon, and making a figure of herself by shedding secret tears over him in her bedchamber and indulging in romantic dreams about him.

And the most shocking thing of all, she thought severely, was how such a girl could transfer her dreams in the twinkling of a bedpost from one subject to another. Certainly she had never thought that she herself would ever possibly fall into that category! And yet during the London Season just past she had been (she saw now in a very shame-making way) excessively silly about the Honourable Mr. Jack Everet, who had never given her a second glance and cared no more for her than he did for his kitchen-maid, if he had one, which of course he hadn't, for being a dashing bachelor he lived in a set of rooms in Jermyn Street and was looked after by a very proper gentleman's gentleman.

And now, she thought, she was proposing to repeat the same folly over Mr. Redmayne, who had been so kind to her but probably still thought of her in exactly the same way as he had when she had been Mr. Smith, and who was, besides, head-over-ears in love with Corinna Mayfield.

"If you had an *ounce* of pride," she told herself, as she looked at herself in her dressing-table mirror and dragged a comb so vengefully through her dark, silky curls that it made her eyes water, "you wouldn't keep falling in love with men who are in love with Corinna Mayfield!"

But her reflections were interrupted at this moment by the entrance of Hilliard, who exclaimed in scandalised tones at the damage she was doing to the coiffure *à la Ariane* she had devised for her.

"I don't care!" said Elyza, rounding upon her in a way that made Sarah, her own abigail, stare, for not even from Mrs. Winlock would Hilliard take what the staff was accustomed to denominate as "sauce." "I shall wear my hair just as I choose! *And* I shan't go about any longer dressed like a Christmas pudding to please Mrs. Winlock; it may be the highest kick of fashion, but it does not suit me in the least! I shall wear the blossom muslin tonight, but before I do, Sarah shall snip all that *odious* Berlin floss trimming off it."

Upon hearing this piece of *lèse-majesté* Sarah fully expected the heavens to fall and earthquakes and floods to occur. But to her amazement Hilliard, who prided herself upon her taste and had for some time been aware of an uneasy feeling that her employer had been going quite the wrong way about it in her attempts to make her young ward appear to advantage, did a complete volte-face and said there might be some sense in what miss said, and she would take the matter in hand herself.

The result, after a quarter hour of concentrated effort, was a simple, almost unadorned frock of palest pink muslin in which Sarah enthusiastically declared miss looked a real picture, and even Hilliard, surveying an Elyza whose small, elegantly formed figure and piquant, vivid face were for the first time unobscured by the ornamentation decreed by fashion, said with a rather sour hint of a smile that miss might set a new mode, she looked so well. Mrs. Winlock, entering in exasperated search of Hilliard, was less complimentary, but when they went downstairs a few minutes later Elyza had the satisfaction of seeing male admiration written large upon Colonel Hanley's florid, foolish face, and suddenly wondered if she was going to have a much better time this evening, unrequited love aside, than she had ever had at a ball before.

Any further doubts she might have entertained on this score were laid to rest a short time later, when she entered the Assembly-rooms of the Castle Inn. The rooms—as she might have seen had she looked about her with any attention—were spacious and elegant, having been designed by John Crunden, a disciple of the famous Robert Adam, and they were already thronged with as fashionable a company as might have been seen at any London *ton* party during the Season. But Elyza had eyes for none of this. Instead, her gaze had flown at once to where Redmayne, in a long-tailed coat of Bath superfine and satin knee-breeches, stood near the door, scanning the new arrivals, and she greeted him radiantly as he at once came up to her party.

"Good evening, Mrs. Winlock," he said, bestowing upon that lady his rare and extraordinary smile, which had the effect of melting slightly even her hauteur. "I have come, as you see, to claim my dance with Miss Leigh."

Mrs. Winlock said something suitably gracious, and asked if she might present Colonel Hanley. The Colonel, who considered that he had brushed tolerably well through his first meeting with Elyza following his recent encounter with her as Mr. Smith, rather boggled the matter now, upon being required to greet Redmayne as if he had never laid eyes upon him before, and jibbed even more noticeably as Mr. Crawfurd came up and joined the group.

"Whatever is the matter with you, Dorsey?" Mrs. Winlock enquired, as she watched Redmayne lead Elyza into the set. "You act as if you expected the constable to take you up at any moment." To his relief she did not wait for a reply and continued instead, "Do you know anything about that young man? He has taken the Duke of Bellairs' house for the summer, which seems to me to mean that he is either quite mad or as rich as Croesus. One of those huge Indian fortunes, I daresay. I wonder what his family is. You must have noted that he seems quite taken with Elyza; he was obviously on the look-out for her arrival, and I am obliged to admit that she is in looks tonight. Still I daresay it is quite useless to hope for anything in *that* direction; he will have half the females in Brighton setting their caps at him if he is as rich as he appears to be. And at any rate, Sir Edward is much more the sort of man to satisfy Sir Robert, and *he* will be making his offer tomorrow."

Meanwhile, Elyza, having been led into the set by Redmayne, sternly quelled the feeling of dizzy happiness that gave her the unusual and highly agreeable feeling of being alone with him upon a lovely pink cloud, surrounded by a magical aura of candlelight and music, and said to him with great propriety, "I am so glad you asked me to dance, because I have never had an opportunity to thank you properly for all you did for me! It all worked out *quite* successfully, and I shall pay you back for everything as soon as I have got my next quarter's allowance."

Redmayne looked faintly amused and, with a slight, warning glance at the dancers beside them, said they might discuss all that at some more suitable time.

"How do you like Brighton?" he asked her, forestalling what was obviously going to be an attempt upon her part to continue the subject, for he already appeared to have grasped a point of her character that had frequently driven her aunt Phoebe and her great-aunt Sephestia almost to desperation—that is, her reluctance to give up on a matter once she had got her teeth into it—and seemed quite able to cope with it in his usual negligently good-humoured manner.

Elyza said she thought she was going to like it much better than London.

"Especially since you and Mr. Crawfurd are here," she confided. "You can't imagine how much better it made me feel about things when he came to call upon us this morning, and later when I saw both of you at Donaldson's Library. It made everything seem *quite* different than it was in London!"

"What beats me is how you can have managed to

85

make such a mull of it there!" Redmayne said, looking with critical approval at the very attractive picture she presented in the blossom-pink gown. "You're a deuced pretty girl, you know, when you're not trying to pass yourself off as a grubby schoolboy! What about that slow-top of a suitor of yours—Mottram, is it? Has he turned up here yet?"

"No, but he is coming tomorrow to pay his addresses to me, Mrs. Winlock says," Elyza replied, for some reason not finding this prospect nearly so frightening as she had in London.

"Well, send him to the right-about," Redmayne recommended. "And if your Mrs. Winlock begins to give you a bear-garden jaw over it, walk out of the room. She can't *make* you marry him, you know."

He broke off abruptly. Elyza was standing at the moment with her back to the door, but, looking into his face, she knew as surely as if she had had eyes in the back of her head exactly what had just taken place behind her. Corinna Mayfield had arrived in the Assembly-rooms.

And what, pray, is that to you? she asked herself severely. But still she felt her suddenly dampened spirits revive a little as she saw the Marquis of Belfort, standing at the opposite side of the room in conversation with Miss Piercebridge, who never missed any sort of social event and made terrifying inroads upon the refreshments at all of them, suddenly excuse himself and go quickly towards the door. Certainly Corinna, with suitors like the rich, handsome (though perhaps rather middle-aged) Marquis and the dashing Mr. Jack Everet to choose from, might decide to bestow her favours on someone other than an unknown admirer from India, no matter how handsome and fabulously wealthy he was.

But the unknown admirer from India, she soon discovered, had no intention of not at least putting his fate to the touch.

"There is Miss Mayfield just come in," he observed, in a voice she recognised as being just a shade too carefully casual. "May I ask you to introduce me to her when the set is over?"

"Yes, certainly!" Elyza said, and put so much false cordiality into her voice that she was certain he would immediately see that she hated Miss Mayfield and would like to scratch her eyes out. No man, she was quite sure, having only seen her, Elyza Leigh, from afar, would carry the memory of her in his heart for two whole years, exactly like the hero in a romance, and then grow pale with emotion at the moment when his eyes fell upon her again. She could not, of course, be precisely sure that Redmayne *had* grown pale, because he was too deeply tanned for it to show if he had, but he looked, she thought, suitably moved and determined — though those emotions, too, owing to the odd inscrutability he seemed to have trained his square, handsome face to express even in moments of stress, she had chiefly to take upon faith.

In a perfect world, she thought, the music would never have ended and she and Redmayne would have gone on dancing together all evening, while Corinna Mayfield was obliged to remain standing on the sidelines in the growing circle of her admirers; but even Brighton in the season was not the perfect world. All too soon the music wound to a close, and Elyza unwillingly walked across the floor towards Miss Mayfield with Redmayne at her side. Corinna, who was looking an enchanting fairy princess that evening in a diaphanous spider-gauze gown strewn with silver spangles, was laughing at the moment at something Lord Belfort had whispered in her ear, and, glancing up, found herself face to face with Redmayne and Elyza. There was a queer little silence, during which Redmayne looked at Corinna and Corinna, with a suddenly arrested expression upon her own lovely face, looked at Redmayne.

"Good evening, Miss Mayfield. May I — may I present Mr. Redmayne?" Elyza said, hoping she did not look as peculiar as she felt.

But she need not have troubled herself about this, for no one was paying the least attention to her. The attention of Miss Mayfield's entire court, in fact, was riveted upon Miss Mayfield herself, who gave a rather breathless, uncertain little laugh as she looked into Redmayne's intent blue eyes.

"Mr. Redmayne," she said. "Is it absolutely true that *you* are the gentleman who has taken the Duke of Bellairs' house? Do you know no one has been talking of anything else all day? I am quite *petrified* with happiness to meet you!"

There were a few rather supercilious smiles exchanged among the gentlemen. Redmayne's eyes flickered over them for a moment and then returned to their steady scrutiny of Corinna's face.

"May I have the honour of standing up with you for this dance, Miss Mayfield?" he said, with his slightly overelaborate formality of manner.

Corinna gave her enchanting little laugh once more, and turned, as if in appeal, to the group about her.

"But, my dear Mr. Redmayne," she said, "here are five gentlemen—no, is it six?—all of whom have been beforehand of you! How can I possibly—?"

"You can possibly," Redmayne said coolly, "because I have been waiting for two years to dance with you, Miss Mayfield."

"For two years!" Corinna looked incredulous but not ill pleased by his audacity. "No, I can't believe that! You are hoaxing me! You have only just come from India, have you not?"

"Yes, but I was in England two years ago and saw you then," Redmayne said. "I shall tell you all about it while we dance."

And as the orchestra struck up the first strains of a waltz he took her hand and drew her gently towards the floor. She cast a glance of helpless, roguish apology at the others, allowed him to slip his arm about her waist, and glided off with him into the waltz.

"Who *is* that fellow?" Mr. Everet, who had been one of the disappointed contenders for the place Redmayne had so cavalierly taken, demanded of the company at large. He was a tall, well-set-up young man, the cadet of a noble family, whose handsome face and dashing reputation both as a Non-pareil in the sporting world and a *chevalier aux dames* had already turned the heads of many young ladies besides the innocent Miss Elyza Leigh's; but during the Season just past his attentions had been directed exclusively towards Miss Mayfield.

His chief rival for that young lady's hand, the Marquis of Belfort, was looking at Redmayne and Miss Mayfield now, his long, dark face saturnine and thoughtful.

"Apparently," he said, "he is a young nabob. But I believe — yes, I do believe I shall have to make a few enquiries."

This statement, slightly sinister-sounding to anyone who knew the Marquis and his usual manner of dealing quite ruthlessly with anyone who stood in his way — and even to Elyza, who did not — was sufficient to produce a faint chill down the spine; but, fortunately for Elyza's peace of mind, Mr. Crawfurd came up at that moment and asked if he might have the pleasure of waltzing with her.

"Cleve — that is, Mr. Redmayne — told me it might be a good idea if I asked you to dance with me several times tonight," he informed her, as they moved off together. Elyza stiffened indignantly. "Here!" said Mr. Crawfurd hastily. "Don't fly up into the boughs. Very happy to dance with you — very happy, indeed! The only thing is, I ain't in the petticoat line, you know! No need for you to go getting ideas —"

Elyza, her irritation vanishing as rapidly as it had come, gave a gurgle of laughter at the sight of his perturbed face.

"No, indeed!" she said. "I promise you I shan't do so! I don't at all wish to be married, you know, but I *should* like you to dance with me, if you please! It is so horrid to be obliged to sit down while everyone else is dancing!"

Mr. Crawfurd, glancing down into his partner's piquant face, which was looking remarkably charming and even happy in spite of her having been convinced only a few minutes before that her heart was broken, said he didn't see why she should have to sit down if fellows had eyes in their heads, and put his opinion to the test at the conclusion of the waltz by introducing to her a pair of young officers from the Cavalry barracks situated just outside the town on the Lewes road, with whom he had become acquainted that afternoon. Each of them promptly asked her to stand up with him for the country dance that was to follow, and she accepted the one who, she decided, after a good deal of laughing argument, had started to speak first, promising the next dance to the other. Mrs. Winlock, who had begun to look around for Colonel Hanley to ask him, as usual, to dance with Elyza so that the girl wouldn't look an utter wallflower, was astonished to find her ward passing from one smart young officer to another, the transfer's not being permitted to be made, however, before the first had exacted a promise that he would be accorded another dance before the evening was over.

After this Mr. Crawfurd reappeared dutifully upon the scene and, as success breeds success, found that he had to stand in line, so to speak, for a second dance with Elyza, for she seemed to have collected around her the entire Cavalry barracks — all young men intent upon nothing but having a good time, who would not have cared a button, even had they known of it, about her being the Product of a Misalliance. To say the truth, she had at last, thanks to Redmayne and Mr. Crawfurd, but also to some extent to her consciousness that for the first time, with her cropped head and unadorned gown, she was appearing to advantage, stepped out of her shell of shyness and contrariness, and the result, as Mrs. Winlock herself remarked in some astonishment to Miss Piercebridge, was quite extraordinary.

"Of course it *means* nothing," she said disparagingly. "I always say it is a great mistake to quarter troops so near a fashionable watering-place, for they *will* attend all the balls and, as they have no local connexions or serious intentions, are apt to pay attention to the first young lady who takes their fancy and quite turn her head."

Miss Piercebridge, who had never in her life had her head turned by anyone, in or out of uniform, said rather spitefully that young girls were very foolish and, if she were in her dear Agatha's place, she would Speak to Elyza for her own good. As Mrs. Winlock had already determined to do this, she made no difficulties about agreeing with her friend, after which they both fell upon Colonel Hanley, who had come up to enquire if Mrs. Winlock would like to dance the quadrille, as the only presently available representative of the perfidious and unreliable male sex, and gave him a very bad time indeed until the music struck up again.

Chapter Eight

Meanwhile, Elyza, in spite of enjoying to the full the heady wine of her first success, had not failed to note that Miss Mayfield had granted Redmayne no fewer than three dances before the evening was yet half over. She was, of course, not the only one who observed this fact, which was the more remarkable because Corinna had been most carefully brought up and, in spite of her great popularity with the male sex, had never previously allowed herself to behave towards any of them in such a way as to bring down censorious comments upon herself.

Lord Belfort, who was far too experienced a hand at the game of love to wear his heart upon his sleeve, showed his annoyance at Miss Mayfield's unusual conduct merely by looking more indifferent than usual and making several cleverly derogatory remarks about the value of a large fortune when one wished to make one's way into Society. But Mr. Everet, who was neither so mature nor so well accustomed to concealing his emotions as Lord Belfort, looked more and more like a thundercloud as the evening progressed, made himself conspicuous by refusing to dance with anyone but Miss Mayfield, quarrelled with her all through the quadrille, and at last, looking thoroughly furious, posted himself in a prominent position against the wall and stood with folded arms, following every move his inamorata made with jealous eyes.

It so happened that Elyza, having just enjoyed a set of country dances with one of her young officers, had sat down near Mr. Everet's station to rest for a moment and fan her flushed face while her partner went off to the refreshment saloon to procure a glass of iced lemonade for her. In her London days it would have been inconceivable that she should be in such close proximity to her then idol without being exceedingly conscious of it, but this evening she had scarcely noticed the handsome young Corinthian, and was considerably startled when, upon hearing a sudden fierce exclamation behind her, she glanced around and saw him standing a few feet away from her. As there was no one else in their immediate proximity she could only conclude that the words were addressed to her, and enquired in a rather puzzled voice, "What did you say?"

"She is dancing with him again!" said Mr. Everet, grinding his teeth and obviously quite unaware to whom he was speaking. "Damnation! I shall—"

He took a hasty step forward, but was startled in his turn when Elyza jumped up and impetuously laid her hand upon his arm.

"Oh no, pray don't!" she exclaimed. He halted, looking down at her, frowning. "That is—I mean—if you are thinking of quarrelling with Mr. Redmayne—" Elyza went on, her voice faltering as she suddenly realised what she was doing. She removed her hand from Mr. Everet's sleeve as abruptly as if she had found it red-hot and stammered, "I—I beg your pardon, but I couldn't help hearing—"

Mr. Everet looked for a moment as if he were about to say, "What the devil business is it of yours?" or something equally unceremonious, but recollected himself and instead said rather stiffly, "I beg *your* pardon, Miss—Leigh, is it? We *have* met, I believe?"

"Oh, yes—at Almack's. Lady Sefton introduced us, but I expect you do not recall it," said Elyza, feeling rather amazed to remember how she had cried herself to sleep one night not a month before because Mr. Everet had walked past her in the corridor of the Drury Lane Theatre with a complete lack of recognition on the evening after that memorable occasion. "And—and you *did* say something just now," she went on defensively, "and as there is no one else about, I thought it was to me—"

Mr. Everet, suddenly becoming acutely conscious that he was not behaving in the cool, ironical, and detached manner of a Brummell in the face of this crisis, all at once became superbly cool, ironical, and detached and said no doubt he had and he begged her forgiveness.

"Well, there is no need for you to do *that*," said Elyza, "unless, that is, you are thinking of quarrelling with Mr. Redmayne because he is dancing so often with Miss Mayfield. That would be *quite* unfair, you know, because after all he could not dance with her if she did not wish him to—could he?"

Mr. Everet, becoming slightly less cool, ironical,

and detached, said rather dismally that he dared say not.

"And I expect he cannot stop asking her to, because she is so very beautiful," Elyza continued ruthlessly. "Dozens of gentlemen keep asking her to dance with them at every ball, and I don't suppose any of them stops after she has danced with him once, or even twice."

Mr. Everet, who had himself importuned Miss Mayfield on more than one occasion to favour him with a third dance after she had granted him two, felt himself being forced into a corner and was obliged to admit that they did not.

"Well, then!" said Elyza triumphantly. "You see how unfair it would be for you to quarrel with Mr. Redmayne. If I were you," she added kindly, "I should simply disregard it. It is by far the best way, for I have often noticed that nothing sets a girl up so much as seeing that a gentleman is jealous of another gentleman's attentions to her. And then, of course, she behaves twice as badly to him as she did before."

Mr. Everet said with some heat that Miss Mayfield, who was perfection personified, would never act in such a reprehensible manner.

"Well, no, I expect she would not," said Elyza soothingly. "But all the same, I should not let her see I was jealous if I were you. It would be much better for you to ask some other young lady to dance, you know, than to let her see you standing here looking so miserable and disagreeable."

At that very moment Miss Mayfield whirled by in Redmayne's arms, her silver-spangled draperies floating out almost to touch Mr. Everet tantalisingly as she passed. Mr. Everet, goaded to desperation, said hastily, "Very well. *Very well!* I shall! Will *you* dance with me, Miss Leigh?"

And before Elyza well knew what he was about he had seized her in his arms and swept her out onto the floor, leaving her young officer, who had just come up with a glass of lemonade in his hand, to stare after her aggrievedly.

For a few moments Elyza, her small gloved hand resting upon Mr. Everet's broad shoulder, his strong arm masterfully clasping her waist, forgot Redmayne, Corinna Mayfield, and everything else and became the Elyza of the dark London days, who had never attracted so much as a glance from the handsome, popular, famous Mr. Jack Everet, and now suddenly found herself miraculously whirling about a ballroom floor in his arms.

I am dancing that Mr. Everet! I am dancing with Mr. Everet! the blissful thought repeated itself in her mind to the gay, lilting cadences of the waltz. She felt like a feather blown about the room in his arms, and in the intoxication of the moment she did not even see Redmayne's face bent close to Corinna's as they circled past, or the expression in his blue eyes as he looked down at her.

Mr. Everet, however, was not so unobservant.

"There they are again," he said, in a tone that gave Elyza the distinct impression that if he was not once more grinding his teeth it was only out of deference to his partner. "Who *is* that fellow Redmayne, Miss Leigh? I believe it was you who introduced him to Corinna, was it not? Have you known him long?"

Elyza, coming down to earth sufficiently to realise

that Mr. Everet was addressing her, recollected herself in time not to admit to any extensive knowledge of Redmayne and said she had been acquainted with him only since that morning, when he had been introduced to her by a mutual friend.

"He has just returned to England from India, I believe, and has taken the Duke of Bellairs' house on the Steyne for the season," she continued, and then, remembering Redmayne's conversation with Colonel Hanley at the fair, said inspirationally, "I believe he is related to the Kerslakes."

"The Kerslakes? Never heard of them," declared Mr. Everet. "And at any rate, no matter who he is related to, it appears to me there is something decidedly *off* about him. Freddy Mandry says he had an Indian servant in full costume following him around the town like a dashed bodyguard this morning."

Elyza would have liked to say indignantly that there was nothing in the least *off* about Mr. Redmayne, but restrained herself, and instead said rather tartly that if Mr. Everet really wished to set Corinna's back up he had only to begin abusing Mr. Redmayne to *her* in that fashion. She then felt like a traitor, because if she gave advice to Mr. Everet on how to remain in Corinna's good graces she was certainly doing a disservice to Redmayne. But such is the perversity of human nature, particularly when it is in the throes of unrequited love, that she told herself in a very Machiavellian way that if Corinna did not prefer Redmayne in spite of anything Mr. Everet might do, she did not deserve him, and therefore whatever she, Elyza, did to aid and abet Mr. Everet, it could really not be considered wrong.

Carried away by the beauty of this logic, she went on to say firmly to Mr. Everet that she had not the least doubt that Corinna had merely been swept off her feet by Redmayne, and that in a few weeks she would probably have forgotten all about him.

"That is, if you don't do anything idiotish in the meantime, such as forcing a quarrel upon him," she said. "Isn't there some other young lady you could pay attention to for a week or two, so that Corinna will see you do not care a button if she dances with Mr. Redmayne or not?"

Mr. Everet said gloomily that the thing of it was that he *did* care a button, and what was more, if he began paying particular attentions to some other girl he would dashed soon find himself in a bumblebath of another sort. Upon Elyza's looking at him enquiringly, he said succinctly, "Marriage!"

"Oh!" said Elyza. "Do you mean they would expect you to—?"

"Yes," said Mr. Everet simply. "That's the deuce of making up to girls. Their mamas don't care for me— I'm too rackety by half to suit them—but girls get ideas into their heads, and then they make tiresome scenes, and—" He seemed to realise abruptly that these revelations were scarcely suitable for Elyza's ears and said austerely, "Well, that is neither here nor there, after all. May I compliment you upon your dancing, Miss Leigh? I have seldom had a more adept partner."

"Oh, thank you!" said Elyza, gratified. "I have not had very much practice, but I do so enjoy it, and the dancing-master my great-aunt procured for me in Bath said I had a great deal of aptitude. But about

99

Corinna," she persisted, with her usual refusal to be deflected from the end in view. "I suppose it would not serve if you paid court to a married lady, because Corinna would know at once then that you were only—I mean that what you had in mind was—was merely—"

Mr. Everet, grinning suddenly, said, here, what would *her* mama say if she heard her talking like that?

"Oh, I haven't got a mama," said Elyza. "There is only Mrs. Winlock, who takes me about, and she couldn't possibly think any worse of me than she already does, no matter what I said." She considered for a moment, and then said abruptly, "I'll tell you what: if you like, you can make up to me, Mr. Everet. I shouldn't in the least expect you to marry me, because, you see, I"—she hesitated, with a sudden odd feeling that she was about to say something of great importance to her whole future life, a feeling that rather surprised her, for in spite of having cried herself to sleep the night Mr. Everet had not recognised her at Drury Lane, she had certainly experienced nothing like this then—"you see," she repeated, "I am already in love with someone else."

"Are you, indeed!" said Mr. Everet, a trifle startled to hear this frank admission from a young lady, and gazing down at his partner for the first time with some attention. As the result of this examination it occurred to him that he had certainly been in error in dismissing Miss Leigh as a shy, rather awkward little creature, always lurking in corners and without a word to say for herself. The Miss Leigh with whom he was dancing tonight was not a beauty in the sense that Corinna Mayfield was, with her cameo profile and silver-gilt hair; but she was certainly an attractive little thing, elegantly gowned, with a pair of enormous dark eyes set in dark-fringed lids and apparently a highly original mind, to say nothing of being the best dancer he had had the privilege of waltzing with for many a month. "Who," continued Mr. Everet, meaning every word he said, "is the lucky man?"

"Oh, I shan't tell you *that!*" said Elyza, colouring up. "I only said it so you would be sure I wouldn't be like the others if you were to show a particular interest in me for a few weeks. But of course if you don't wish to—"

"On the contrary," said Mr. Everet, casting a vengeful glance at Miss Mayfield and Redmayne as they again revolved into view, "I think it may be an excellent idea! But what about *your* young man? Isn't *he* likely to be jealous?"

"I only wish he might be," said Elyza candidly, "but to tell you the truth, I don't think he will mind in the least. You see, mine is what might be called a Hopeless Passion." She tried to look suitably mournful, but found it so difficult, what with her enjoyment of the waltz and the excitement of actually dancing with Mr. Everet, that she gave it up. "No," she said judiciously, after a moment, "I think it is very likely that the only person who will resent it at all will be Sir Edward Mottram, because he is to make me an offer tomorrow and of course I shall refuse him, and he *may* take it into his head that it is because of you. But I expect he will not do anything but stand about looking grave and censorious."

"Mottram? I should think not!" said Mr. Everet scornfully. He looked down at her curiously. "Do you tell me *he* has a *tendre* for you?" he enquired. "That is odd! I mean—you scarcely seem the sort of girl—"

"Oh no, I am not in the least the sort of girl he admires!" Elyza agreed cordially. "It is only his mama who wishes him to marry me, and *she* does not admire me, either, only I am to have quite a large dowry, you see, and they are very much purse-pinched—I daresay I ought not to have said that!" she broke off, suddenly conscience-stricken by her frankness.

Mr. Everet assured her that it did not matter in the least, as everyone knew the Mottrams hadn't a feather to fly with, and added that he would be willing to lay odds on it that she could do better than Edward Mottram.

"Oh, do you think so?" said Elyza, tremendously pleased by this tribute from her former idol, and on the crest of the wave of euphoria engendered by it found the music ending, and herself and Mr. Everet, by the peculiar machinations of Fate, standing directly beside Redmayne and Corinna.

It would have required a far less acute observer than either Elyza or Mr. Everet, with their perceptions sharpened by the pangs of jealous love, not to have noticed that both Redmayne and Miss Mayfield appeared to be in a state of peculiar exhilaration and even exaltation. There was, in fact, an almost dazed expression upon Redmayne's bronzed face, as if he could not quite believe in his own good fortune, while Corinna, appearing quite unconscious of Mr. Everet's scarcely encouraging expression, invited him

102

to share her pleasure in the remarkable fact that Mr. Redmayne, having seen her once two years before, had never forgotten her, and in fact had come to Brighton now solely in the hope of meeting her.

"It was at Harrogate," she said, "before I was out. Mama took me there that summer because I had had scarlet fever and the waters are said to be very healthful, but I found them quite revolting and Harrogate the dullest place imaginable. And I can *almost* remember him, too, because he says he was staying at the same hotel and picked up my sunshade once when I had dropped it. Isn't that extraordinary?"

Mr. Everet, with what he apparently hoped was an air of complete detachment, said he didn't see anything so very extraordinary about a fellow's picking up a lady's sunshade when she had dropped it.

"Sort of thing anyone would do," he said, eyeing Redmayne with disfavour, and then, recollecting himself, resumed his detached air and asked Elyza if he might have the pleasure of standing up with her for another dance before the evening was over.

"Perhaps the boulanger—?" he suggested.

Elyza gladly accepted, and Corinna, finding herself in the unusual position of being obliged to recall to Mr. Everet's mind the fact that she was engaged to him for the set of country dances just then forming, went off with him, leaving Redmayne to return Elyza to her chaperon.

Instead of performing this duty, however, he asked her to stand up with him, and upon her agreeing with some alacrity, enquired rather absently how she was getting on.

"Splendidly!" said Elyza. "I have danced every

dance!"

But her boast, she saw with a sinking heart, fell upon deaf ears. Redmayne, it seemed, had not even heard it; his eyes were fixed upon Corinna, standing farther down the set with Mr. Everet, and there was an expression in his eyes very like that of a man who, after years of searching for a fabulous gold mine, suddenly finds its treasures poured into his lap.

"She really is the—the most wonderful—What I mean to say is, isn't she the loveliest—?" he began suddenly, obviously quite unconscious that he was talking to anyone but himself.

"If you mean Corinna Mayfield, of course she is. Everyone knows *that*," said Elyza, not very sympathetically, for, though ordinarily a good-tempered girl, she was beginning to find it more than a little trying to have partners who did nothing but sing another girl's praises to her.

Redmayne coloured up suddenly and returned his attention to her with some slight self-consciousness.

"I beg your pardon!" he said. "I'm afraid I wasn't attending."

"Well, I don't mind, really," Elyza said charitably. "Of course you are tremendously excited about seeing her again, after wishing to for all this time. She seemed glad to see you, too," she added, heroically twisting the knife in the wound.

Redmayne's face brightened with elation. "Oh—do you think so?" he said. "I thought—I wasn't sure—"

"Of course she was," Elyza said firmly. "Mr. Everet noticed it at once. He is *quite* jealous."

Redmayne, making an obvious effort to come down to earth and think and talk of more mundane things, said with a sudden grin that if he was, he had a queer way of showing it, for it had seemed to him a few moments ago that Mr. Everet had been more interested in the partner he was just relinquishing than in the one with whom he was walking off.

"Oh, no!" said Elyza, blushing guiltily as she remembered the conspiracy into which she had entered with Mr. Everet, and which, if the truth had to be told, she herself had instigated.

But she comforted herself once more with the thought of Miss Mayfield's potential unworthiness as a bride for Redmayne if she did not perceive how infinitely he was to be preferred over Mr. Everet, no matter how much jealous-making attention Mr. Everet bestowed upon another young lady; and as she found it more than a little exhilarating to display to Redmayne the fact that a Nonpareil of Mr. Everet's standing was paying court to her, she managed to gloss over her traitorous behaviour very satisfactorily in her own mind and even to enjoy to the fullest the remainder of the ball.

Chapter Nine

By the end of what had begun as a very ordinary
ball at the Castle Inn Assembly-rooms that evening it
was perfectly plain to all the members of the *ton* that
two rather extraordinary events had occurred during
the four or five hours of its duration. In the first
place, Corinna Mayfield, obviously smitten to an extent that she had probably never felt and had certainly never displayed before, had transferred her
favour from Mr. Jack Everet to a totally unknown
young man from India, who appeared to have
dropped from nowhere endowed with all the gold of
Croesus. And in the second place Mr. Jack Everet,
far from appearing to resent this fact, had begun to
pay violent court to Miss Elyza Leigh, who seemed
suddenly to have blossomed from a shy girl no one
could remember into a dashing young charmer with
her own coterie of admirers.

"It is the dowry, I expect," Mrs. Winlock said disparagingly over her morning chocolate to Miss
Piercebridge, who, as she frequently did after a ball,
had come to talk over the events of the previous

evening. "Everyone knows that Jack Everet is all to pieces, and as he seems to be making no progress in carrying off Corinna Mayfield, no doubt he has come to the conclusion that he will try for easier game. Which makes me all the more thankful that Edward Mottram is to make his offer in form without delay. That tiresome girl is already sufficiently contrary, without having her head turned by being made the object of the gallantries of a man like Jack Everet."

Miss Piercebridge, drawing her black eyebrows together over her nose, said that for her part she would always pity a girl who was foolish enough to encourage the attentions of a rake, and was going on to recite a heart-rending account of a young lady of her acquaintance who had been led astray and ultimately abandoned by one of those monsters in pleasing masculine form when a heavy rap on the knocker was heard.

Miss Piercebridge and Mrs. Winlock exchanged pregnant glances.

"Sir Edward?" whispered Miss Piercebridge conspiratorially.

"I should certainly think so," said Mrs. Winlock. "Will you excuse me, Adelina?"

She hurried upstairs, where she found Elyza, who had breakfasted in her bedchamber on chocolate and rolls, engaged with Hilliard, who was trying the effect upon her of an azure-blue promenade frock from which she had ruthlessly removed its yards of silk braid trimming.

"Heavens! What have you done to that dress?" said Mrs. Winlock, in high disapproval. "But it cannot signify now. Elyza, you must go down to the drawing

107

room at once! Sir Edward is come. And I *do* hope you will remember what your papa expects of you. I wish to hear of no missish temporisings or refusals! Sir Edward is an excellent *parti,* and I am sure you should be exceedingly grateful that he is doing you the honour of paying his addresses to you."

Elyza, like the soldier hearing the long-anticipated summons to battle, had turned slightly pale at Mrs. Winlock's words, but, remembering Redmayne's statement that, after all, no one could *make* her marry Sir Edward, merely said in a quite calm voice that of course she would see Sir Edward. She then allowed Hilliard to put the finishing touches on her coiffure and walked down the steps behind Mrs. Winlock, who entered the drawing room and greeted Sir Edward with the greatest cordiality.

"Good morning, Edward! So you have arrived in Brighton at last! I am sure I know someone" — with an arch glance at Elyza — "who has been counting the hours! And how is your dear mama? Eliza, come and make your curtsey to Sir Edward!"

Sir Edward, a very tall, thin, serious young man who looked at the moment as if he wished he were dead, managed a rather ghastly smile, hastily transferring the large bouquet he was holding from his right hand to his left and taking Elyza's small, slightly trembling fingers in his own clammy clasp. He then again transferred the posy to his right hand and stood looking at it with as much terrified indecision as if it had sprouted there that instant and he could not think what to do with it.

"What lovely flowers!" said Mrs. Winlock encouragingly. "For Elyza? How charming of you, Edward!

I shall just go and see that they are put into water."

And taking the bouquet from Sir Edward's nerveless fingers, she walked out of the room, leaving the unfortunate couple alone.

Eliza, who had decided on the way downstairs that the best thing she could do would be to allow Sir Edward to make his offer and have it over with once and for all, recovered first from the shock of realising that the dread moment was now upon them and asked her suitor to sit down. He thanked her and made as if to do so, but then, apparently determining, as she had, to face the peril from which he could not fly, suddenly coloured up all over his preternaturally serious face and trod towards her across the carpet.

"M-may I say how h-happy I am, Miss Leigh," he stammered, obviously reciting a set speech, "to see you so well recovered from your indisposition? I have missed our almost daily encounters in London; indeed, I may say, with the poet, that absence m-makes the heart grow — grow —"

"Fonder," said Elyza in desperation, seeing that Sir Edward, over whom the sudden horrid realisation had evidently come that he was actually launched upon his declaration, had grown quite incapable of completing his sentence.

"Fonder," repeated Sir Edward, gritting his teeth and proceeding. "For I had not previously, I believe, understood the — the *d-depth* of my f-feeling for you, Miss Leigh!"

And at this point, apparently also by prearranged plan, he plunged forward and was in the act of flinging himself upon his knees before her when Satterlee's tall, portly figure suddenly loomed in the doorway.

"Mr. Crawfurd!" announced that imperturbable functionary, looking as bland and disinterested as if the sight of a scarlet-faced young baronet scrambling hastily back to his feet from a reverential position before Miss Leigh's chair was a sight he was accustomed to viewing every day in the week. To say the truth, however, as he confessed later to Mrs. Bradden, the housekeeper, it had given him such a turn that, being of a sensitive disposition, he had almost swooned dead away. He had expected, he explained to her, to find both Mrs. Winlock and Miss Elyza in the drawing room with Sir Edward, having unfortunately failed to see the Missus leave that apartment, owing to having been summoned to sit in judgement upon the slapdash way the pantry boy had polished the knives, so that he had naturally had no inkling that a scene involving the Tender Passion was being played out upon the drawing-room stage.

"If I had been kept *oh currant* of the situation, as they say in France," he remarked, in dignified disapproval of this lapse on the part of his usual informants among the lower echelons of the staff, "I should of course have detained the other young gentleman below. As it was, it was too late. Miss was obliged to request me to show Mr. Crawfurd upstairs, and if she never becomes Lady Mottram I fear there are those of us belowstairs who will forever have it upon our consciences."

Meanwhile, Elyza, quite unaware of the shock she had given Satterlee's sensibilities, saw Mr. Crawfurd enter the room with all the gratitude of a condemned

110

criminal for a messenger bearing a reprieve, for in spite of her good resolutions to have the inevitable scene with Sir Edward over with, she found herself grasping in a very cowardly fashion at the opportunity to postpone it. When Mr. Crawfurd came in she greeted him effusively, and accepted the enormous bouquet of roses he bore with exclamations of pleasure that caused Sir Edward, remembering her far cooler reception of his own tribute, to regard him jealously. It was not that Sir Edward, in less stressful moments, would have cared a rush whether Miss Leigh preferred Mr. Crawfurd's posies to his or not, but when a man has nerved himself to make a proposal of marriage to a young lady, it is naturally somewhat irritating to him to find her preferring the offerings of another man.

Sir Edward glared at Mr. Crawfurd. Mr. Crawfurd, who had never met him and had not the least notion that he had interrupted what Satterlee had termed a scene involving the Tender Passion, looked puzzled and enquiring. Finally Elyza, glancing up at the two of them from the roses in which she had buried her face, came to a somewhat belated realisation of her responsibilities as a hostess and said, "Oh! I daresay you do not know each other! Sir Edward Mottram — Mr. Crawfurd."

The two young men exchanged bows, exceedingly stiff upon Sir Edward's part and somewhat startled upon Mr. Crawfurd's. Now that Sir Edward had been made known to him, he recalled Redmayne's having explained to him that the reason for Miss Leigh's appearance on the Bath Road as Mr. Smith had been a desperate attempt upon her part to escape the attentions of a young baronet whom she was being importuned to marry against her will. Undoubtedly, he thought, this must be the man, which explained his having found Elyza alone with him, and also the obvious air of mingled discomposure and relief in her welcome to him.

Mr. Crawfurd, no hero but a true champion of a damsel in distress, immediately determined to outstay Sir Edward, and settled himself in a chair beside the window with a challenging glance at the obviously less than pleased baronet.

The somewhat halting conversation that ensued did little to make his self-imposed task the easier. When the previous evening's ball had been extensively and somewhat repetitiously commented upon, and Mr. Crawfurd, in the teeth of Sir Edward's marked disapproval, had rallied Elyza in a very man-of-the-world way on her having been singled out for Mr. Everet's particular attentions upon that occasion, no one seemed to have a further subject to introduce. At last Elyza, in desperation, enquired of Mr. Crawfurd if he had yet seen the house Mr. Redmayne had taken.

"Seen it? Oh—didn't you know?" said Mr. Crawfurd, in some surprise. "I am staying there. He wouldn't hear of anything else." He added, in a sudden burst of confidence, "Splendid sort of place, you know. A bit fusty to begin with—marble statues standing about, that sort of affair. But he's brought in a lot of new things. You'll be surprised when you see them."

Elyza said she would love to see them but she didn't quite know how.

"Oh, you'll see them," Mr. Crawfurd assured her. "Believe he's sending out cards of invitation today for an evening-party on Friday. You're sure to get one."

Sir Edward, looking superior, said might he enquire of whom they were speaking.

"Oh, I forgot. You weren't at the ball last night so you didn't meet him," Eliza said, thus innocently causing Sir Edward to formulate more bitter thoughts about the irony of proposing to a girl who hadn't even the decency to remember whether or not she had seen one the evening before. "Well, he is just come from India, and has taken the Duke of Bellairs' house on the Steyne. He is excessively agreeable; I am sure you will like him," she said, upon which Sir Edward immediately determined not to, and to add his name to Mr. Crawfurd's under the heading, *People To Be Avoided.*

Redmayne's value as a conversation piece being effectually ended by the unencouraging silence with which Sir Edward greeted this information, Elyza was racking her brains for another subject when Satterlee once more appeared in the doorway.

"The Honourable Mr. Everet!" he announced, in tones of strong disapproval.

His disapproval, however, had little effect upon the trio in the drawing room, for Eliza looked pleased, Mr. Crawfurd, scenting reinforcements, looked relieved, and only Sir Edward appeared to share his sense of the marked impropriety of yet another gentleman's intruding in this offhand way upon the peculiarly sacred intimacies of a marriage proposal.

Mr. Everet, receiving *via* Satterlee Elyza's cordial invitation to join the company in the drawing room,

113

came in at once, bearing a third floral tribute in the form of a bouquet of carnations in a silver holder.

"Good morning!" he said, bowing over Elyza's hand with the graceful ease that was so much admired in feminine circles, and acknowledging the presence of Mr. Crawfurd and Sir Edward with a careless nod. "I am come to ask if you will do me the honour of driving out with me, Miss Leigh. It's the deuce of a fine morning, and I have my curricle outside."

"Oh," said Eliza fervently, "I should love to, Mr. Everet! That is," she added punctiliously, once again belatedly recollecting her duties as a hostess, "I shall be very happy to, when — when I am free."

Upon hearing this broad hint, Mr. Crawfurd immediately declared that he was just leaving, but as he was about to rise discovered that Sir Edward, with a mulish expression upon his face, was showing not the least sign of budging from his position and sank back into his chair again. In truth, however, had he known what was going on in the unfortunate baronet's mind he would have pitied rather than censured him, for Sir Edward, having received strict instructions from his mama to make his offer that morning, was terrified of returning to her without having done so, with the inevitable result of a fit of the vapours upon Lady Mottram's part, tearful accusations of his wishing to drive them both into the poorhouse, and dagger-glances cast at him by all the servants as a monster of filial ingratitude.

Mr. Everet, for his part, appeared not a whit cast down by Sir Edward's obstinacy, but took a chair close to Elyza's and said cheerfully that there was no need for haste, as the day promised to remain fine.

At that point Mr. Crawfurd, whose own seat beside the window enabled him to cast an eye over the street below, glanced down and saw the magnificent team Mr. Everet had been driving.

"By Jupiter, are those your chestnuts?" he exclaimed enthusiastically. "What a splendid team! Prime bits of blood, ain't they? Complete to a shade!"

Mr. Everet said negligently that he would back them against any team in town, a statement to which Mr. Crawfurd unexpectedly took exception.

"Fancy I know a team that might beat them," he said diffidently. "Welsh-bred, stand a little over fifteen hands—as bang-up a set-out of blood and bone as you could wish for."

"Indeed?" said Mr. Everet, his brows going up. "And who is the owner of these paragons?"

Mr. Crawfurd said they belonged to a friend of his named Redmayne.

"Had them brought down from London only yesterday," he said. "Hasn't had them long, of course, but if they ain't sixteen-mile-an-hour tits, I miss my guess."

Mr. Everet, whose good spirits seemed to have suffered a sudden check at this introduction of Redmayne's name into the conversation, remarked somewhat uncharitably that to his notion a team of horses was no better than the pair of hands that was driving them, and, never having seen Mr. Redmayne handle the ribbons, he was therefore not in a position to give an opinion on what his horses could do, even if they were all winged Pegasuses.

"I have never," said Sir Edward, entering the conversation at this point out of the outraged feeling that when a man's proposal of marriage had degenerated into a discussion of the merits of various representatives of the equine species it was time for the worm to turn, "I have never, I repeat, been able to understand this mania for speed in transportation. To *my* way of thinking, a steady, reliable pair is far to be preferred, and I flatter myself that the bays I drive answer perfectly to this description." He turned to Elyza. "You, Miss Leigh," he said, "may rely upon it that when I invite you to drive with *me* — which I hereby do — you need be under no apprehension of the sort of accidents that commonly occur in vehicles drawn by what Mr. Crawfurd denominates as prime bits of blood."

Elyza began to say hastily that she must regret not being able to take advantage of Sir Edward's kind invitation, as she had already accepted Mr. Everet's, but was interrupted by the reappearance of Satterlee.

"Mr. Redmayne!" he announced, with the resigned air of a man who finds Fate against him, and so far forgot what was due to his position as to bend a commiserating glance upon Sir Edward.

That unfortunate lover, finding himself now, as it appeared to him, surrounded by a positive horde of lusty young men, all bent upon seeking the favours of his chosen bride, gave up in despair. Flesh and blood, he felt, could bear no more, and he sprang up, making his adieux to Elyza in the tone of a man who strongly feels that he has been unpardonably ill-used, and stalked out of the room, almost colliding with Redmayne in the doorway.

As he descended the staircase he met Mrs.

Winlock, who was coming up, having finally succeeded in getting rid of Miss Piercebridge. At sight of his angry, disappointed face she checked abruptly.

"Sir Edward! You are not leaving?" she said sharply. "What has that tiresome—what has Elyza said to you?"

"She has said n-nothing, ma'am!" said Sir Edward, so overcome by a sense of the ill-usage to which he had been subjected that he forgot his usual punctilious politeness. "And do you know *why* she has said nothing? Because *I* had no opportunity to say anything to *her,* ma'am! I had been under the impression up to this time that Miss Leigh was a quiet, modest young female, not given to keeping—as I understand the saying goes—half a dozen young men dangling at her shoe-strings. But when I find her, on a single morning, entertaining no fewer than *four* male callers in your drawing room, of whom I had the misfortune to be one—"

He broke off as the rat-tat-tat of the knocker sounded again below them. The door was opened by Satterlee, just returned from showing Redmayne upstairs, to reveal a pair of the young Cavalry officers whose acquaintance Elyza had made the night before.

"Is Miss Leigh at home?" they chorussed hopefully, in unison.

Satterlee, bearing up with some difficulty, said he would ascertain and what names should he say? Meanwhile, Mrs. Winlock, with great presence of mind, dragged Sir Edward into a small sitting room opening off the half-landing.

"My dear boy," she said, in tones as soothing as a

very strong-minded female can manage when she is addressing a young man who she feels has made a maddening mull of something that any moderately sensible schoolboy could have managed without difficulty, "you will not, I hope, hold our sweet Elyza responsible for something that the poor child is in no way to blame for? I see you understand what I mean," she went on, though in point of fact Sir Edward's own mother could not have said at that moment that he looked as if he understood anything at all. "Elyza is an heiress. I have always done my best to protect her from the consequences of this fact, and hitherto I believe I may flatter myself that I have been successful. But how, alas! is one always to be able to shield her from the advances of young men whose only interest in her—so unlike *your* genuine feeling for her, dear Edward!—is her fortune?"

Sir Edward looked a trifle mollified, though still very sulky.

"Is that indeed so, ma'am?" he said rather pompously after a moment. "Now that I recollect, I *have* heard it said that Everet is monstrously in the wind, and must marry well to recoup his fortunes."

"Exactly!" said Mrs. Winlock. "I assure you, you have nothing to fear. Elyza, like all young girls, is somewhat volatile, and I will not attempt to deny that she is capable of having her head momentarily turned when she is made the object of the attentions of a young man such as Everet. But the assertion of your own steady attachment, dear Edward, is certain to prevail in the end. Indeed, you must not grow discouraged! Only approach her again at some more suitable time, and you will see that she has, at heart, a genuine appreciation of the solid worth of your character."

Sir Edward, no more immune to flattery than another man, upon this recovered his spirits so far as to preen himself slightly and observe that he *did* rather fancy there was more to him than to a frippery fellow like Jack Everet. Mrs. Winlock, seeing him go off down the stairs a few moments later with a moderately self-satisfied expression upon his face, said, "Idiot!" under her breath, and then turned her attention at once towards the drawing room, from which Elyza at that very moment emerged, bent upon going upstairs to don hat and gloves in preparation for her drive with Mr. Everet. Mrs. Winlock proceeded rapidly up the stairs after her and came upon her in her bedchamber as she was setting a flat-crowned Villager hat of satin straw at a jaunty angle upon her dark curls.

"And where, miss," she enquired awfully, "do you imagine you are going?"

Elyza turned about from the mirror and said she was going for a drive with Mr. Everet, picking up a frivolous little Chinese sunshade as she did so and moving towards the door. Mrs. Winlock barred her way.

"You little fool!" she said acidly. "Do you fancy for one moment that Sir Robert will ever consent to your marrying a man like Jack Everet, who has been under the hatches almost from the moment he came on the town and has gotten himself into every sort of scrape and scandal one could well imagine? If you will whistle Edward Mottram down the wind for *that — !*"

The pretty colour of excitement faded suddenly from Elyza's face, but she said steadily, in an extremely sedate and grown-up tone that surprised her almost as much as it did Mrs. Winlock, "I wish you will understand, ma'am, that I shall *never* marry Sir Edward. It has nothing to do with Mr. Everet; it is only that I do not care for him in the least, and never shall. And now, if you please, Mr. Everet is waiting, and I must say good-bye to Mr. Redmayne and Mr. Crawfurd and the other gentlemen."

She moved again towards the door, and Mrs. Winlock, who had never before seen this determined, self-composed Elyza, this time unwillingly made way for her. Looking over the bannisters, she saw Eliza run downstairs, enter the drawing room, and emerge a few moments later escorted by five young men, all of whom seemed to be upon excellent terms with her and with one another, though to say the truth Redmayne's disclosure to Mr. Everet in Elyza's absence that he had only looked in for a brief call upon her on his way to keep an appointment to take Miss Mayfield for a drive had caused Mr. Everet to experience a strong desire to murder him.

But, remembering the part he was schooling himself to play, he restrained himself and was very attentive to Elyza instead, venting his spleen only by making one or two disparaging remarks about the team of Welsh-bred greys Redmayne was driving; but as the latter gentleman was in a state of extreme euphoria that morning, owing to his appointment with Miss Mayfield, no immediate harm came of that.

Chapter Ten

As Mr. Crawfurd had predicted, an elegant cream-laid gilt-edged card of invitation to a *soirée* to be given by Mr. Cleve Redmayne on the Friday evening following the ball at the Castle Inn did indeed arrive in the Marine Parade for Elyza and Mrs. Winlock that very afternoon. Though they were of course unaware of it, similar cards reached a great many other members of the *ton* at the same time, occasioning rather heated discussions in certain households, a considerable number of satirically lifted eyebrows in others, and comments ranging from, "Encroaching young mushroom!" (from a retired general with strict ideas of protocol) to, "I shall certainly give Mama no rest until she agrees to take me. Did you *ever* see such *divine* blue eyes — exactly like ice! I am sure he has had a *dreadful* past!" — from one romantically inclined young lady to another.

As it happened, however, in almost all these cases the results of the various discussions, raised eyebrows, and romantic imaginings were the same — namely, a universal resolution to visit the Duke of Bellairs' house on the evening named and view upon his home grounds the young man who had succeeded, in the space of no more than a few days, in making himself the most talked about person in Brighton.

For as if his taking of the largest house in the town, outside of the Royal Pavilion, and his whirlwind courtship of the Beauty of the Season were not enough, a stream of subterranean information concerning his ménage on the Steyne daily trickled, by way of servants' quarters and other equally reliable sources, into Brighton drawing rooms. Several large and mysterious crates and packages with outlandish foreign markings upon them had arrived, it was said, at Mr. Redmayne's house. Ditto twenty dozen of the best champagne to be had in London. Ditto parcels from the tailors, bootmakers, hatters, hosiers, and snuff merchants patronised by the leading exponents of male fashion in the *ton*. The Regent's perfumers, Bourgeois Amick and Son, had despatched flagons of the eau Romaine, essence of bergamot, eau de miel d'Angleterre, and jasmin pomatum favoured by the Prince; John Weston had supplied eighteen fine waistcoats ranging from fancy lilac double-breasted to brown nankeen striped Marseilles quilted; rich gold spotted muslin handkerchiefs at twelve guineas each had arrived in batches of three dozen; and from Messrs. Schweitzer and Davidson of 12 Cork Street had come a half dozen elegant dressing gowns of handsome French brocade and several fine white coating bathing suits—jackets, vests, and trousers lined throughout with Welsh flannel—of the exact pattern of those ordered by the Regent.

As for the huge quantities of the finest fruits, sugar, flour, and condiments ordered from delighted Brighton grocers in preparation for Friday evening's *soirée*, the staggering salary (a rumoured three hundred pounds a year) that had lured one of the most famous French chefs in England from the service of a noted and titled gourmet, and the tales of frenzied activity by florists and decorators inside the house — it scarcely needed all this to ensure the arrival at Mr. Redmayne's residence on the Friday evening of all but the starchiest members of the *ton* who had received those gilt-edged cards of invitation. By nine o'clock the musicians seated upon a small dais in the Grand Saloon were sedately rendering Haydn and Handel to the first curious guests; by ten the orchestra in the ballroom upstairs was playing gay waltzes and quadrilles for a romping crowd of young people; and by midnight Redmayne's guests, encouraged by liberal potations from the twenty dozen of the best champagne and the fifty bottles of vintage port that had followed them into the house, were discussing their host and his ménage with a freedom they would not have dreamed of using in more orthodox surroundings.

"Fantastic!" said Lady Jersey, who had lent even her gilded presence to the occasion, as she looked about her at the yards of ruby-red silk that had been draped to form an opulent sort of tent in the Grand Saloon, investing what had been a rather cold Palladian box with something of the exotic glamour of the Arabian Nights. The effect was heightened by the rich odour of the roses that bloomed everywhere throughout the house, by Kashmir carpets and Moradabad brass, and by the large pieces of extraordinary Indian statuary that loomed rather menacingly over the guests in the recesses where cool white Dianas and Apollos had formerly chastely gleamed. "Utterly fantastic!" repeated Lady Jersey. "The poor Duke would undoubtedly believe he had walked into a phantasmagoria if he were to step inside his own front door. I shan't speak of the Duchess: her health is quite uncertain, you know. Someone *should* drive over to Worthing and tell her on no account to come here while this extraordinary young man is in residence. The shock, I am *quite* certain, would be entirely too much for her."

Lady Mayfield, Corinna's mama, who was ordinarily a rather placid, dull woman but looked anything but placid just now because she had just come downstairs from the ballroom where she had seen the perpetrator of the phantasmagoria leading her daughter onto the floor for the third time that evening, said rather fretfully that she could not think why they had all come.

"I am sure I should not have done so if you hadn't, Sally," she said to Lady Jersey. "But what was I to do when Corinna told me you had decided to accept, so that there was really no reason that we should not, too? We hardly *know* this young man, after all."

One of the romantically inclined young ladies, a Miss Exton, who had been dragged downstairs, metaphorically speaking, by her mama with an early departure in view, said darkly at this point that if Lady Mayfield could hear the things that were being said about him upstairs, she wouldn't think she knew him at all.

"What sort of things?" asked Lady Mayfield, looking alarmed. "Good gracious, he *is* related to the Kerslakes, isn't he?"

"Well, I don't know anything about *that*," said Miss

Exton, enjoying the sense of having collected an attentive audience. "But Freddy Mandry says he has it on the very best authority that the reason Mr. Redmayne was sent to India was because he had killed someone in a duel and had to fly the country"—at which romantic phrase she shuddered deliciously.

"A duel? Nonsense! It was nothing so tonnish," a satirical voice drawled behind her. The company looked up and saw Lord Belfort entering the room, his tall, elegant figure, in a superlatively cut black coat, a cravat tied with restrained artistry, and black satin knee-breeches, forming a startling contrast to the exotica among which he stood. "His father," continued the Marquis, flicking open a buhl snuff-box with his left hand in the style perfected by Mr. Brummell and raising a delicate pinch of Messrs. Fribourg and Treyer's finest King's Martinique mixture to his nostrils, "a highly impecunious Yorkshire clergyman, was, I understand, delighted to seize the opportunity to find employment for him, when he was a lad of thirteen, through the good offices of a relation modestly employed in the East India Company. I cannot vouch, however," he concluded, as he brushed a quite imaginary grain of snuff from his sleeve with a fine cambric handkerchief, "for Mr. Redmayne's not having pursued a course quite as bloodthirsty as any Miss Exton may have imagined while he was in India, although in a manner frowned upon by Society—and indeed by the authorities—to a far greater extent than the practice of duelling."

Lady Jersey, her curiosity now thoroughly piqued, looked at him, her eyes sparkling.

"Why, what on earth are you saying, Basil?" she enquired. "Do you mean to tell us he has done murder?"

"Not to put too fine a point upon it, Sally, I should not be surprised if he had," said the Marquis, calmly surveying his spellbound audience. "One hears such very alarming rumours, you see, when one begins making enquiries of people who are in a position to know. It is quite certain, at any rate, that he inherited this enormous fortune of his from an unscrupulous old nabob named Macquoid, who was famous—or should I say notorious?—for fifty years in the Bombay area before his demise some six or eight months ago. Mr. Macquoid, I understand, had a penchant for—er—direct methods in gaining his ends in his business dealings, and apparently found young Mr. Redmayne so useful to him and so much a man of his own kidney that he embraced him, so to speak, as a son, even to the extent of leaving him his entire fortune when he died."

There was an awed silence as he completed his speech, broken by the retired general (who had decided to grace the occasion with his presence, after all, because by Gad, sir, everyone else seemed to be going: no one interested in keeping up the tone of Society these days!). "Pshaw!" he said. "Knew the fellow was a commoner from the start! Look at this room, now! Shocking taste! Shocking!"

The romantic Miss Exton, who had had the honour a few days before of an invitation to a musical evening at the Royal Pavilion, said pertinaciously that for her part she couldn't see a ha'porth of difference between the way the Prince had decorated that remarkable edifice and the changes Mr. Redmayne had made in the Duke's house.

"Except that the Prince's things are mostly Chinese," she said. "All those dragons and water lilies and life-sized figures of mandarins leering at you in corridors and holding lanterns on poles!"

The General said with dignity that he believed connoisseurs found the Chinese Corridor very *recherché*, but Lady Jersey laughed and remarked that he knew very well that many people considered poor Prinny's ideas to be quite as outlandish as Mr. Redmayne's. As she was well known to have enjoyed an agreeable connexion with the Regent, which she now enjoyed no longer, no one felt capable of entering into a proper discussion of the subject with her, and at any rate the conversation was immediately diverted into other channels by Lady Mayfield, who enquired rather distractedly what she ought to *do*, because Corinna had already stood up to dance with him three times that evening.

"To say nothing of his having sent her only this morning the most enormous diamond I have ever laid eyes on," she said piteously. "It was set in a brooch, and seemed to me very much the sort of thing gentlemen are said to give to their *chères-amies*. Of course I obliged her to return it, but one really never knows what he may do next—"

"My dear Emily, if you are worrying that Corinna may be enticed into throwing her cap over the windmill for Mr. Redmayne, you need not," replied Lady Jersey, cynically but kindly. "He is most assuredly bent upon lawful matrimony, and a fortune will buy one almost anything nowadays, you know—even a title, I have heard it said!"

"But if he has killed people—!" said Lady Mayfield,

unconsolably. "You may say what you like about his being so rich, Sally, but, really, I couldn't *ever* bring myself to think of him as a son!"

Lady Jersey, thinking what a silly woman Emily Mayfield was, laughed and said it was early days still to be talking of sons, and glanced rather enquiringly at Lord Belfort, who said, "Just so, Sally," with a lazy, appreciative smile.

"But not so early that you had best not be taking time by the forelock, Basil!" she warned him mockingly, as she rose, trailing azure blue draperies. "Had you not best betake yourself upstairs to join the dancers and spread your interesting little tale of Mr. Redmayne's past? Even if the hint of his having played hired bravo to the wicked Macquoid does not give Corinna pause, perhaps the boyhood spent in impecunious drudgery may do the trick for you."

And she wafted herself out of the room and out of the house without troubling herself to make her adieux to her host, no doubt reflecting that, since she had satisfied her curiosity concerning him and had every intention of cutting him the next time she met him, it would be a work of supererogation.

She was not the only one of Redmayne's guests that evening to entertain similar sentiments, once Lord Belfort's tale of their host's past had made its way like wildfire through the throng of guests enjoying the dancing in the ballroom upstairs. Mrs. Winlock heard it from Miss Piercebridge, as she sat on one of the rout chairs lining the walls of that stately apartment, which, like the Grand Saloon, had undergone a rather startling transformation, due in this case to yards of gold satin and the display of several colourful tapestries of remarkable size, depicting what were apparently exotic scenes of high life in ancient India. She, turned an exasperated glance upon Elyza, who was waltzing for the second time that evening with Mr. Everet.

"Well!" she said crisply. "If *that* doesn't put a period to her career as a belle here in Brighton, nothing will! Of course *she* will be held responsible for introducing him into Society! He had scraped an acquaintance somehow, you know, with the Crawfurd boy, who introduced him to Elyza and me the other day in front of Donaldson's Library — and what must that tiresome girl do but proceed to present him to everyone in sight at the Castle Inn that same evening! I am sure that Emily Mayfield, for one, will be furious with her!"

She sat tapping her fan angrily upon her knee for a few moments and then, summoning Colonel Hanley, instructed him to bring Elyza to her the moment the music ended. The Colonel, also full of Lord Belfort's disclosures, enquired a trifle nervously if she had heard the latest *on-dit* about that fellow Redmayne.

"Yes, I have!" said Mrs. Winlock curtly. "It is precisely why I wish you to bring Elyza to me! We shall be leaving at once, Dorsey!"

The Colonel, looking more unhappy than ever, automatically said very well, because that was what he was accustomed to say in reply to all Mrs. Winlock's dictates, but added, with a heroism born of the uneasy conviction that Redmayne, if he chose, might make certain disclosures concerning the Colonel's expedition in search of Elyza that would make things more than a little uncomfortable for him, that there was no need to set the fellow's back up.

"And why should it concern *you* whether it is set up or not?" Mrs. Winlock retorted, and both she and Miss Piercebridge looked at him so piercingly that he beat a hasty retreat and said of course it didn't concern him in the least—no, no, ha! ha!—not in the least.

This apparently satisfied Mrs. Winlock, whose mind was preoccupied with Elyza; but Miss Piercebridge, who had long ago learned to detect the signs of an uneasy conscience—more than one cosy stay at a country house or other small favour highly welcomed by a maiden lady in straitened circumstances having come her way as a result of a discreet hint dropped in guilty ears—looked at him more piercingly than before, so that he was glad to hear the music winding to a close and betake himself in quest of Elyza.

Elyza, brought back flushed with the triumph of another most successful evening, during which she had not been obliged to sit out a single dance, looked very much surprised on being told that they were to leave immediately.

"But I can't!" she protested. "I have promised this dance to Mr. Redmayne! I *must* stay."

Mrs. Winlock, in a few pithy sentences, acquainted her with Lord Belfort's tale of Redmayne's antecedents.

"And *that,*" she concluded, "as you will immediately understand, is why it is necessary for us to leave at once. Oh, good God! Here is the creature approaching us now. Come along, Elyza!"

She put her hand upon Elyza's arm to draw her away, but Elyza, her face flushing up vividly, stood her ground.

Redmayne came up and bowed. "Our waltz, I believe, Miss Leigh?" he said.

Mrs. Winlock, with a sudden tinkling, artificial little laugh, began to say something rapidly about being so sorry, but they were really just about to leave. Redmayne, his expression suddenly more remote than ever, looked at Elyza. Elyza looked at him.

"Of course we shall have our dance first, Mr. Redmayne," she said very steadily, and stepped towards him, raising her hand to place it upon his shoulder. His arm encircled her waist; they swept out onto the floor.

"What is it?" he enquired abruptly, as soon as they were out of hearing of the others.

Elyza raised an indignant face to meet his gaze.

"Oh, it is Lord Belfort!" she said. "He had made enquiries about you, it seems, and—and he is saying some perfectly horrid things!"

"I see." Redmayne's gaze made a swift survey of the room; the sight of mamas bundling reluctant daughters out the door, of middle-aged peers and their elegantly gowned wives looking as if they had been caught red-handed buying made-up clothes in Cranbourne Alley and were explaining to everyone who would listen that they had got into this place quite by mistake, was plain to be seen now. "What sort of things?" he asked rather grimly.

"About—about someone named Macquoid," Elyza said, a trifle breathlessly. "And about your being quite dreadfully poor, and being sent to India to be a clerk, and—and perhaps having killed people—"

"Well, I haven't killed anyone except in a fair fight, when it was his life or mine," Redmayne said, even more grimly than before. He looked down at her, his face quite unreadable now. "Perhaps, Miss Leigh," he said formally, "you would wish me to take you back to your chaperon?"

"Oh, *don't* be silly!" said Elyza impatiently. "Of course I don't believe the murdering parts, and I *can't* see what difference it makes that you have been poor, any more than it matters about your being rich now. Besides, you have been very kind to me and — and I *like* you!"

Redmayne's face lightened suddenly in his extraordinary smile. "And I like *you*, Mr. Smith!" he said. "Very well, then! We shall have our waltz, and if it ruins your reputation, at least it will mean that Mottram will leave off wishing to marry you. Has he made his declaration yet?"

"No! That is, he has tried to three times, but something always occurs to interrupt him! It is becoming quite ridiculous, and I am thinking of writing him a letter to tell him please not to try any more. Only I expect if I were to do that it would shock him more than anything." She broke off, seeing, as he turned her in the dance, Corinna Mayfield just going out the door with her mother. She cast a quick glance up at his face, and it was obvious to her at once that he too had seen that unceremonious departure.

"It is — it is no doubt only because Lady Mayfield obliges her to go," she said, reduced by love to pleading her rival's cause, which after all is the only thing one can do when one is convinced one has no chance oneself. "She danced with you three times, you know."

Redmayne did not say, "Before she knew," but perhaps he thought it for a moment, before the hope that

is always quick to accept any plausible — or even im-
plausible — excuse for reprehensible behaviour on the
part of the beloved object sprang up again.

By the time the waltz had ended the population of
the ballroom, now thinning fast, had been reduced
chiefly to the orchestra, a number of rather fast young
matrons who considered the whole thing a great lark
and would plume themselves in the morning upon
having danced with a man whom they were quite willing to think of as being as delightfully hardened a
criminal as Captain Macheath, and a group of young
Bloods who were either partnering them or lounging
against the walls, discussing their host. Elyza, puncti-
iously brought back to Mrs. Winlock at the end of the
dance by Redmayne, was at once snatched away by
her wrathful chaperon and hustled out into the fresh
seaside darkness, to be scolded for her rash disobedi-
ence all the way back to the Marine Parade.

For his part, Redmayne imperturbably strolled over
to where Mr. Crawfurd, his face very much flushed,
was apparently engaged in a spirited defence of someone or something in the midst of a group that included Mr. Everet and Lord Belfort. At Redmayne's
approach he left off speaking abruptly, as did everyone
else, and Redmayne was left facing a silent group,
some with faint, supercilious smiles upon their faces
and all, it appeared, looking at him expectantly. Redmayne stood regarding them; the quiet, rather chill-
ingly dangerous look that Elyza had observed at the
fair had appeared upon his face.

"Well, gentlemen?" he enquired almost negligently,
after a moment.

Mr. Crawfurd, as if forestalling something, burst

133

suddenly into speech.

"We were talking about those greys of yours," he said quickly. "Have you seen Everet's chestnuts? He thinks they could give the greys the go-by."

Redmayne looked at Mr. Everet. "Do you, indeed?" he said equably. "Would you care to lay a wager on that?"

"A race?" asked Mr. Everet.

"If you like."

"Over what course?"

"Any you care to name."

A slight smile passed round the circle. Mr. Everet had not attained his membership in the Four-horse Club or his reputation as one of the premier whips among that illustrious group of Nonpareils without cause, and it was obviously the universal opinion that he had only to give his assent to Redmayne's proposal to lighten that gentleman's pocket of the sum to be named in the wager, to say nothing of teaching him a much-deserved lesson for his presumption. These considerations were also not absent from Mr. Everet's mind, but it must be stated in fairness that the chief reason for his uttering an instant agreement was the thought of being able publicly to best his rival for Miss Mayfield's hand. No doubt crossed his mind of his being able to do so; he had never seen Redmayne handling the ribbons, but it seemed to him that a young man who had passed the greater part of his life as a clerk in a Bombay counting house, or in doing bloodthirstily illegal things in the back-country or the upcountry or whatever it was they called it in India, must be almost embarrassingly ill-qualified for competition in the gentlemanly sport of curricle-racing.

Someone was suggesting Epsom as the scene of the race, but he was overridden by the majority opinion that a longer course — say, from Brighton to Horley, on the New Road — would provide a better test. Mr. Everet, with an eye to the fact that Corinna might be present at the start of the race if it were held over the latter course, promptly plumped for it, and, the following afternoon being agreeable to both parties, the time and the conditions of the contest were at once fixed.

"And the amount of the wager?" enquired Lord Belfort, addressing Mr. Everet. "I should advise you to make it a large one, Jack, since Mr. Redmayne" — with a satirical glance at the stupendously decorated ballroom — "is obviously not only willing, but anxious, to part with his blunt."

Mr. Everet hesitated. He would dearly have liked to take Lord Belfort's advice, for he was quite sure both of his horses and of himself, and was, as usual, in pressing need of funds. But an inherent regard for fair play, which was one of the qualities that endeared him to his friends, made him feel qualms against naming too large a sum.

"Shall we say a monkey?" he enquired after a moment, using the cant term for five hundred pounds.

"Paltry, dear boy — paltry!" protested Lord Belfort. "You are insulting Mr. Redmayne; I am quite certain he had no such trifling sum in mind. Am I not correct, Mr. Redmayne?" he enquired, with the sweet insolence for which he was noted. "When one has succeeded in amassing — never ask me how — the gold of the Indies, one has naturally the laudable desire to display one's opulence upon every possible occasion."

Mr. Crawfurd, flushing up hotly, opened his mouth to speak, but Redmayne laid a restraining hand upon his arm. His face, as usual, was quite impassive.

"As you say, old boy," he said. "But since Mr. Everet, I believe, does *not* possess the gold of the Indies, it may not be convenient for him to lose a large sum."

"Ah, but *will* he lose it?" murmured Lord Belfort. "Turned squeeze-crab of a sudden, Redmayne?"

"Not at all," said Redmayne. "I'll give him odds." He looked at Mr. Everet. "Ten to one?" he suggested.

Mr. Everet, looking rather uncomfortable, said that if anyone should be giving that kind of odds it was he, but he was overruled by his friends, who were able in this way to experience the agreeable sensation of giving him a handsome present without being obliged to reach into their pockets to do so. The group then proceeded to melt away like the rest of the company, leaving Redmayne alone in the huge, deserted ballroom except for Mr. Crawfurd, the orchestra, still dubiously playing, and two or three gentlemen with wellknown reputations for toad-eating and sponging, who were eyeing him hungrily from the far end of the room. Redmayne looked at young Mr. Crawfurd.

"If you would care to leave, too—" he said evenly.

Colour swept warmly into Mr. Crawfurd's fresh young face. "W—what do you take me for?" he stammered. "I'm not like that s-set of d-detestable—"

"They're all wrong about it, you know," Redmayne interrupted him, speaking suddenly and very seriously. "Angus Macquoid was like a father to me. He was a remarkable man; I knew that the first time I ever set eyes on him. Many people have criticised him, but if he ever engaged in any unethical practices it was all before I knew him. 'I don't want you to get involved in any Greeking transactions, my boy,' he used to say to me. 'Then when I die you can go back to England with a clear conscience and mingle with the *ton*.' " Redmayne's eyes went slowly over the huge, empty room. "He would have liked this place," he said. "I was thinking I might buy it, as a sort of memorial to him, but now—"

One of the toad-eaters, still at the other end of the room, made a sudden, tentative move forward.

"My God, let's get out of here," said Redmayne hastily. "We'll go into the library; they won't follow us there."

Which, as young Mr. Crawfurd was burning to ask if Redmayne would take him, instead of a groom, in his curricle for the race, suited him exactly, and they went off together, amicably discussing the Great Race, as Mr. Crawfurd had already begun to call it in his mind—or at least Mr. Crawfurd discussed it and Redmayne did nothing to halt the flow of his eager discourse, though he looked remarkably as if he had something else on his own mind.

Chapter Eleven

Naturally Lord Belfort's revelations concerning Redmayne's past formed the chief topic of discussion at breakfast tables all over Brighton the next morning. Several persons of uncertain social status said how shocked they were to find they had been lured into lending consequence to the pretensions of a person of no social status by their presence in his house. A number of dowagers remarked ominously that they had always said that blood would tell, and it was no doubt to have been expected that a person introduced into Society by Miss Elyza Leigh would turn out to have a background that was distressingly low.

And an even larger number of much younger ladies, who had come under the spell of that quiet, indefinable, but sometimes, as Elyza knew, faintly chilling recklessness expressed in Redmayne's bearing, made up their minds that, mamas to the contrary, they would find the opportunity to explore more deeply into what went on behind those cool blue eyes and that aloof manner.

But the events of the previous evening were at once

eclipsed when they emerged a little later to take advantage of a rather windy but quite warm and sunlit morning to stroll along the sea-front, or to walk to North Street to do some shopping, or to stop in at Donaldson's Circulating Library to change a book. Donaldson's, in particular, was buzzing with news of the Great Race; wagers were being freely laid, and all the young ladies were cajoling their mamas into allowing them to be present that afternoon on the Steyne, where the start was to be made.

"I daresay no harm can come of it if they only *watch*," said Lady Mayfield nervously, when appealed to by one of her contemporaries who had three daughters and was looking for someone to legitimise her failure to stand up to their determination to see the contestants set off. "Not that Corinna has been at all difficult about it, for she has said it is all one to her whether she goes or not. I think she has the headache a little this morning," she said, looking anxiously at her lovely daughter, who, with a listlessness quite unusual in her, was turning over the pages of one of the many periodicals displayed upon a table nearby.

Mrs. Winlock, coming up just then with Elyza, who was looking remarkably pretty in a yellow chip hat tied under her chin with long yellow ribands and a frock of pale lemon-yellow muslin with bishop sleeves, said that for her part she had no intention of dignifying a race in which Mr. Redmayne was to be one of the participants by *her* presence.

"Oh," said Elyza, "then I must find someone else to go with, for I promised Mr. Crawfurd just now, while you were talking with Colonel McMahon, that I should be there. Mr. Redmayne is taking him up with him instead of his groom, you know, and he is so excited about it that I think he is likely to burst before the race begins!"

Mrs. Winlock gave her a dagger-glance of disapproval, but Lady Mayfield, who had a rather confused feeling that she ought to be grateful to Elyza for drawing off Mr. Everet, her chief worry before Redmayne had come upon the scene, said kindly, "Oh, you may come with us if you like, Miss Leigh." She then wished she hadn't said it and looked in anguished appeal at her daughter, but Corinna only looked slightly surprised and then indifferent.

"That will be very nice," she said colourlessly.

Lady Mayfield and Mrs. Winlock fell into conversation, and Elyza unobtrusively moved to stand beside Corinna, who was still flicking over the pages of the latest issue of *The Mirror of Fashion*.

"What a perfectly horrid dress!" said Elyza, pointing to a gown ornamented down its entire front with a double row of knots of ribbon, and worn with a very high-crowned bonnet trimmed with yards of thread net. Corinna idly assented. "But that is not what I *really* wish to talk to you about," Elyza went on in a lower voice, wondering greatly at her own unselfishness, but then she had remained awake for almost an hour the night before having angry, worrying thoughts about what had happened at Redmayne's evening-party, and had come to the conclusion that it was her duty to do everything in her power to set things to rights for him. "It is about Mr. Redmayne," she went on. Corinna started slightly and a faint rose flush crept into her perfect face. "Those things that Lord Belfort said about him last night simply are not true,"

Elyza stated firmly. "At least, some of them are true, but only the nicer ones, about being poor and working for the East India Company. And he has never done anything dishonest, or killed anyone at all who wasn't trying to kill *him* first."

At this hint of a violent and dangerous existence quite outside the scope of her own experience Corinna looked alarmed but also, with the perversity of her sex, intrigued. But she recollected almost at once that she was a properly brought up young lady and said rather coldly that she was sure Mr. Redmayne's affairs were no concern of hers.

"Oh, *don't* be missish!" begged Elyza impatiently. "*I* am not your mama, or Mrs. Drummond Burrell, or anyone starchy of that sort. You can speak *quite* frankly to me."

"About what?" enquired Corinna, still wary and unbending.

"It's not about *what;* it's about *who.* No, I expect I mean *whom,*" said Elyza, considering. "At any rate, I mean about Mr. Redmayne. You *aren't* going to drop him — are you? I have heard three people say this morning that they intend to, and I think it is *quite* abominable of them."

She looked so pink as she spoke that Corinna, who was in that very difficult mood that comes when one is — or at any rate thinks one is — in love with perfection and then suddenly discovers that there is no such thing, all at once wondered if she ought to be jealous. She then reminded herself of Mr. Everet's recent marked attentions to Elyza and that young lady's complaisant reception of them, and, quite forgetting Redmayne for the moment, was, somewhat to her surprise, jealous all over again. She had become so accustomed to Mr. Everet's devotion to herself that it had somehow seemed to her that it could no more be withdrawn from her than could the light of the sun, and now when it came over her clearly for the first time that it really had been, she was not sure that she liked the sensation. She had, indeed, a sudden feeling that life, which had been so agreeable up to this time, full of balls and bouquets and admirers, had all at once grown very complicated and difficult. A slight frown overspread her lovely face, and she said rather petulantly to Elyza that she could not conceive why she should think that Mr. Redmayne's affairs were of any particular concern to her.

"Oh!" said Elyza reproachfully. "You know very well why! You have been encouraging him in every possible way, and he—you *know* he is in love with you!"

Corinna's face flushed, and her eyes flew to see if any of the many other fashionable patrons thronging the library had been standing near enough to overhear Elyza's rash statement. To her confusion, her gaze encountered Lord Belfort's calm, satirical one.

"My dear Miss Mayfield," he said, bowing to her, "you are divinity itself, but even divinity, one feels, must sometimes be led astray by appearances. Let us say that Mr. Redmayne gave a plausible imitation of being a gentleman, admit we were taken in, and so dismiss the whole affair."

"He *is* a gentleman!" said Elyza indignantly. "Just because he once was poorer than you think he ought to have been, and now is richer than *any* of you—"

"Elyza!" said Mrs. Winlock, roused from her conversation with Lady Mayfield by the sound of her young ward's imprudently raised voice.

Elyza, suddenly conscious of being the cynosure of amused or scandalised attention, coloured up and fell silent.

"Cannot you understand, you wretched girl," said Mrs. Winlock angrily, as she hurried her out of the library, "that you are already in the briars because it was you who introduced Mr. Redmayne into Society here? Are you quite determined to ruin yourself completely by making yourself his champion now?"

Elyza did not reply. It was undoubtedly horrid of her, she thought, but she could not help feeling quite foolishly happy at the thought that perhaps Corinna did not care so much for Redmayne, after all. Not that that made one's own prospects any brighter, because in most of the novels she had read gentlemen suffering from an unrequited passion wore the willow all their lives and never so much as looked in the direction of any other young lady. But at any rate it seemed to leave the door open for hope.

So she looked forward with a good deal of anticipation to the afternoon, when she would see Redmayne again, fended off Sir Edward Mottram's advances outside a shop in North Street, where Mrs. Winlock had taken her to make some purchases, by the simple expedient of casting her eyes in the direction of a passing young officer of her acquaintance in such a way that he immediately crossed the road to make a third in their tête-à-tête, and paid so little heed to the lecture Mrs. Winlock attempted to read her all the way back to the Marine Parade that that formidable female was almost glad when Lady Mayfield and Corinna arrived to take her off with them to the Steyne to see the start of the race, much as she disapproved of her going.

The day, which had begun by being breezy and fine, had now turned sultry under a cobalt-blue sky, and a glowing sun lent a somewhat lurid brilliance to the scene at the starting-point when Elyza and the Mayfields arrived there that afternoon. The pale, modish colours of the ladies' wispy muslins and broad hats, the scarlet uniforms of the many young officers present, seemed to shimmer a little in the still air. There were a great many smart curricles and phaetons jockeying one another for position in the roadway, for those of the younger men of sporting proclivities who had not driven on ahead to Horley to see the finish of the race had the intention of following the two contestants until — as they freely admitted it undoubtedly would — the pace became too hot for them.

But the centre of all attention in this colourful scene was a pair of lightly built, well-sprung racing curricles, each drawn by a magnificent matched team, and each driven by a young man whose sartorial elegance fully equalled that of his equipage. Mr. Everet's curricle, which had been built to his own design by Hatchett of Longacre, was already well known to most of the gathered throng, but the gentlemen took a great deal of satisfaction in examining and commenting knowledgeably on Redmayne's less familiar vehicle, from its smart yellow body, complete with splashing-board, lamps, and silver moulding, to its silver-mounted harness.

Most were obliged to agree that it quite cast Mr. Everet's into the shade, but they were of the unanimous opinion that not all Redmayne's enormous fortune had enabled him to find a team superior to Mr.

Everet's famous chestnuts. As they were also well acquainted with Mr. Everet's skill in handling the ribbons, he was the odds-on favourite among the bettors, and indeed the many gentlemen — and even ladies — eager to put their money upon him were finding it difficult to discover takers.

Elyza and the Mayfields, owing to the assiduity of Corinna's usual court of admirers, found a position quite at the forefront of the throng, where they could not fail to be noted and greeted by both contestants. Elyza saw that Redmayne looked quite calm, but perhaps too calm, as she put it to herself, in view of the fact that he must know he was the subject of invidious comment by most of the onlookers, and she noted as well the intentness of his gaze as his eyes fell upon Corinna, and fancied she saw a slight pallor creep into his bronzed face as Miss Mayfield gave him a quick, careless greeting and then allowed herself at once to be drawn into animated conversation with Lord Belfort. Mr. Everet looked cheerful and determined, and as if he was quite enjoying himself, as indeed he would have done, except for the sight of Lord Belfort's dark, saturnine face beside Corinna.

The hour for the start of the race having now arrived, the gentleman to whom the duty of giving the signal had been entrusted was about to take his place when a sudden diversion was caused by the appearance of an extremely elegant high-perch phaeton driven by a stout, florid, still handsome gentleman of some fifty years, for which room to approach the starting-point was hastily being made. It did not require the Royal crest on the panel to inform the throng that the Prince Regent was among them, for the Prince and his phaeton were a familiar sight in Brighton in the summer, as they were in the Park in London during the Season.

The Prince, looking affable and handling the reins of his perilously high vehicle with a great deal of aplomb, had his secretary, Colonel McMahon, a little bustling, spotty, red-faced man, up beside him, and as he brought the phaeton to a halt near the starting-line said something in his ear. It was impossible, in the crush, for the two contestants to leave their vehicles and pay their devoirs to the Prince who had done them the honour to come to see the start of their race, but Mr. Everet, who was a favourite of the Regent's, bowed deferentially to him, and Redmayne, colouring up slightly under his tan as he saw the Prince's eyes fall upon him, did the same. The Prince again spoke to Colonel McMahon, who forthwith called out jovially to Mr. Everet, "Hallo, Jack! As you see, His Highness has come to see you off, like all the rest of the world! Quite a pageant, eh? Like one of those tournaments of old. Only you ought to be wearing your ladies' favours, both of you!"

As it was obviously the Prince, who was highly romantic at heart and enjoyed nothing so much as interfering in matters that were no concern of his, from whom the suggestion came, everyone within hearing of the Colonel's voice began saying what a splendid idea it was, except the two contestants, who looked rather red and said nothing at all. It was plain that the Prince was unacquainted with the recent turn of events regarding the two gentlemen and Miss Mayfield, for he now said something to Colonel McMahon which resulted in his secretary's casting a questing glance over the throng gathered at the starting-line. Seeing Corinna standing with her mama and Elyza almost directly below him, beside the phaeton, he leaned down and said to her with a meaning smile upon his remarkably ugly face, "My dear Miss Mayfield, I appeal to you! May not Mr. Everet carry your favour into this contest?"

Corinna, turning quite pink, cast an agonised glance at her mama and curtseyed to the Prince, almost in one motion, and then, sensing encouragement on all sides, began in a rather mesmerised way to draw off the light, filmy scarf that she wore about her shoulders. Willing hands passed it to Mr. Everet, who was now quite as flushed as his inamorata, and could only bow his gratitude to her as he bound the scarf silently around the sleeve of his exquisitely tailored coat.

An even more embarrassing pause now ensued. Obviously it was necessary for Redmayne also to receive some young lady's favour; equally obviously, although there were several present who would have jumped at the chance had they not been held in check by stern glances from their mamas, no damsel was willing to fly in the face of propriety to the extent of offering a token of her regard to a man who had just been so publicly cold-shouldered by the *ton*.

A pregnant hush fell over the throng, during which the only sound to be heard, except for the impatient shifting of hooves upon the glazed red-brick roadway and the subdued jingle of harness, was a nervous feminine giggle. Then Elyza stepped suddenly forward, jerking at the yellow riband that passed over the crown of her flat satin-straw hat and was tied in a coquettish

147

bow under her chin.

"Here!" she said, pulling the riband free and handing it, with a very flushed face, up to Redmayne. "Do have this!" She then further compounded her shocking behaviour by calling out in a clear voice the sporting phrase of encouragement, "Go it, Redmayne!"—which so discomposed the starter that he dropped the handkerchief prematurely, and the two curricles set off with a great clatter of hooves and a cheer from the crowd, Redmayne's slightly in the rear because he had paused to bind Elyza's yellow riband about his sleeve.

"Oh, Miss Leigh! Really! What will Mrs. Winlock say?" moaned Lady Mayfield, looking quite overcome by Elyza's rash act and the resulting notoriety to her party. "Oh, dear! Oh, dear! I *do* think we had best return at once to the Marine Parade! Dear Lord Belfort, how very kind! Yes, I *should* like the support of your arm! I don't know *what* I shall find to say to Mrs. Winlock!"

Elyza, in disgrace, fell in behind her with Corinna. Corinna did not look at her, which was perhaps as well, for if she had Elyza might have said what she thought of her having been weak enough to have given her favour to Mr. Everet rather than to Redmayne, thus leaving the latter in the embarrassing situation from which she, Elyza, had been obliged to rescue him. Neither hints from Royalty nor public obloquy, she was quite sure, would have caused *her* to behave in such a fashion towards the man she loved—and then, stealing a glance at Corinna's perfect profile, still at the present time indicating discomposure though it is well known that it is very difficult for a profile view to express anything at all, she wondered again, with that hopeful thump of the heart, if Corinna was not in love with Redmayne, after all.

Still, that could not alter the fact that *he* was in love with *her,* so she pushed hope firmly down and prepared herself for the storm that would break over her head when Lady Mayfield told Mrs. Winlock what she had done—which, as she was a very silly woman, it was undoubtedly certain that she would.

Chapter Twelve

So great was Mrs. Winlock's displeasure upon hearing from Lady Mayfield the news of her ward's shocking behaviour that she utterly refused to chaperon her to the ball to be held that evening at the Assembly-rooms of the Old Ship Inn, where Elyza had been tolerably certain she would be able to receive intelligence of the outcome of the Great Race. It would be far better, Mrs. Winlock acidly observed, to allow people at least to expend the first fury of their gossip about her before she must appear the following day at the evening-party at the Royal Pavilion to which they had been honoured by an invitation.

As a result of this decision, Elyza was compelled to spend the evening in the Marine Parade, which she felt to be the greatest deprivation, for they had no visitors, so that she was left in total ignorance of what had transpired after Redmayne and Mr. Everet had driven out of Brighton in a cloud of dust. On the following morning, however, to her great delight, Mr. Crawfurd made an early call, and one glance at his jubilant face told her the news she had been longing to hear.

"Oh!" she gasped, flying up out of her chair to greet him as he was shown by Satterlee into the drawing room where she and Mrs. Winlock had been sitting. "He *did* win, didn't he? How perfectly *splendid!*"

Mrs. Winlöck, casting a glance of disapproval at her, held out her hand rather coldly to Mr. Crawfurd, for his intimacy with Redmayne, she felt, quite overbore the advantage of his being an eligible and agreeable young man.

"How do you do, Mr. Crawfurd?" she said. "Have you come to tell us about that tiresome race? Really, I cannot conceive how it is that you young men set such store on these sporting contests of yours! It is quite absurd of you!"

Under ordinary circumstances young Mr. Crawfurd would have been so daunted by this greeting that he would have become entirely mute, have sat for a quarter hour in the drawing room counting the moments until he could decently take his departure, and then precipitately have fled. But today, conscious that he, Nicholas Crawfurd, had had a part, if only a very humble one, in scoring a stunning upset victory in the Great Race, he was made of sterner stuff.

"Oh, do you think so, ma'am?" he said incredulously, and forthwith launched into a Homeric account of the race, including such details as the magnificent skill with which Redmayne, faced with the prospect of following a very slow Accommodation-coach all the way down the hill from Pease Pottage to Crawley, had dropped his hands and let his greys shoot, with only inches to spare, between the coach and a gig going in the opposite direction, and the splendid neck-and-neck race they had had with Mr. Everet's curricle down a straight stretch of road outside Hand Cross.

"You know, of course, that Everet took the lead at the start," he said, his cheeks flushed with remembered excitement. "He held it all the way to Hand Cross, which had me in a pucker, but Cleve said it would do no harm to let him set the pace, as we should have plenty of time to pass him between there and Horley. You never saw anything so cool as he was! Even when we lost sight of Everet entirely in that hollow road beyond Cuckfield it didn't put him about in the least, though we hadn't the least notion, of course, how far ahead of us he might have drawn. But, sure enough, at Hand Cross we came up with him, and then Cleve, who had no notion, you know, of eating his dust, gave him the go-by as neat as you please, and he never headed us again. Everet says himself—we all supped together at the Chequers at Horley afterwards, and he is the best of good fellows!—that he had never seen such driving. There were a good few times, I can tell you, when I made certain we should end up in splinters, but we never so much as grazed a wheel on another vehicle, no matter what hairsbreadth escapes we had!"

Elyza, who had been listening to all this with rapt attention and glowing eyes, at this point declared enthusiastically that she would have given anything to have been in Mr. Crawfurd's place, perched up in the groom's seat between the springs and able to see the whole race at first-hand.

"My dear Elyza!" said Mrs. Winlock. "Pray do not

be wishing anything so improper! In point of fact, if I were in *your* place, I should do everything in my power to forget that unfortunate race entirely!"

This oblique reference to Elyza's imprudent act in drawing attention to herself at the start of the race by bestowing her yellow riband upon Redmayne had the effect of halting Mr. Crawfurd's spate of reminiscence.

"Oh!" he said, blushing slightly. "I had almost forgot—I am charged with a message for you, Miss Leigh. Cleve—Mr. Redmayne, that is—says he will call upon you to express his gratitude for the honour you did him at the start of the race if it is convenient, but if it is not, he will understand." He saw that Mrs. Winlock, without waiting for Elyza to speak, was about to express *her* opinion of the matter and hurried on, "But of course it is probable that you will meet him at the Royal Pavilion this evening, at any rate. Did you not tell me that you have received cards?"

"*We* have received cards," said Mrs. Winlock, with a slight, superior smile. "I cannot think, however, that Mr. Redmayne has had that honour."

"Oh, but he has!" retorted Mr. Crawfurd proudly. "And so have I! They were brought by messenger this morning, and Colonel McMahon, whom I met as I was coming here, says the Prince has heard the whole story of the race and is most anxious to meet the man who was able to beat Jack Everet and those chestnuts of his! You know everyone says he is quite mad about horses!"

This statement, as Mrs. Winlock knew, was all too true, for, although the Regent had not patronised

Newmarket for almost a dozen years now, ever since the unfortunate scandal over the race in which his favourite jockey, Chifney, had failed to bring Escape in a winner, he still took an avid interest in the turf and kept a large and notable stable. Indeed, his horses, the Prince was accustomed to jest, were better housed than he was himself, for thus far the only plans drawn up by Repton for enlarging and remodelling the Pavilion that had been carried through to completion were those for the construction of the Royal Stables and Riding House, a magnificent mosquelike structure in the Moslem Indian style. This had cost the Prince over fifty-five thousand pounds to build and provided, under a huge central cupola, stalls for fifty-four horses set around the great circle of its interior, with harness rooms and grooms' quarters on a sort of balcony above and a central fountain for watering the horses.

With all these facts Mrs. Winlock was well acquainted, and she was aware as well that the Prince, far from being a high stickler concerning the people he honoured with invitations to Carlton House in London and the Pavilion in Brighton, was apt to choose his companions more on the basis of their being amusing raconteurs or famous sportsmen than upon the more socially accepted foundation of blue blood. It was, in fact, she informed Elyza somewhat waspishly after Mr. Crawfurd had left, exactly like the Prince to have invited Redmayne to the Pavilion merely because he had chanced to come in first in a curricle-race with Jack Everet.

"But I hope," she continued repressively, "that you will accord him no more than the merest civility in your greeting to him this evening, Elyza. If the Prince wishes to take Mr. Redmayne up, that, of course, must make him acceptable wherever he goes, in spite of his background, but it is not in *your* place to put yourself forward in that regard. Thank heaven, this invitation will at least serve to make your *most* unbecoming behaviour at the start of the race appear in a less scandalous light. But you must be very careful not to give further fuel to the tattle-mongers by appearing to bestow any particular attention upon Mr. Redmayne. I am glad that I made it clear to Mr. Crawfurd that his plan to call upon you was *quite* unacceptable, at any rate."

Elyza, who had been feeling very rebellious upon this point, said she could not see why, if the Prince received Redmayne, she should not; but she was too happy over Redmayne's victory in the curricle-race and the certainty of seeing him at the Pavilion that evening to dwell long upon that subject.

The prospect of being entertained by Royalty naturally caused both Elyza and Mrs. Winlock to take unusual care over their toilette that evening. When they came downstairs to the drawing room, where Colonel Hanley was waiting to escort them to the Pavilion, he found Elyza looking particularly charming in a very simple gown of palest blue that set off her dark eyes and cropped black curls to full advantage, and Mrs. Winlock superb in puce satin draped with Brussels lace.

"Wind's changed. Coming on to rain, I expect," said the Colonel, looking appreciatively at his pair of ladies. "By the bye, I told Adelina we'd stop for her — d'ye mind?"

"Adelina? Has *she* a card for tonight?" enquired Mrs. Winlock rather sharply, for invitations to the Pavilion did not come in Miss Piercebridge's way often, despite her high connexions. "The sly thing—she said nothing to me about it!"

"Been sucking up to McMahon, I expect," said the Colonel. "Devilish slippery piece of goods, that woman, Agatha! Turns you inside out before you know where you are! Can't think why you have her for a bosom-bow!"

Elyza, glancing at him as they all left the room together, thought that he appeared rather uneasy, and for an instant wondered what Miss Piercebridge could have done to make him look that way; but she was too much caught up in the excitement of the moment to speculate long upon the matter.

There was a mutter of thunder and a gust of soft, sultry air to greet them when they stepped out of the house to enter the closed carriage that was to take them the short distance to the Royal Pavilion. Miss Piercebridge, taken up at her lodgings, was in black, with a lace mantilla, also black, draped over a large opera-comb set in her black hair, and looked so much, with her beaky profile, like a bird of doom that Elyza found the unwinking stare she fixed upon her as she sat opposite her during the brief drive almost unnerving.

But she forgot Miss Piercebridge and everything else except the honour that was in store for her when, the carriage having halted before the fairytale domes and towers of the Royal Pavilion, gleaming palely now under a fugitive moon appearing and disappearing behind black, scudding clouds, she stepped across the threshold of that extraordinary edifice to find herself in an octagonal vestibule, lit by a large Chinese lantern, and from thence was ushered into the entrance hall, where Colonel Hanley gave their names to one of the liveried servants standing beside the door.

The next moment she found herself entering the famous Chinese Gallery, an immensely long apartment in which the rumble of the thunder clearly heard from outside—for a great part of its ceiling consisted of a stained-glass skylight—seemed to echo and reverberate like an orchestration of kettle-drums set against the flutes and violins of the ladies' voices and the trumpets or cellos of the gentlemen's. In the center of the Gallery the Regent, his corpulence unfortunately emphasised by a gorgeously coloured waistcoat and the prevailing fashion for wasp-waisted, skin-tight coats, stood affably receiving his guests. Elyza, sinking into a deep curtsey before him as Mrs. Winlock begged leave to present her ward, found her hand being taken very cordially in the Regent's own.

"Well, well, Miss Leigh, so you are Sir Robert's daughter," he said genially. "A remarkably good fellow, extraordinarily capable—I have known and valued him any time these twenty years. But," he added, regarding Elyza with a rather arch twinkle in his blue eyes, "I fancy I have seen you before, too, my dear! Eh? Yesterday, on the Steyne?"

Elyza, blushing rosily, could find nothing to say for herself. The Regent smiled at her approvingly.

"And very prettily done by you!" he said. "Amazing fellow, this young Redmayne—I don't wonder all you young ladies are taken by him. Coxeter — you will remember Sir Oswald Coxeter, Hanley," he went on, turning to include the Colonel in the conversation, "who is an old Indian hand himself, as you know, was telling me some quite remarkable tales of him last evening. It seems he has been of exceptional service to the East India Company — devil of a fellow in dealing with those Mahratta horsemen who are constantly terrorising the countryside over there. Not surprising, I daresay, that he was able to handle his cattle well enough to beat Jack Everet yesterday. I recollect Wellington's telling me, *à propos* of the Mysore horse, that he considered them the finest of their type he had ever encountered. I am quite looking forward to having a chat with Mr. Redmayne on the subject this evening."

The approach of a new party of arriving guests put an end to the conversation at this point as the Regent turned to greet them, and Elyza, swelling with vicarious pride over the Prince's praise of Redmayne, passed on with Mrs. Winlock, the Colonel, and Miss Piercebridge down the long Gallery, where a footman offered them a tray of refreshments. Elyza, whose awed attention had now been attracted by the extraordinary *décor* of the apartment in which they stood, with its ironwork trellises painted to resemble bamboo, its Chinese canopy hung round with bells, and its looking-glass doors, all set beneath the huge stained-glass skylight depicting — most appropriately, at the moment — the Chinese god of thunder, was startled suddenly to find Miss Piercebridge's black presence close beside her and her voice whispering something in her ear.

"May I have a word with you in private this evening, *Mr. Smith?*"

A particularly loud clap of thunder at that instant, and the sudden drum-rattle of raindrops beating on the skylight above them, all but drowned out the last words. Elyza, unable to believe that she had heard them properly — for how could Miss Piercebridge know anything of young Mr. Smith's adventures on the Bath Road? — looked round at her, startled and a good deal discomposed. But before she could utter any of the questions that sprang to her lips Mr. Crawfurd came up, glowing, with the news that the Regent had borne Redmayne off into the Yellow Drawing-room so that he could converse with him for a short time uninterrupted there. Elyza was obliged to speak to him, and when she turned again to Miss Piercebridge she found her gliding away to pay her devoirs to the Duke of Cumberland, who had just then come into the Gallery.

Then Mr. Everet appeared at her side, rueful over his defeat of the previous day, but enquiring eagerly whether she did not consider it an excellent sign that Corinna had bestowed her scarf upon him so readily at the start of the race.

"You were with her, were you not?" he asked. "Did she — did she make any comment on the matter to you?"

Elyza, still preoccupied with Miss Piercebridge's strange and ominous words, said in a slightly *distrait* tone that she had not. Mr. Everet looked rather crestfallen.

"Oh!" he said. "I thought perhaps — well, since she seemed so ready to bestow the scarf upon me —" He broke off to vow in a tone of romantic fervour, "I shall never part with that scarf, Miss Leigh! I have it on me now, just over my heart"—which words quite impressed Elyza, for she had learned enough during her London Season to know that nothing less than an overmastering passion would have induced a dandy of Mr. Everet's standing to wear under his coat any superfluous object that might mar the sleek perfection of its fit.

"I am afraid," she said, rousing herself from her own disturbed thoughts to speak kindly to a young man so far gone in love, "that we did not speak of the matter at all, Mr. Everet. I—I daresay she felt too deeply about it to discuss it."

Mr. Everet said gloomily that he hoped it might be so and, finding no further comfort to be obtained from Elyza, went off to drink wormwood and gall in discussing his previous day's defeat with some of his sporting friends. Elyza, who wished very much to be left alone for a few minutes so that she could think about Miss Piercebridge's strange request for a private word with *Mr. Smith,* pretended to be absorbed in contemplation of a porcelain pagoda set in a recess of the room, but was at once seized upon by one of her officer friends, who recounted to her enthusiastically the complete history of the race as she had already had it from Mr. Crawfurd.

Then Redmayne himself, released from his private interview with the Prince, came up. The young officer, having warmly expressed his congratulations on his victory and his regret at not having been able to be in at the finish, took himself off, and Elyza said happily to Redmayne, "And *I* should like to congratulate you, too. I think it was *famous,* and I have heard all about it from Mr. Crawfurd and from Lieutenant Graham, but I should like it ever so much if *you* would tell me, too, because you will know *why* you did things and not just *what* you did."

Having concluded this speech, she looked up expectantly into his face, but Redmayne only smiled and said he had had quite enough of that race, and what he really wanted to do was to thank her for coming to his rescue with her yellow riband.

"Oh, *that!*" said Elyza, blushing deeply. "Anyone would have done *that!*"

"The point is that *anyone* didn't; *you* did," said Redmayne. "And I am deuced sorry if it got you into trouble — as I expect it did — with Mrs. Winlock."

"Oh, yes — but she will forget all about it, now that the Prince has been so very cordial to you!" Elyza said, wondering if anyone had ever been happier than she was at that moment, with Redmayne thanking her for rescuing him as he had once rescued her, and looking down at her out of his blue eyes in a way that it seemed to her he had never looked at her before.

But then there was that sudden, familiar stir behind her, the voice of the Prince himself saying jovially, "And here, at last, is Miss Mayfield!" — and Lady Mayfield's voice flutteringly apologising for a carriage that had most provokingly broken down just as it was being driven round to their front door. Elyza saw Redmayne stiffen, saw his eyes go swiftly across the room to where Corinna, looking breathtakingly beautiful in a toilette of white spider gauze over a pink satin slip, was curtseying to the Prince.

The rain beat down savagely upon the stained-glass skylight where Lin-Shin, the thunder god, flew above them. Redmayne, standing rigid beside Elyza, watched as Corinna, having exchanged a few words with the Prince, turned away when a new group of guests engaged his attention. Her eyes, rapidly scanning the brilliant scene before her, came to rest upon his face and she made a sudden, impulsive movement, as if to come towards him.

"Will you excuse me?" said Redmayne in an odd voice, and strode across the room to her.

Elyza, with a sudden very hard lump in her throat, turned blindly to examine with an appearance of intense interest the glass tulips and lotus-flowers adorning one of the three mantelpieces in the Gallery.

Determinedly, she did not look in Redmayne's direction during the few minutes that elapsed before the Prince led his guests into the adjoining Music Room, where they were to hear a concert by the Prince's own Wind Band. Mr. Crawfurd, who took upon himself the duty of finding a suitable seat for her in this huge and quite overpoweringly magnificent apartment, could only ejaculate, "By Jupiter! *By Jupiter!*" as his awed gaze took in a dazzle of crimson and gold, dragons and serpents and water lilies writhing and bursting in gilded effulgence on carpet and window draperies and walls. But Elyza was scarcely conscious of the Oriental splendour about her, because she saw now — she could not help but see — Corinna Mayfield smiling up at Redmayne as she entered the room upon his arm.

Mr. Crawfurd was going on reverently, "I say! Did

you *ever* see anything like it, Miss Leigh? This beats even the Chinese Gallery all hollow! They say those yellow and crimson panels on the walls are twelve views of the neighbourhood of Pekin. Will you be comfortable here?" he broke off to ask, as he piloted her to a sofa upholstered in yellow satin.

"Oh, yes! Quite comfortable!" Elyza heard her own voice saying brightly.

She sat down; Mr. Crawfurd placed himself beside her, and she saw, with a peculiar feeling of dread, that Miss Piercebridge was taking a chair set very near the sofa on her other side. Miss Piercebridge was leaning towards her, a slight, meaning smile upon her dark face.

"So difficult to arrange for even a few words in private — don't you agree?" she said, in a voice just above a sibilant whisper. "But perhaps I may take advantage of this opportunity to speak now. I should be so very glad, Miss Leigh, if you could arrange to have the headache, or some slight indisposition of that nature, when dear Agatha goes — as I am persuaded she quite intends to — to Donaldson's Library tomorrow morning. I have something, you see, of the most *particular* importance to say to you."

Elyza, looking into the smiling face under the black mantilla, was wondering somewhat bemusedly if she could actually have heard its owner address her as "Mr. Smith" only a half hour before. But even as she wondered, Miss Piercebridge bent closer towards her and her voice whispered meaningly in her ear, "Of *most* particular importance, *Mr. Smith!*"

A loud clap of thunder rattled the enormous cut-glass lustre, made in the shape of a pagoda, above them. The Wind Band broke into an impressive march by Handel; the Prince, as annoyed as a child to find his concert being upstaged by the storm, looked suddenly peevish; and Elyza whispered to Miss Piercebridge, with her heart sinking in a most unpleasant way, that she would certainly remain at home on the following morning to hear what she had to say, though she did not understand in the least what she could mean by addressing her as "Mr. Smith."

Chapter Thirteen

After a most disagreeably wakeful night, disturbed both by the torrents of rain beating against her window and by a mystified dread of what Miss Piercebridge could have to disclose to her in the morning (to say nothing of having had one's heart broken all over again by the sight of Corinna's renewed cordiality towards Redmayne), Elyza came downstairs to find Mrs. Winlock, as Miss Piercebridge had foretold, about to set off to change her book at Donaldson's Library.

"Come along, Elyza," she said impatiently. "I promised Augusta Mottram we should be quite early at the Library, as there is something I particularly wish to discuss with her. The rain appears to be over, and I am sure the walk will do you good. You are looking quite hagged this morning!"

"Yes, I—I am afraid I am not feeling quite the thing," said Elyza, seizing upon this remark and attempting to look as woebegone as she felt. "I think I have the headache, a little. If you will not mind, ma'am, I believe I should really like better just to stay quietly at home."

Mrs. Winlock looked at her sharply, for it was not like the new Elyza to neglect any opportunity to go abroad. But seeing nothing suspicious in her appearance she merely recommended that she take some camphorated spirits of lavender and lie down upon her bed, and forthwith went off to Donaldson's.

Elyza, left alone, sought out Satterlee and told him somewhat nervously that if Miss Piercebridge were to call he was to show her up to the drawing room at once. She then went upstairs to the drawing room herself, but she had scarcely sat down before there was a knock at the front door and Miss Piercebridge herself appeared, with a promptness suggesting she had been lurking somewhere to watch for Mrs. Winlock's departure.

"Well, Miss Leigh!" she said, advancing across the room with her customary rapid, gliding step and giving Elyza her black-mittened hand. "How good of you to have taken my suggestion! I am so very glad! *So* much better to discuss these matters quite in private — don't you agree?"

Elyza, inviting her to sit down, said in a somewhat breathless voice that she was sorry, but she didn't quite know what there was to discuss.

"Oh, come now, Miss Leigh!" said Miss Piercebridge, suddenly turning arch in a rather terrifying way and shaking one finger at Elyza. "You and I know very well — do we not? — that that wee indisposition of yours just before you left London was not really an indisposition at all. As a matter of fact, we were not in London during that time, were we?" she enquired, suddenly endowing Elyza with a plural personality in the way that a well-remembered nanny Elyza had once been inflicted with had done, as if one small girl could not possibly account for all the naughtiness she had perpetrated.

"I am afraid I don't—" began Elyza uncertainly.

The black-mittened finger was raised once more, impressively.

"My *dear* Miss Leigh!" said Miss Piercebridge. "Or had I better say *Mr. Smith?* It *was* under that name—was it not?—that Colonel Hanley discovered you on the Bath Road, dressed—I really blush to say it!—in breeches and coat, and in the company of a gentleman with whom you were apparently travelling—"

She paused significantly. Elyza felt the colour draining out of her cheeks, or if she could not actually feel it she felt something else so queer inside her that that was the only way she could describe it. Colonel Hanley! she thought. This, then, had been the reason for his uneasiness the evening before when he had mentioned Miss Piercebridge's name. Miss Piercebridge, with her usual uncanny perspicacity, had managed to discover that the Colonel had something to hide in regard to Redmayne and herself, and to a person of her acknowledged skill in ferreting out secrets, turning the Colonel inside out like a sack, shaking him to make quite sure he was empty of further information, and turning him briskly right side out again would have been mere child's play.

And now the Colonel, Elyza thought, who was certainly rather terrified of Redmayne, besides, she suspected, entertaining hopes of future favours to be bestowed upon him as a reward for his silence on the subject of the peculiar events he had recently witnessed on the Bath Road, was living in dread of what might happen if Redmayne were to discover he had been lured into revealing the secret of those events. The question now was, she considered, did Miss Piercebridge intend to disclose what she had learned, and if so, why? And the answer was not long in coming.

"I see," Miss Piercebridge was saying, looking quite satisfied with the effect of her statement upon Elyza, even though Elyza herself had not uttered a word, "that you quite understand me, Miss Leigh. *So* clever of Mr. Redmayne to have sent you back to London under the care of a respectable female, so that even dear Agatha was deceived as to what actually occurred after you ran off from Green Street! Such adventures can have a really ruinous effect upon a young lady's reputation if they get about, don't you agree? So I *do* think the thing for us to do is to put our heads together and see what we can do to make sure that it *doesn't* get about."

Elyza was seized with a sudden violent distaste for her visitor. Miss Piercebridge, she decided, was like a spider, a very large, primly smiling, black-browed spider spinning webs of intrigue instead of gossamer. But since one could not simply ignore her, or put her out the window, as one might a real spider, the best thing to do, she thought, was to get any unpleasant negotiations one was obliged to transact with her over as soon as possible.

"What is it that you want, Miss Piercebridge?" she asked bluntly. "You *do* want something, don't you? So you had better tell me at once."

Miss Piercebridge gave her a slight, unconvincing

smile and again looked arch.

"Now, now," she said. "We mustn't lose our tempers, must we?"

"No, we mustn't," said Elyza, at the same time feeling the queer sensation inside herself of being a champagne bottle just about to pop and realising for the first time in her life, with some astonishment, that she was her roaring father's daughter, after all. "But I shall, if you don't tell me at once why you have come here!"

Miss Piercebridge, with a rapid change of front, suddenly assumed a melancholy air and smoothed out her mittens.

"Dear Miss Leigh!" she sighed. "How can I explain to you—? You, who have been reared, so to speak, in the lap of luxury, who are able to look forward to a life of ease and comfort as heiress to your father's—I am given to understand—considerable fortune—"

"Is it money?" Elyza interrupted her incredulously. "Do you actually mean to tell me that you wish me to give you money to hold your tongue?"

"Only a thousand pounds, dear Miss Leigh!" said Miss Piercebridge apologetically. "Such a comparatively trifling sum to *you*, I am persuaded!"

"A trifling sum!" Elyza gasped. "Well! You must have an odd idea of my allowance, Miss Piercebridge! I assure you, it will not run to a quarter of that amount in a twelvemonth!"

"Ah, but you are such a *great friend* of Mr. Redmayne, are you not?" Miss Piercebridge suggested, looking primly down at her folded hands. "Surely, if you put it to him, *he* would not object to—shall we say?—lending you a sum that will certainly appear trifling to *him*."

Elyza looked at her in astonishment. "Good heavens!" she thought. "I think she really does believe I was engaging in some sort of intrigue with Mr. Redmayne when Colonel Hanley discovered us on the Bath Road!"

And the idea seemed so absurd to her, in view of the entire lack of interest Redmayne had displayed in young Mr. Smith, even after he had learned that the hall-boy's bottle-green coat and breeches were a disguise for Miss Elyza Leigh, that she was nearly betrayed into a most unsuitable gurgle of laughter.

The next moment, however, she was reminding herself severely that this was no laughing matter. If Miss Piercebridge were indeed to carry out her hinted threat of spreading the tale of Mr. Smith's adventures, she, Elyza, would not be the only one to suffer. Corinna Mayfield, she thought, was a very carefully brought up young lady, and although carefully brought up young ladies, she was aware, had been known to forgive even quite notorious lapses on the part of the gentlemen in whom they were interested, provided those lapses had taken place in the past, she did not think that Corinna would be easily brought to forgive a suitor who had been caught out less than a fortnight before in what would be made to appear a sordid intrigue with one of her friends.

"And what is it to you if she doesn't forgive him, and goes and marries someone else?" Elyza's worser self basely suggested, with what she was sure would have been a sinister leer of satisfaction if one's worser self had a face.

But her better self prevailed at once, because, being

170

truly in love with Redmayne, she could not bear to see him made unhappy, and by dint of telling herself very sensibly that even if Corinna did marry someone else it would not make Redmayne fall in love with *her*, she came to an almost instant conclusion that at any cost Society in general and Corinna Mayfield in particular must not learn of that compromising incident on the Bath Road.

"But I can't simply ask him for a thousand pounds!" she exclaimed, involuntarily speaking her thoughts aloud. "I *couldn't!* What could I say to him?"

"My dear Miss Leigh, nothing could be easier!" said Miss Piercebridge smoothly. "You have only to tell him, you know, that you have imprudently allowed yourself to be led into playing whist, or loo, for higher stakes than you can afford, and that you find yourself, quite at a stand, with gaming debts that you cannot meet."

"Gaming debts!" repeated Elyza in astonishment. "But I don't—"

"Oh yes, my dear, but unfortunately so many other ladies do, you know," Miss Piercebridge said encouragingly. "I assure you, Mr. Redmayne will see nothing in the least odd about it. You must be aware that even at *ton* parties ladies sometimes lose considerable sums, and there are a number of private houses in London, maintained by females of perhaps not the *first* degree of respectability but of very tonnish antecedents, where ladies as well as gentlemen may engage in play almost as deep as the gentlemen enjoy at Watier's or White's. There is Lady Wimsatt's house, for example, in St. James's Square—"

Elyza , who had been shaking her head in a decid-

171

edly negative way all during this speech, now made her disapproval of this scheme even more evident by uttering a determined, "No!" She went on, "I have no claim on Mr. Redmayne, Miss Piercebridge, whatever you may think! My meeting him on the Bath Road was the sheerest accident, and he only offered to take me up in his travelling-chaise because he thought I was a boy, and had lost my purse, so that I had no way of continuing my journey to Bath." Miss Piercebridge looked skeptical. "It is the truth!" Elyza said desperately. "He would think it very peculiar indeed, I am sure, if I were to apply to him."

"Nonsense!" said Miss Piercebridge. "I am quite certain he will oblige you if you will only put it to him properly. Gentlemen are very selfish creatures, my dear, but if you were not so inexperienced you would know that most of them are prepared to pay for their pleasures, provided it is made clear to them that they will be placed in an exceedingly uncomfortable position if they do not. It is not in Mr. Redmayne's interest, you must understand, any more than it is in yours, to have this story get about, since it would then reach the ears of a certain young lady to whom he has been paying very particular attentions." She rose. "And now," she said composedly, "I must take my leave, before dear Agatha returns and finds me here. But I shall be in touch with you again, of course— shall we say, in eight-and-forty hours? By that time you will have had an opportunity to speak to Mr. Redmayne, and I am persuaded that if you put it to him properly, he will certainly comply with your request."

And, smiling in a self-satisfied way, she glided silently and rapidly from the room, looking more than ever, Elyza thought with loathing, like a spider.

Left alone with her problem, Elyza for a few moments gave way to despair. It was all very well for Miss Piercebridge to tell her to apply to Redmayne for the thousand pounds that would buy her silence, but how could she possibly bring herself to do so? He might, indeed, give her the money — she knew his careless generosity — but whether he did or not, was it not highly probable that he would believe it was she, and not Miss Piercebridge, who was selling her silence about that compromising incident on the Bath Road for a thousand pounds? Her cheeks flushed hotly at the thought, and as she pressed her hands to them Satterlee entered the room.

"Sir Edward Mottram!" he pronounced.

Elyza stared at him, aghast. It had not occurred to her, when she had instructed him to show Miss Piercebridge up to the drawing room as soon as she arrived, to tell him that she would not be at home to other callers; and now here was Sir Edward, of all the unwelcome people in the world, coming to intrude upon her when she so much needed time to think about the dilemma into which she had been pitchforked by Miss Piercebridge.

"Tell him —" she began hastily; but it was too late. Sir Edward, with a very flushed face and a determined air, strode into the room on Satterlee's heels, and thrust into her hands a large bouquet of yellow roses.

Satterlee discreetly and reluctantly withdrew.

"I have come, Miss Leigh," Sir Edward began at once, in the rather loud and almost angry voice of a man goaded beyond endurance by enforced delay in doing something he does not at all wish to do but knows he is going to have to do in the end, "because I can no longer bear not to speak my true sentiments to you. It is now some five days since I first endeavoured to lay open my heart to you, and in that time I have never once succeeded in seeing you alone. Now I must—I *shall* speak!"

And to Elyza's horror he got down carefully upon one knee before her, laid one hand over his heart, and launched into a very long and flowery speech, which dwelt chiefly upon the sacredness of his feeling for her and his wish to shield her throughout life from the harsh winds of misfortune. Elyza, having attempted without success to interrupt him twice, resigned herself to hearing the whole of it with what patience her jangled nerves allowed her to command, but her mind, do what she would, insisted upon returning to the distressing problem Miss Piercebridge had left her with—when suddenly an idea darted into it of such hopeful brilliance that she almost burst in upon Sir Edward's speech with it then and there.

Why, this brilliant idea posed itself to her, why should she not ask Sir Edward for the thousand pounds she so urgently needed? If he were really even half so devoted to her as he was fervently professing to be, he would be overjoyed to have the opportunity of shielding her from at least this one of life's vicissitudes. She saw herself, in a haze of romantic self-sacrifice, bestowing her hand upon him in melancholy gratitude for his generosity in enabling her to rescue Redmayne from having all his hopes of happiness dashed by Miss Piercebridge's revelations; and in after years, her heart eternally Redmayne's although her troth had been plighted to another, she would receive the reward of her nobility by seeing him happy in marriage to the one woman he had always loved. . . .

"And so, Miss Leigh," Sir Edward's voice intruded unwelcomely upon this affecting vision, "I offer you my heart and hand, asking nothing better than to be able to go through life as your bulwark against its storms. If there were but some way in which I could prove my eternal devotion—"

"Oh, but there is!" Elyza pounced upon him, still in the grip of her romantic dream. "There really is, Sir Edward! You see, I am in the most dreadful trouble!"

"In trouble? You, Miss Leigh?" Sir Edward, looking knocked quite out of his reckoning by this unexpected interruption, stared up at her, still in his kneeling position.

"Yes!" said Elyza. "I cannot explain it all to you at present, but I am in the *greatest* need of a thousand pounds at once. And to whom," she went on, carried away to speak in terms almost as exalted as those in which he had been addressing her, "shall I turn if not to you, Sir Edward? If you could possibly see your way to save me—"

"To save you? But from what?" enquired Sir Edward, now looking totally bewildered. "And why must you have a thousand pounds?" He slowly uncoiled his tall, thin figure into a standing position and stared down at her. "You must know," he said rather severely, "that that is a very considerable sum of money to put one's hands on in a moment, Miss Leigh! Indeed, I might say it would be quite impossible—"

"Oh, it wouldn't be *impossible*," Elyza said, glad to exhibit some of the new-found knowledge she had picked up during her sojourn in London. "I have heard people say that there are very obliging gentlemen who will lend you quite enormous sums upon security, without the least difficulty in the world! I should apply to them myself except that I have no notion how to go about it, and, besides, I daresay I have not got any security, whatever that is. But I am sure that if you—"

"Me! Apply to money-lenders!" Sir Edward appeared quite petrified with horror at the idea. "My dear Miss Leigh, you cannot know what you are saying!" he exclaimed. "Indeed, the whole matter bewilders me! What need can you possibly have for a thousand pounds?"

"Well, there is nothing so very odd about it!" Elyza said glibly, recalling Miss Piercebridge's suggestion. "It is merely that I—I have been led into some rather deep play, and now I cannot pay my debts—"

"Into deep play!" Sir Edward looked as if he could not believe his own ears. "No, I cannot credit it! How can such a thing have happened?"

"It is quite simple, really!" Elyza persevered, ploughing desperately forward, though already with the distinctly uneasy feeling that she was not doing the right thing. "It was—it was at Lady Wimsatt's house in St. James's Square—"

"Lady Wimsatt's house!" Sir Edward recoiled. "Do you tell me that Mrs. Winlock would countenance your going to so disreputable a place?"

"She did not know of it!" Elyza floundered on, inventing with her usual facility, though conscious that that horrid sinking feeling somewhere inside her was growing more pronounced. "She—she thought I was gone to Drury Lane with Mrs. Lymburn and her party—only I went to St. James's Square instead with a—a lady with whom I am acquainted—"

A sensible man, seeing Elyza's flushed, uncomfortable face and hearing her faltering words, would have realised at once that he was listening to a Banbury tale, concocted upon the spur of the moment; but Sir Edward, unfortunately, was not a sensible man. He took Elyza's heightened colour and stumbling speech as clear proof of a guilty conscience, and looking at her like a judge pronouncing sentence said awfully that he considered gaming, of all vices, the most dangerous, and particularly reprehensible in a female.

"Had I known, Miss Leigh," he said solemnly, "had I had the least conjecture that you were addicted to play, I assure you I should never for a moment have contemplated marriage with you! I take it very unkindly of Mrs. Winlock that she did not inform me of this! A man in my position, she must be aware, requires of all things prudence and respectability in a wife! Had I but known—"

"Well, you know now!" said Elyza, who had been rapidly losing her temper as she listened to this homily. "And I daresay *I* should have known that you wouldn't lend me a thousand pounds, or even a thousand pence! And as for your not wishing to marry me," she continued, feeling almost with exhilaration that the champagne cork really had popped now and all the fizzing contents of fury and frustration inside her were gloriously exploding, "I am exceedingly glad of it, for you are the very last man I should wish to have as a husband! Indeed, I have been teased to death these past weeks with the idea that you might make me an offer! And now that you know," she concluded, picking up the bouquet of yellow roses and thrusting it upon him quite as unceremoniously as he had upon her, "I wish you will take your roses and *go away!*"

During this speech Sir Edward's countenance had gone from splotchy red to furious white. Being the only son of a doting mama, he had been brought up to think very well of himself, and rage at this unceremonious dismissal so overcame him now that he had difficulty in recalling that he was a gentleman and Miss Leigh a lady, though by her behaviour scarcely within the definition of one of those delicate, well-bred creatures.

"V-very well, ma'am!" he stuttered, with an assumption of as much dignity as his own discomposure and the sight of Elyza's scornfully flashing eyes would allow him. "I shall t-take my leave of you, since it appears we can now have no more to say to each other! But let me t-tell you," he could not prevent himself from adding darkly, as he moved ignominiously towards the door with his despised roses, "that if you are so much addicted to this vice, Miss Leigh, I think it h-highly improbable that you will find any respectable gentleman willing to make an offer for your hand! Your f-fortune, as anyone can see, would be as nothing in the face of this ap-ap-*appalling* extravagance!"

Having delivered himself of this really outrageously ill-mannered speech, he trod out of the room and down the stairs, unfortunately encountering James, the footman, on the landing, who regarded the rejected roses with great interest and later reported to an attentive audience in the Servants' Hall that, by the look of things, Miss Elyza had sent Sir Edward away with a flea in his ear and he fancied they wouldn't see that maggotty looby in the house again.

As for Elyza, she paced up and down the drawing room for some moments after Sir Edward's departure with feelings of mingled high exhilaration over having at last got rid of him and righteous fury over his parting shot, basely hinting that her fortune was the only basis on which she could hope to obtain a husband. But reflection on both subjects was soon banished by the anxious realisation that her greatest problem still remained unsolved—namely, how to obtain a thousand pounds.

The arrival back in the Marine Parade of Mrs. Winlock with the news that she and Lady Mottram, to whom Sir Edward had obviously not confided his resolve to put his fortune to the touch with Elyza that morning, had settled it between them that he would call to make his offer in form on the following morning merely confirmed her in the impression that life was now so much at sixes and sevens that nothing she could do would ever be able to put it to going on properly again. Feeling quite unable to cope with a third major scene that morning, she refrained in a cowardly manner from informing Mrs. Winlock that Sir Edward had already made his offer and been dismissed. Mrs. Winlock, she was convinced, would learn of that *contretemps* soon enough, and meanwhile she really *must* do some concentrated thinking on how to deal with the situation in regard to Miss Piercebridge, which at the moment was of far greater importance to her than any past or future actions of Sir Edward.

Chapter Fourteen

But not even the most concentrated reflection, doggedly engaged in during the entire afternoon, was sufficient to suggest to Elyza's mind any respectable means of obtaining the thousand pounds needed to stop Miss Piercebridge from spreading her tale of scandal. In despair, she decided at last that if she saw Redmayne that evening at the Assembly-rooms at the Castle Inn—which she confidently counted upon doing, as Corinna was to be there—she must take the opportunity to confide the whole story to him, and hope to be able to do so in such a way that he would believe her when she told him it was for Miss Piercebridge, and not for herself, that she wanted the thousand pounds.

"Because I really do not think I shall be able to bear it if he thinks I am low enough to take advantage of the kindness he showed me by getting money from him," she thought forlornly, as she sat at her dressing table watching Hilliard thread a cherry-coloured ribbon through her dark curls. "Of course he will never be in love with me, because he is so very much in love with Corinna, but still I don't wish him to *despise* me."

She was looking so woebegone, in fact, when Mrs. Winlock came into her bedchamber a little later that that sharp-eyed female said if she still had the headache they had best not go to the Assembly that evening. Elyza, seeing her opportunity to talk with Redmayne going glimmering, looked alarmed.

"But I am quite well now, ma'am!" she protested.

And to prove her point she ran downstairs and greeted Colonel Hanley with such a bright smile that that portly military gentleman, who had been rather apprehensively awaiting his meeting with her, looked relieved and told himself that there was nothing to worry about, after all, for Adelina Piercebridge could be as close as an oyster when she chose.

Not many minutes later they were all three entering the elegant Assembly-rooms of the Castle Inn. Here, however, Elyza's hopes received a setback, for almost the first person she encountered upon stepping across the threshold was Mr. Crawfurd, who, having engaged her hand for the country dance that was just forming, led her into the set and informed her at once, with considerable pride, that Redmayne had been invited by the Regent to dine at the Pavilion that evening.

"Oh, dear! And I particularly wished to see him!" Elyza said, looking so disappointed that Mr. Crawfurd, slightly surprised, enquired if anything were the matter.

"Well, actually — yes!" Elyza replied frankly.

She looked speculatively at young Mr. Crawfurd, wondering if she might confide her difficulties to him, but almost at once decided not to. Although he was older in years than she was herself, he was, she well knew, both ingenuous and impetuous, and she rather fancied she would do better to rely upon her own judgement than upon any advice he might give her. What was more, as he lived, she knew, upon quite a modest allowance, it would be impossible for him to come to her aid financially upon his own account.

So she parried the questions her admission elicited, said with what she hoped was a careless smile that she was sure matters would come about, and began to cudgel her brains afresh as to how to arrange a meeting with Redmayne.

Towards the end of the set, however, as she was going down the dance, she saw Sir Edward and his mother enter the ballroom, and at once her thoughts flew to another of her difficulties — namely, how to inform Mrs. Winlock that Sir Edward had made his offer and been rejected. With some apprehension she observed Mrs. Winlock, who had apparently also espied the Mottrams as they came into the room, approach them with her most cordial smile and greet them gaily. The greeting was returned, but so stiffly by Sir Edward, so icily by Lady Mottram, that she saw Mrs. Winlock's face grow rigid with astonishment.

The movement of the dance unfortunately obliged her to turn her back upon this interesting scene at that moment, but when she was again able to cast an anxious glance at Mrs. Winlock she saw her, with a heightened colour, moving rapidly away, tapping her fan angrily upon her open palm, while Sir Edward stood looking both self-conscious and self-righteous, and his mama, who had sunk down on one of the rout chairs at the side of the room, appeared to be inviting the world to admire the melancholy fortitude with which she was suffering the slings and arrows of outrageous fortune.

"Oh, dear!" thought Elyza, her heart sinking. "I daresay they have told her all about it!"

But when Mr. Crawfurd dutifully returned her to Mrs. Winlock at the end of the set, she found her chaperon to be suffering rather from indignant puzzlement with the Mottrams than from disapproving fury with her.

"I cannot conceive what sort of maggot Augusta Mottram has taken into her head!" she declared, looking very hard at the object of her conjecture, who had now roused herself from a lachrymose enjoyment of her own misfortunes to engage in animated conversation with a broad-faced and rather loud-voiced young lady with large hands and feet, got up in a pink frock with far too much ruching and Berlin silk floss ornamenting it. "She all but cut me dead just now, and Edward was almost rude!" She suddenly transferred her gaze to Elyza. "Have you—?" she began suspiciously.

But Elyza was turning thankfully to Mr. Everet, who, coming up just then, was bowing to them and requesting her hand for the next dance.

She moved off with him, conscious that the fat

was in the fire now and that an explanation would have to be made to Mrs. Winlock as soon as they were alone together. But there was no use in crossing *that* bridge, she thought, until she came to it, so she flung herself into conversation with Mr. Everet as one dancing on the edge of a precipice, and asked him how he was getting on with Corinna.

Mr. Everet, looking more romantically handsome than ever with a frown upon his ordinarily pleasant face, said gloomily that he was getting nowhere at all.

"I think she likes playing the lot of us one against the other," he said, with a flash of extraordinarily sound insight for a young man in love. "Did you see her last evening at the Pavilion? I was within amesace of calling Redmayne out when I saw the way she looked at him, but then Belfort came up and began talking to her in that smooth way he has and I'll swear she was every whit as cordial to *him!* Still, when I thanked her for letting me wear her scarf in the race she gave me a glance that—Well, she really *is* an angel, you know!" said Mr. Everet, carried away by the memory of a pair of melting blue eyes raised to his own. "Only what I mean to say is— dash it all, Miss Leigh, if she goes on like this, I shall simply have to blow my own brains out, or someone else's!"

Elyza said severely not to be so silly, but added that if he really *had* to blow someone's brains out she would much rather they were Lord Belfort's than his own or Redmayne's.

"He really is an odious man," she said, "always

184

looking at one with that satirical little smile, as if one were *quite* beneath his notice. I wonder Corinna can endure him! Of course he is a marquis, but if it is any comfort to you I will tell you that I don't think she will have him in the end, no matter how much she is urged by her relations. I am almost sure she holds him in dislike, and only shows him as much civility as she does upon Lady Mayfield's account. And what is more," she added sagaciously, "I think Lord Belfort knows that, too, only he is not the sort of man to be put off by it. In fact, I should think he rather enjoys it."

Mr. Everet, almost audibly grinding his teeth, said he should not at all wonder if that were true, adding that he had heard more than one story to Belfort's discredit when it came to his dealings with women.

"His own wife!" he said. "You did not know he had been married? I daresay not; the lady has been dead a dozen years, but the tale is he made her so wretched that she ran off from him and took refuge with her only near relation, her sister, who was married to a respectable country squire. Belfort is said to have forced a quarrel upon this man, and to have killed him in the ensuing duel. Of course the matter was hushed up," he went on bitterly. "Belfort is a very rich man, and has powerful friends. But if Lady Mayfield believes she can force Corinna into a loveless marriage with him while I have breath in my body, she has sadly mistaken the matter!"

And he glowered so darkly at Lady Mayfield, just then entering the room with her daughter, that she was moved to remark to Corinna that she wondered what little Miss Leigh could have said to Mr. Everet to put him into such a dreadful temper. Corinna, seized with the distinctly disagreeable thought that, for a man who professed such devotion to herself, Mr. Everet appeared to spend a remarkable amount of his time dancing with Elyza Leigh, said coldly that she dared say they were having a lovers' quarrel.

"Oh no, my dear!" said Lady Mayfield seriously. *"Not* Miss Leigh and Mr. Everet! I have it from Agatha Winlock herself that Elyza is all but promised to Edward Mottram."

"Well, if she is," Corinna said a trifle spitefully, "it isn't stopping him from paying violent court to that dreadful Spraggett girl at this very moment. I know she has sixty thousand pounds, but *really,* mama!"

Lady Mayfield's eyes, following her daughter's, were at once transfixed by the sight of Sir Edward dancing with the broad-faced, pink-satin-clad heiress, and ogling her with an earnestness that, in Sir Edward, could not but denote serious intent.

"Good heavens!" said Lady Mayfield, who liked the hint of a broken romance as well as any mother with a daughter whom she has not yet successfully married, although she would have scorned Sir Edward for Corinna, who might have had offers from a dozen more desirable *partis* at any moment if she chose. "I must certainly find out all about this from Agatha Winlock!" she went on. "Or perhaps it would be even better if I asked Augusta Mottram, for if Edward *has* cried off it will have put Agatha into a miff, and she can be most disagreeable when she chooses."

And, having seen her daughter engulfed by her usual throng of admirers, all vying for the privilege of leading her into the next set, she took herself off to the opposite side of the room, where Lady Mottram was uttering confidences, with a lugubriously saintly air, into the eager ear of a turbaned dowager.

Mr. Everet, meanwhile, having followed Lady Mayfield's progress across the room with a rather direly threatening expression upon his face, appeared to be recalled by the sight of Lady Mottram from thoughts of his own romantic difficulties to Elyza's.

"By the bye," he remarked abruptly, "what has happened between you and Mottram? I thought you had told me he was to have offered for you. Has he put his fortune to the touch?"

Elyza blushed and looked highly uncomfortable.

"Well, I daresay you won't answer that," Mr. Everet said approvingly. "But I think I should tell you that he is taking his rejection badly. To say nothing of paying very pointed attentions to that appalling heiress in pink," he said, gazing at the giggling Miss Spraggett and closing his eyes momentarily in pained indication of his revolted sensibilities, much in Mr. Brummell's style, "he is, it would appear, going about spreading some remarkably unlikely story of your being involved in difficulties over gaming debts. Shouldn't think anyone would be gudgeon enough to believe such a Canterbury tale, but there you are. Fellow's a bit of a commoner, I think."

Elyza said, "Oh! How very odd!" in a hollow voice that she felt did not carry the least conviction, but Mr. Everet, obviously more interested still in brooding over his own troubles than over Elyza's, did not appear to notice anything peculiar. After a few moments, again wrenching his mind with difficulty, it seemed, from the bitter sight of his inamorata surrounded by admirers and smiling up at Lord Belfort, he remarked rather absently that no doubt Mottram would think twice about spreading his unpleasant tales if Elyza had a male relation in Brighton.

"I understand your father is out of the country?" he said.

"Yes. In Morocco." Elyza looked slightly alarmed. "You *don't* mean to say that if he were here he would — ?"

"Call him to account? I should certainly think so!" said Mr. Everet bluntly. "I know I should if you were one of my sisters. Deuced bad for a girl's reputation, to have that sort of thing said about her!"

Elyza, remembering Miss Piercebridge, thought with a feeling of rather forlorn frivolity that, if Sir Edward continued in this vein, that enterprising lady might well find she was too late with her scheme to extract a thousand pounds from her as the price of keeping her reputation intact, since there would be no reputation left to save.

"At any rate, if *he* ruins my reputation with his tales, I shan't be obliged to find the money to keep *her* from doing it," she told herself; but it was poor

188

comfort. More than ever now did she wish that the Regent had not invited Redmayne to dine at the Pavilion that evening, for in the face of this new difficulty she felt in direst need of counsel.

The set ended, and to her great relief her hand was claimed for the ensuing waltz before Mrs. Winlock, who by this time had also heard the story being industriously circulated in the Assembly-rooms by both the Mottrams, had time to utter more than the single ominous sentence, "Elyza, I wish to know exactly what you have done to cause Edward Mottram to behave in this *most* peculiar fashion!" It was young Lieutenant Graham, one of her officer admirers, who led her onto the floor, and he too, it appeared, had heard those disagreeable rumours being spread by the Mottrams, or else he had something else on his mind that prevented him from speaking easily and freely to her. He carried on a halting and rather uncomfortable conversation with her as they danced, was betrayed on one occasion into remarking hotly, *apropos* of nothing in particular, that *he* thought she was a regular right 'un, and would tell anyone so, no matter what they said, and ended by treading, to his great confusion, upon the flounce of her frock and tearing it slightly. Elyza was obliged to retire from the ballroom floor to pin it up, which she was very glad to do, as there was no one in the anteroom and she was able to afford the luxury of allowing tears of frustration and unhappiness to well up in her eyes for a few moments before she winked them resolutely away.

At that moment she heard the music wind to a

close in the ballroom. There was the usual outburst of conversation and movement that always follows the end of a dance, and, hearing footsteps approaching the door of the room in which she stood, she slipped out, upon impulse, into the garden.

It was a fine moonlit night, with a soft sea breeze that just ruffled her hair and stirred the heavy summer leaves of the trees visible as black, graceful shapes against a dark sapphire sky. A setting for romance, one would have said—but the voices that struck upon her startled ears as she entered this peaceful, rose-scented scene were far from being those of lovers. In point of fact, they were distinctly unfriendly, and they belonged, as she instantly recognised, to young Mr. Crawfurd and Sir Edward Mottram.

"What *are* they quarrelling about?" she thought, with a sinking feeling that she already knew the answer to this question.

She moved stealthily a little further along the wall of the inn towards the spot where the two young men were standing facing each other in angry colloquy. Their voices now came more clearly to her ears, though the breeze still carried some of the words away.

". . . action of a blackguard . . . defenceless girl. . . ."

That was Mr. Crawfurd's heated voice, and then Sir Edward's reply, self-exculpatory and equally furious, came to her ears.

". . . speaking no more than the truth. . . . I myself was shocked beyond words to learn . . ." And, more peevishly, "At any rate, I quite fail to see, sir, that it is any concern of yours!"

There was a pregnant pause before Mr. Crawfurd's voice, rather too high now, and sounding very strained and young, came to Elyza's ears.

"Then, Sir Edward," it said resolutely, "I may tell you that I make it my affair, since Miss Leigh has no male relation of her own present in this place to take you to account for your actions. Either you will desist from bandying her name about in this public fashion or you will answer for it to me!"

Sir Edward made a contemptuous sound, snapped his fingers, and began to walk away. But he did not get far. As Elyza watched, horrified, Mr. Crawfurd's right hand shot out and, grasping Sir Edward by the shoulder, swung him around to receive a valiantly meant but rather futile blow which merely grazed its intended victim's ear, but startled him so much that he staggered momentarily and almost fell down.

"You young p-puppy!" he exclaimed furiously, when he had recovered his balance. "You—you shall answer to me for this!"

"By all means, sir!" said Mr. Crawfurd promptly, and Elyza realised fatally that, now that matters has progressed this far, he was rather enjoying the high drama of the moment, just as she herself would have done in his place. "I am quite at your disposal," he went on grandly. "Name your friend, sir, and mine shall call upon him in the morning!"

Sir Edward seemed, as far as Elyza could discover by his attitude, rather taken aback for a moment, but then, apparently recognising that the matter had gone too far for him to retreat, began to speak stiffly just as Mrs. Winlock's voice called impatiently from the window, "Elyza! Elyza! Where is that tiresome girl? Elyza! Is that you?"

Elyza turned, distracted. "Oh, do, pray, be quiet, ma am!" she said. "I cannot hear—"

"And what is there to hear, may I ask?" enquired Mrs. Winlock tartly, stepping into the garden and looking severely at Elyza.

The two young men, startled by the sound of feminine voices, cast one dismayed glance at each other and walked rapidly off in opposite directions. Mrs. Winlock came up to Elyza.

What on earth do you mean by it, Elyza, walking out here alone?" she scolded. "Lieutenant Graham told me you had torn your frock and I came to find you, but as usual you are up to some mischief! Have you been eavesdropping on a pair of love-birds out here? *Quite* a vulgar thing to do—but then I daresay I might have expected—"

She led Elyza back into the inn, still scolding. Elyza, feeling quite numb, did not utter a word. It was perfectly plain, from the scene she had just witnessed, that Mr. Crawfurd and Sir Edward intended to fight a duel, and in the whirl of thoughts occasioned by this knowledge one remembrance stood out with dreadful clarity—Sir Edward's boasting to her at Almack's one evening of having spent the entire afternoon at Manton's Gallery, and of the astounding number of wafers he had culped while there.

"I pride myself upon being a crack shot, Miss Leigh," he had said. "Of all things I abhor such brutal sports as pugilism and fox-hunting, but a gentleman should know how to handle firearms in a respectable fashion."

And then there had been an interminable listing of the numbers of unfortunate birds and beasts he had slaughtered on various hunting expeditions—all of which led Elyza to the horrid conclusion that if he did indeed wish to kill Mr. Crawfurd when they met, he would not have the least difficulty in doing so.

"And it will be all my fault if he does!" she thought wretchedly. "Oh, *why* did I ever tell Sir Edward that stupid taradiddle about my having gaming debts? None of this would have happened if I had not!"

Of one thing she was certain—she must prevent the meeting from taking place, no matter to what lengths she had to go. It might be, she was aware, extremely difficult to do so, for she had a confused remembrance of having once heard it said that, by the Code of Honour which so rigidly ruled gentlemen's behaviour in situations of this sort, no apology could be accepted after a blow had been received. And Mr. Crawfurd *had* struck Sir Edward—not very successfully, it was true, but then that probably did not signify, she thought, as long as the intention had been clear.

She supposed she was looking peculiar, with all these unpleasant thoughts jostling one another in her mind, for when they came into the brilliantly candle-lit ballroom Mrs. Winlock glanced at her sharply and enquired if the heat was making her ill.

"Oh, no! No!" Elyza disclaimed quickly, for of all things she did not wish to be bundled off to the Marine Parade before she had had the opportunity of dancing again with Mr. Crawfurd. Perhaps, she thought, if she explained to him that the whole thing had been a hum she could persuade him to apologise to Sir Edward. But this, she knew, was a forlorn hope, and it seemed to her even more unlikely that Sir Edward, who was such a high stickler for all formalities, would accept an apology even if it were given.

As it happened, however, she had no opportunity to put her powers of persuasion to this test, for neither Mr. Crawfurd nor Sir Edward made an appearance in the Assembly-rooms again that evening. She was obliged to give up all hope of doing anything about the projected duel until the morning, and at last began formulating a plan instead for arranging the meeting with Redmayne that she already desired upon her own account; only now an urgent consultation with him as to how they might prevent Sir Edward from putting a period to Mr. Crawfurd's existence must take precedence over her own difficulties.

In her worry over the duel she had all but forgotten those difficulties, even though she was made aware, by a series of dark hints cast out by the young officers with whom she danced during the remainder of the evening, that the tale spread by Sir Edward had reached their ears and that they stood ready to constitute themselves her champions against the unpopular baronet in any manner she desired. This was gratifying but not very helpful, for she knew that their partisanship would do little to turn the balance of public opinion in her favour, judging by the cold looks being cast in her direction by the starchier matrons in the room.

Still, none of this, she felt, really mattered at the moment, in the face of Mr. Crawfurd's mad determination to get himself killed upon her account, and she managed to retain a satisfactory detachment about her own troubles even when Miss Piercebridge, coming up just as she and Mrs. Winlock and Colonel Hanley were leaving, whispered in her ear with an air of ladylike contempt, "What a fool you are, Miss Leigh, to have approached Edward Mottram, of all people, for help with that story of gaming debts! He will never marry you now! And if you wish to retain the least hope that any gentleman will, you must be prepared to keep your part of our bargain very shortly! May I remind you that you can afford less than ever now to have the true story of your adventures exposed—*Mr. Smith!*"

"What," Mrs. Winlock enquired, as Miss Piercebridge glided away and she and Elyza moved towards the door, "was Adelina saying to you so confidentially just now?"

"It was—it was n-nothing—" Elyza began.

"And *don't* think," Mrs. Winlock continued, bearing down explanations in her usual masterful way, "that you are going to lay your head upon your pillow tonight before you have given me a *full* account

195

of this affair with Edward Mottram, because you are not! Gaming debts, indeed! If you have ever played anything more dangerous than Speculation I shall confess myself a fool, and so I have told Augusta Mottram! As it is, I also told her, she may take *that* appellation to herself, and very green she turned when I said the words, you may believe me! 'If you wish to whistle thirty thousand pounds down the wind, my dear, that is *your* affair,' I said to her. Then she cast Susan Spraggett into my teeth, and *I* said, 'All very well, my dear, *if* you think you can get her! But sixty thousand pounds going for a baronetcy and that tumbledown barracks of a house in Northumberland! I think *not*, my love!' I have been thinking, Elyza, that it would be as well if you saw rather more of that nice Crawfurd boy in future. They have a very pretty place in Wiltshire, I am told, and he will have ten thousand a year when he inherits. I am sure Sir Robert would be pleased!"

Chapter Fifteen

Fortunately for the happy outcome of at least one of Elyza's problems, Mrs. Winlock's quarrel with Lady Mottram had reconciled her to the demise of her hopes of arranging a marriage between Elyza and Sir Edward, and upon their return to the Marine Parade, Elyza was allowed to escape to her own bedchamber after having given only a very sketchy account of her interview with Sir Edward. Following this, she spent a decidedly unquiet night, and before Mrs. Winlock had so much as thought of ringing for Hilliard in the morning she herself had dressed and scribbled a note to Redmayne, urgently requesting him either to call in the Marine Parade that day or to suggest some other rendezvous where they might meet.

Having sealed the note with a wafer, she went off downstairs in search of her friend James, the footman, to whom she entrusted it with strict instructions to deliver it personally into the hands of Redmayne himself and to wait for an answer. James, scenting romance, winked and said mum was the word and she could trust him to keep his chaffer close, and added approvingly, before he went off, whistling, down the street, that Mr. Redmayne was a right-down proper man.

A suspenseful half hour followed, at the end of which time Elyza, who had been on the watch from the window, saw him returning with what appeared to her a rather crestfallen air. Her heart fell. She ran down to meet him at the door.

"Well?" she enquired urgently, as soon as he had entered the house. "What is it? Were you able to see him?"

James shook his head. "Nay," he said in his slow Devonshire drawl, looking quite as disappointed as she was herself. "He'm gone off to Cuckfield already, Miss Elyza, along with the other young gentleman, to see a mill."

"A mill? Oh — you mean a prize-fight," Elyza said. "But — but if it is to take place in the morning, as I believe they usually do, won't he be back, perhaps, later in the day?"

James, in spite of his obvious sympathy with her disappointment, could not prevent himself from grinning at these hopeful words.

"Nay, miss, *that's* not likely," he said. "Thurr's that much excitement, you see, at a mill that it takes a man a bit of time after to quiet himself down to ordinary living again. Happen they two young gentlemen'll make a day of it — *and* a night," he added reflectively. "I wouldn't look to see neither of 'em back here in Brighton before the moon's high."

"Oh, *dear!*" said Elyza, and went off upstairs again

to her bedchamber to think what she could do now.

It seemed to her, after half an hour of wrestling with the problem, that there was nothing she *could* do. If Redmayne and Mr. Crawfurd had gone off to Cuckfield, she could not follow them there, nor, apparently, by James's reckoning, could she hope to see either of them at the Assembly-rooms of the Old Ship that evening. And meanwhile, she suspected, Sir Edward's second and Mr. Crawfurd's would have made all the arrangements for the duel, which, from what she knew of such matters, would then take place as soon as possible, probably on the following morning.

Of course, there *was* the possibility that Mr. Crawfurd had confided the whole story to Redmayne and had even asked *him* to be his second. But on the whole she was of the opinion that it was far more likely that Mr. Crawfurd, suspecting that Redmayne would take a disapproving view of his rash action in challenging Sir Edward, would have enlisted the services of one of his hot-headed young officer friends instead.

The possibility remained of going herself to see Sir Edward, explaining to him that the story she had told him concerning her gaming debts had been nothing but a Banbury tale, and begging him not to go through with a duel based entirely upon it. But even the briefest consideration of this step was enough to convince her that it would be quite useless, as Sir Edward's reaction to it would undoubtedly merely be outrage both at the notion of his having been made the victim of a hoax and at her presuming to meddle in such a purely masculine matter as an affair of honour.

But meddle she must and meddle she would, and before the morning was out she had laid her plans.

These involved a brief colloquy with James, who disappointed her by taking the same tiresomely male view of the utter inappropriateness of her interfering in the matter that she had attributed to Sir Edward. But with James she could use authority, and after futilely arguing with him for some minutes in an attempt to bring him round to her way of thinking, she abandoned cajolery and reason and ordered him, in somewhat heated terms, to bring her the hall-boy's bottle-green coat and darned Inexpressibles that night.

James, scandalised, said that it was one thing for her to go about dressed as a boy in London, where there were so many people that she might hope to be unnoticed, but it was a far different matter in Brighton.

"Gammon!" said Elyza scornfully. "At five o'clock in the morning I shall certainly see no one I know! And I simply *can't* call at Mr. Redmayne's house at that hour as Miss Elyza Leigh! That *would* appear very odd, and if people should hear of it, it would cause any amount of trouble for both of us, I am sure! All the same, I *must* get Mr. Redmayne to try to do something about stopping the duel before it happens, and as there is no possible way for me to be sure of seeing him except by going to his house, I shall certainly go there!"

She added optimistically that she was certain that

if she kept her hat—or rather the hall-boy's—well down over her eyes, not even Redmayne's butler would be able to recognise her, upon which James became so involved in explaining to her that no respectable butler in his right mind would think of answering the door at five o'clock in the morning that the substantive part of the argument was quite forgotten and Elyza, blithely assuming that it had been decided in her favour, thanked him for his prospective assistance and went off.

So it was that, as the earliest light of dawn broke over the peacefully sleeping streets of Brighton, the door of a house on the Marine Parade was opened and the figure of a slim youth in a bottle-green coat crept stealthily out and off down the street in the direction of the Steyne. The figure, having encountered no living creature other than a large and self-satisfied black cat, who was strolling homeward after a night of illicit revelry, arrived shortly afterwards at the magnificent mansion of the Duke of Bellairs, pulled the bell, and waited rather nervously for some response from within its tranquil and imposing bulk.

Somewhat to his—or rather her—surprise, for the slim youth was of course Miss Elyza Leigh in the hall-boy's lendings, the door swung open almost immediately. Ram, resplendent in his usual scarlet and gold, appeared in the aperture and regarded her with, it seemed, faint indications of surprise beneath his monumental impassivity.

"Ah—Miss Leigh!" he remarked noncommittally, after a moment.

"Oh" said Elyza, disappointed. "You recognised me!"

Ram bowed.

"But, of course," Elyza recollected, somewhat consoled by the thought, "you have seen me dressed in these clothes before. May I come in?" she added, seeing that Ram was making no move to admit her.

Ram looked doubtful.

"If," said Elyza persuasively, "you are thinking of my reputation, it would really be much better to let me in, because I *must* see Mr. Redmayne, and someone may recognise me if I stand out here. He is in, isn't he?" she asked, in sudden anxiety.

Ram, admitting her somewhat reluctantly, said he was in, but sleeping.

"Well then, you must wake him up," Elyza said. "It is a matter of life and death," she added urgently, upon which Ram, apparently coming to some decision, showed her into a large, deserted saloon, still shuttered against the night, and, lighting a lamp in the shape of a water lily that stood upon a ornate buhl table with crocodile feet, himself went off up the stairs.

Elyza, left alone with the water lilies, the crocodiles, and the dragons that seemed to surround her on every side, sat down rather nervously on the edge of a chair opposite a large, frowning statue of a many-legged goddess, who seemed to resent her intrusion. To her relief, she had not long to wait. In a very few minutes Redmayne, in shirt and breeches, his crisp fair hair still tousled from sleep, strode into the room.

"What the *devil*—!" he exclaimed, as she rose to greet him and his eyes took in "Mr. Smith's" bottle-green coat and breeches and ill-tied cravat. "Have you lost your senses?"

"No—but I simply *had* to see you," Elyza said, feeling for some reason suddenly unaccountably shy in her male attire before those raking, unsmiling blue eyes, "and—and I thought it would perhaps not seem quite so odd if a boy came to call upon you at this hour instead of a girl. It is about Mr. Crawfurd," she hurried on, anxious to get away from these personal matters. "He is going to fight a duel with Sir Edward Mottram, probably this very morning, and it is all my fault, and as Sir Edward is a crack shot, you see I *had* to come and try to get you to stop it."

It required some minutes of persistent enquiry upon Redmayne's part to elicit from his visitor a clear picture of the series of events, beginning with Miss Piercebridge's threats and Elyza's own fruitless application to Sir Edward for the thousand pounds that lady had demanded, that had led to the impending duel and the presence of "Mr. Smith" in his house at this peculiar hour of the morning.

"Pair of gudgeons!" was his succinct comment upon the projected heroics of Mr. Crawfurd and Sir Edward. "If either of them had ever seen a man killed, they wouldn't be so eager to come to standing up at a dozen paces and letting off pistols at each other. And *you*," he went on, looking accusingly at Elyza, "deserve to be shot yourself for setting on the affair. Why didn't you come to me if you were in difficulty, instead of trying to cozen Mottram with that outrageous pack of lies?"

"Well, *he* believed it!" Elyza said, with some spirit. "And I *have* come to you now, but as far as I can see, you are doing nothing but scolding me, which will not help to mend matters in the least!"

But at that moment, perhaps fortunately for the maintenance of friendly relations between them, there was the sound of carriage wheels outside. They looked at each other and then Redmayne, moving swiftly, extinguished the water-lily lamp that Ram had lit, leaving the room in the grey, pallid dawn-light that enveloped the rest of the house. The next moment pebbles rattled suddenly in a harsh shower against an upstairs window. This was followed almost immediately by the sound of cautious footsteps on the stairs.

"Oh!" squeaked Elyza breathlessly. "It is Mr. Crawfurd! They are going to fight this morn—"

A hand clapped over her mouth cut the last syllable short. When the footsteps had passed the door of the saloon the hand was removed.

"What are you *doing?*" she sputtered indignantly. "Don't you see he is leaving? Are you going to let him—?"

"Stay here," said Redmayne briefly, and strode into the hall.

Of course she followed him, and reached the front door in time to see him walk down the steps and enter into conversation with a startled Mr. Crawfurd, who seemed just about to step into a smart new cabriolet with its hood up, the reins of which were being held by Lieutenant Graham. As Elyza and the lieutenant watched, fascinated, Mr. Crawfurd exhibited obvious signs of finding the conversation not at all to his liking, listened with an appearance of great reluctance to perhaps a dozen words, said—"No! Dash it, I'm going!"—in a very loud voice, and turned stubbornly towards the cabriolet again.

The next moment, before Elyza's dazzled eyes, the same extraordinary phenomenon occurred that she had seen once before, in a ring of cheering spectators at a fair on the Bath Road. One moment Mr. Crawfurd was standing, quite conscious and able to talk and move like everyone else, beside the cabriolet, and the next, after a series of movements by Redmayne so rapid that they seemed to take effect with the suddenness of a lightning bolt, he was lying peacefully on the ground, snuffed, as Lieutenant Graham pronounced in an awestruck voice, like a candle.

"Oh! What have you *done* to him!" Elyza shrieked, tumbling out the door and down the steps in her zeal to give succour to the stricken Mr. Crawfurd.

"That's all right, then," said Redmayne in a businesslike voice. He looked down at his recumbent friend, nursing a slightly bleeding knuckle on his right hand. "Ram!"

Ram appeared from the house and came down the steps.

"Carry him inside and put him to bed, will you?" said Redmayne. He turned to Lieutenant Graham. "Just wait a moment until I get my coat, old boy," he said.

He walked into the house as Ram, ignoring the ministrations by which Elyza was attempting to revive the unconscious Mr. Crawfurd, picked him up as easily as if he had been a baby and followed Redmayne into the house. Elyza and Lieutenant Graham stared at each other.

"Miss Leigh!" said the lieutenant after a moment, in the strangled voice of one who has seen too many wonders in one day and is seriously beginning to doubt his senses. "It *is* you! But what—?"

"Oh, that does not matter!" Elyza said impatiently. "The thing is, what will Sir Edward do now? Poor Mr. Crawfurd *can't* meet him this morning, and though I was very angry for a moment with Mr. Redmayne for knocking him down, I quite see now that it is far better this way than letting him go off and have Sir Edward shoot him."

Lieutenant Graham, still in the same shocked voice, managed to say that it wasn't done, really it wasn't.

"Yes, I know, old boy," said Redmayne, once more emerging from the house, this time wearing a coat of dandy russet and a Belcher handkerchief knotted round his neck. "But I'm afraid I've been out of England for too long to have much patience with this sort of foolery. However, we shan't deprive Sir Edward of his fun, if he likes to have it. Is that a pair of duelling pistols you have there?" he demanded, nodding towards a long slim leather case lying on the seat beside the lieutenant.

Lieutenant Graham, looking more dazed than

ever, said that it was, upon which Redmayne picked up the case, opened it, and carefully examined the pair of wicked-looking, silver-mounted pistols that lay inside. "A nice pair," he said approvingly. "Swiss, I see. They'll do."

Lieutenant Graham, who now appeared to be wavering between a case of the same sort of violent hero-worship that had beset young Mr. Crawfurd upon his first meeting with Redmayne and a strong feeling that an unforgivable social lapse was about to be committed in which he would be forced to participate, enquired in an incredulous voice if it was Redmayne's intention to fight Sir Edward in Mr. Crawfurd's place.

"If he likes," said Redmayne. "Fair enough, don't you think? I daresay you won't mind acting as my second, old boy, as it might be a deuced awkward business to try to find someone else at this hour of the morning."

Lieutenant Graham stammered that he would be honoured, and then looked as if he wondered why he had said it.

"But—but, look here, sir," he tried to formulate the whirling thoughts that were pinwheeling in his mind like a rocket gone berserk and exploding in all the wrong places, "what if he doesn't—I mean, what if he won't—?"

"As a matter of fact, I don't think he will," Redmayne said coolly, "but at any rate he won't be able to say he wasn't given the chance. And now—" he began, turning to Elyza.

But before he could go any farther she interrupted him violently, her face suddenly going very red, like a child's when it is about to cry.

"*No!*" she said. "I won't let you! I *never* meant, when I asked you to stop it—I mean, it will be *just* as bad if he shoots *you*—"

"Don't be a widgeon, Elyza," said Redmayne, but quite kindly. "It's as unlikely as anything that anyone will be shot. Now you go back to Marine Parade—"

"*No!*" said Elyza, even more determinedly than before. "I won't! You can't make me. I am going with you!"

Lieutenant Graham looked as if for two pins he would throw the whole thing up and drive away in the cabriolet, but the thought of Sir Edward awaiting an opponent whom he, Lieutenant Graham, had pledged himself to produce upon the field of honour deterred him.

"Really, Miss Leigh—" he expostulated in despair.

Elyza paid no heed to him. She was standing, her feet very firmly planted in the hall-boy's boots and her face still quite pink, before Redmayne.

"If you don't take me with you," she said in a clear, threatening voice, "I shall walk about Brighton all morning in these clothes till everyone has seen me! You can't stop me!" she went on, retreating strategically a few hasty paces as it seemed Redmayne was about to make a movement towards her. "You won't be able to, because you won't be here. And if I go with you I shall—I shall be able to look after you if—if you are hurt," she added, in a much lower and rather wavering voice, as a vision of Redmayne lying senseless and bleeding upon the greensward rose horridly in her mind.

Lieutenant Graham, looking scandalised, said there would be a surgeon for that. It was quite unheard of, he added severely, for a lady to be present at a duel!

"Well, if I know Mottram, there won't be a duel," Redmayne said, suddenly reversing his stand and coming down upon Elyza's side. "I'll tell you what, Elyza—you may come with us if you'll give me your word you won't let Mottram or his second see you. You're to stay in the cabriolet—sit on the floorboards and keep yourself hidden under the rug, do you understand? It will be better, at any rate, than having you parading all over Brighton in those clothes!"

Elyza said rather rebelliously that she would stay out of sight as long as Sir Edward didn't shoot him, which cavil did not appear to bother Redmayne, as he only laughed and helped her up into the cabriolet. It was rather crowded when he had got in too, but not uncomfortably so, as Elyza was small and Lieutenant Graham a very slender young gentleman.

"Would you like me to drive?" Redmayne enquired after a moment, observing that the lieutenant was sitting in his place as if paralysed, the reins motionless between his fingers.

"No! That is—well, really, sir, I *can't*—" said the lieutenant, growing quite as scarlet as Elyza had a few moments before and looking at Redmayne imploringly. "I mean to say—it isn't *done!*"

209

Elyza said warmly, "I think you are quite right! We had all much better stay here, and then when Sir Edward is tired of waiting he will go away."

But the horrible picture conjured up by these words was sufficient to cause Lieutenant Graham to give his horse the office to start, and in a few moments they were moving off briskly up the Steyne. At any rate, the lieutenant was reflecting miserably, it was better to bring *someone* on the ground to face Sir Edward and give him satisfaction for the insult he had received than to bring no one at all.

Conversation did not flourish during the drive. It was by this time beginning to grow quite light, and the cheerful sounds of a midsummer dawn — the stir and twitter of birds, a cock's clarion crow, the soft ripple of a morning breeze in the tops of the trees — had the day all to themselves, as far as the occupants of the cabriolet were concerned, except for the rattle of wheels and the steady *clop-clop* of the horse's hooves. Lieutenant Graham drove out past the town in the direction of Woodingdean, and before long turned the cabriolet off on a broad woodland ride. At a clearing a closed coach came into sight, and then Elyza had an unwelcome view of Sir Edward, standing with a young gentleman in spectacles who had once been introduced to her as Mr. Titcomb, and a middle-aged man in the black frock-coat of a physician, all three clustered in an uneasy knot beside the coach.

"Now," said Redmayne to Elyza, "down on the floorboards you go, Mr. Smith — and if I so much as catch a glimpse of that revolting hat, I promise you

I'll have your liver and lights!"

And with a slight grin of encouragement for her, which somewhat mitigated the effect of this ferocious threat, he cast the rug over her as she curled up obediently at his feet. The cabriolet having come to a halt near the waiting group, he then swung down from it lightly and approached Sir Edward and his companions, followed — as soon as he had secured the cabriolet's reins — by a reluctant Lieutenant Graham.

In spite of Redmayne's threat, Elyza had not the least notion of remaining in such a position that she could not see what was going on, so when she heard the sounds of masculine conversation and deemed that the attention of the participants would be centred elsewhere than upon the cabriolet, she peeped out cautiously from under the rug. She was at once able to see that an animated discussion was taking place, chiefly between the bespectacled Mr. Titcomb and Lieutenant Graham, on the unusual circumstances that had led to Redmayne's appearing upon the field of honour as surrogate for Mr. Crawfurd.

"Most irregular . . . preposterous . . . quite unheard of!" came huffily from Mr. Titcomb, while Lieutenant Graham, looking unhappy, endeavoured to stem the tide of his indignation and Redmayne, apparently content to let the storm run its course before attempting to speak himself, stood calmly by.

As for Sir Edward, he was obviously torn between outrage at this flouting of the rules of proper etiquette concerning a duel and a feeling of desperate hope that now the duel need not take place at all. If only, Elyza thought, her heart bumping uncomfortably against her ribs with the suspense of the moment, someone like Mr. Brummell or Lord Alvanley, whose opinion as to the proper social conduct under the circumstances Sir Edward could rely on, would come along and tell him it was quite unnecessary for him to fight Redmayne, he would no doubt be as relieved as anything and not do it. But the possibility of either of those gentlemen appearing was quite remote and it would be just like Sir Edward, she thought in despair, to insist upon killing Redmayne merely because he thought convention demanded it of him.

In this reading of her erstwhile suitor's sentiments she was not far wrong. As Mr. Titcomb, having expressed his indignation to the fullest, at last fell silent, Elyza saw Sir Edward address Redmayne in a stiff, formal way, and obviously he was doing exactly what she had feared he would—suggesting the necessity of their going forward with the duel.

"Very well, if you like," Redmayne's voice rang out cheerfully. "But it seems a pity; I haven't the least wish to put a bullet through you, old boy. Graham, have you those pistols handy?"

The lieutenant, who was carrying the case under his arm, looked alarmed at this sudden request, but allowed the case to be opened and one of the pistols selected by his principal, whereupon a very peculiar scene—at least to Elyza's eyes, and certainly to the outraged Mr. Titcomb's—took place. It appeared that certain targets, all of which seemed to Elyza ridiculously small and at a phenomenal distance, were being proposed, first by Redmayne and then with increasing enthusiasm by Lieutenant Graham and with incredulous discomfort by Sir Edward. The pistols were primed, loaded, and fired; twigs from incredibly distant trees broke and fluttered to the ground; and finally Sir Edward, stung, it seemed, into competition, seized one of the pistols and failed miserably, on several tries, to emulate his opponent's feats. The firing ceased; the small group stood for a moment, as if irresolute, and then drifted back in the direction of the cabriolet.

"An idiotish business, upon all accounts," Elyza heard Redmayne's voice remarking pleasantly to Sir Edward. "A hot-headed halfling like Crawfurd—he is hardly more than a boy, you will admit—and a young lady with a taste for spinning Banbury tales; you will not like to be made an object of ridicule by appearing to take all this seriously, old boy! Far better to go quietly home and forget the whole affair. Which I assure you I am prepared to do as well, provided you are willing to make amends to the young lady in question by telling anyone to whom either you or Lady Mottram repeated that remarkably silly story about gaming debts that you had mistaken the matter and there is no truth in it. Naturally, however," he added, as Sir Edward sulkily said nothing, "if that course of action doesn't appeal to you, I stand quite ready to put a bullet into you here or at any other time and place you care to set."

There was an odd, dangerous note in these last words that Elyza had heard before. Evidently Sir Edward heard it, too, for his sallow face suddenly coloured up in alarm (one could scarcely blame him for *that*, Elyza thought, feeling charity with all the world at this exalted moment, when she had just heard Redmayne offer to shoot Sir Edward for her sake, because if Redmayne had not missed the twigs he would certainly not miss *him*) and he said very quickly and stiffly that to cast an undeserved slur upon a young lady's name was the last thing in the world he desired to do.

"She is perhaps rather—rather *overvolatile*," he said in a self-justifying sort of way; but Redmayne looked so unencouraging that he added hastily that of course he would see to it that the story was contradicted, upon which Elyza felt as if she would have liked to set up three cheers, but dutifully restrained herself.

There was no need for restraint, however, once Redmayne and Lieutenant Graham had returned to the cabriolet and Sir Edward and his companions had driven away, and both she and the lieutenant were so loud in their praise of the way in which Redmayne had managed the matter that he was obliged to quell their enthusiasm by reminding them that if Elyza were not returned immediately to the Marine Parade his managing Sir Edward would be of no avail in preserving her reputation.

"My reputation!" thought Elyza guiltily. "Oh, dear! But there is still Miss Piercebridge!"

But as this was obviously not the time to discuss that matter, with Lieutenant Graham seated beside them in the cabriolet, she resolved to wait until they had arrived back in the Marine Parade and then hope to exchange a word with Redmayne in private upon that subject.

In this, however, she was doomed to disappointment. Brighton was stirring and waking under a golden morning sun as they entered its streets once more: a butcher's cart rattled over the cobblestones; maidservants were flinging up windows; and on the deserted beach a solitary early-morning bather in a scarlet-striped suit was just about to enter a lazy, sparkling sea.

Redmayne said, "Time you were safely home, Mr. Smith. Can you get into the house without calling up a servant to admit you?"

"Oh, yes!" Elyza said proudly. "I had thought of that. James has left the service door open for me, and he will be on the look-out and warn me if there is anyone about."

Redmayne nodded. "Well then," he said, "when Graham stops the carriage I want you to nip out like lightning and into the house. It's not likely that anyone you know will be strolling down the Marine Parade at this hour, but still it won't do to take chances."

"But—but—!" Elyza stammered protestingly. "I haven't really talked to you as yet about what we are to do about that—that *other* matter—"

"That's all right," Redmayne said calmly. "I'll take care of it, and see you later in the day. Do you go to the Lymburns' moonlight picnic tonight?"

"Yes! Do you?"

"Well, I haven't a card yet, but I shall get one," Redmayne said, so matter-of-factly that Elyza almost expected him to add, "Quigg will attend to it," as she had heard him do more than once in the past.

It was comforting, at any rate, to feel that the matter of Miss Piercebridge and her threats might now be left in his hands, and it was with a considerably lighter heart that she entered the house on the Marine Parade than she had left it with a few hours before. Mr. Crawfurd had been rescued from a untimely death at Sir Edward's hands; Redmayne, she did not doubt, would now give her the thousand pounds she needed; Miss Piercebridge would be silenced; and Corinna, in happy ignorance of the fact that her lover had all too recently been discovered under highly compromising circumstances travelling on the Bath Road with Miss Elyza Leigh, would consent to marry him and they would live happily ever afterwards.

But at the thought of this extremely satisfactory end to the story such a lump came into her throat and such a prickling to her eyes that she felt obliged to run up the stairs very fast to try to get away from them—a wholly inadvisable thing to do, as it only made her stumble in the hall-boy's ill-fitting boots and practically fall into her bedchamber, banging her knee painfully against her dressing table, which was as good an excuse as any for having a bout of very unrestrained and undignified tears.

Chapter Sixteen

Owing to James's assiduity in collecting the hall-boy's clothes before Elyza's maid entered her bed-chamber that morning, Mrs. Winlock remained in happy ignorance of her ward's early-morning excursion, and expressed surprise only at the unaccountable drowsiness Elyza displayed at breakfast, for as that enterprising young lady had stayed awake the better part of the night for fear she would not be up at a sufficiently early hour to save Mr. Crawfurd, she was understandably very sleepy.

Mrs. Winlock, still full of her recent falling-out with Sir Edward and his mama, was now pressing forward diligently in her pursuit of Mr. Crawfurd, and suggested when breakfast was over that they might walk to Donaldson's in the hope of meeting him there.

"I should really feel you were far safer if he were to escort you to the pic-nic tonight instead of your going with the Mayfields," she said. "Lady Mayfield is careful enough, certainly, in looking after Corinna, but she is quite unreliable in all other respects, and I cannot like her being the only other chaperon present, outside of Mrs. Lymburn. These *al fresco* parties are so apt to turn into romps when they are given after dark!"

Elyza, remembering her last view of Mr. Crawfurd as Ram had carried him into Redmayne's house a few hours before, was quite willing to wager a considerable sum that they would not find him at Donaldson's that morning, but as it was impossible for her to inform Mrs. Winlock of her reason for thinking this, she held her tongue and was presently carried off to the library. As she had anticipated, there was no sight of Mr. Crawfurd there or anywhere else, and Mrs. Winlock was equally disappointed in not seeing Miss Piercebridge, with whom, she declared with some irritation, she had made a particular appointment for that hour.

Elyza, however, could only be grateful for Miss Piercebridge's absence, which relieved her of the necessity of endeavouring to explain to her why she had not yet succeeded in obtaining the thousand pounds she had demanded. She went home to take a much-needed nap that lasted most of the afternoon, and caused Mrs. Winlock to demand with some asperity why the quiet day she had spent yesterday should have left her so fatigued.

But she was quite restored to her normal self by the time the Mayfields' carriage arrived at the door, and looking very fetching in jonquil muslin with double scallop work round the bottom—though she could not, as she was the first to confess, hope to compete with Corinna's dazzling fairness, set off by a frock of the palest blue *mousseline d'Inde*. The sight of Miss Mayfield, indeed, was sufficient to bring back all the disagreeable thoughts that had darkened her morning, about that ravishing young lady's living happily ever after with Redmayne, while she, a forlorn Cinderella, went back to a mundane existence among the ashes again.

It was all very melancholy, and even the excitement of the large and rather elaborate *fête champêtre,* that had been contrived by the famous Mrs. Lymburn, a young matron of unexceptionable antecedents but dashing habits, to lend *éclat* to what she considered the boring round of Assemblies at the Castle and the Old Ship, failed to delight her as it would ordinarily have done. She looked with indifference upon the fairyland of a grove lit by innumerable coloured lanterns—a vista of exotic light in a silvery, moonlit landscape, with the pale, transparent gowns of the ladies moving like winking glowworms against the dark, obscuring coats of the gentlemen beneath the overarching trees—seeing only that it was Redmayne to whom Corinna, with her light laugh and radiant face, appeared to drift irresistibly as she left the carriage.

Mr. Crawfurd unexpectedly materialised before her out of the darkness.

"Oh!" said Elyza, regarding him in some surprise. "I didn't expect *you* would be here tonight."

"Well, I am," said Mr. Crawfurd incontrovertibly. He looked at her rather truculently, somewhat self-conscious, it seemed, of a large purple bruise, showing livid and ghastly even under a hopeful plaster of powder, upon his jaw. "I'm dashed if I'm going to stay cooped up like a moulting pigeon till I'm fit to be seen again. Besides, it doesn't show much in this light, does it?" he asked anxiously.

Elyza, with splendid mendacity, assured him that it scarcely showed at all.

"I'm telling anyone who asks that I fell down the stairs," he said, glowering at her gloomily. "They'll think I was bosky; that's all." He added, in an accusing tone, "I daresay you think you've been very clever!"

"Well, I *couldn't* let Sir Edward kill you — could I?" Elyza asked reasonably. "Especially as it was all my fault for telling him that hum about my gaming debts. But I *do* think it was very noble of you," she continued earnestly, "to offer to fight him for my sake."

Mr. Crawfurd, looking somewhat mollified by these words, said magnanimously that it was nothing.

"Oh, but it was!" said Elyza. "Indeed, it was excessively brave of you, for he is a crack shot, you know, and I daresay there are not many men who would like to go out with him!"

Upon hearing these words of praise Mr. Crawfurd so far forgot the animosity occasioned by Elyza's unwarranted interference in his affairs as to ask her to stand up with him for the set of country dances about to form upon the broad platform that Mrs. Lymburn had caused to be built upon the greensward for this purpose.

"I should love to," Elyza said, allowing him to

lead her into the set. "I think I should tell you, though," she continued punctiliously, feeling that she had already caused far too much trouble in Mr. Crawfurd's young life to let him in for any more, "that you had best not show me a great deal of attention tonight. You see, since it is out of the question now for Sir Edward to marry me, Mrs. Winlock has had to look out for someone else, and I am awfully afraid you are the one."

"Me?" Mr. Crawfurd looked at her, aghast. "But I don't—I mean, I'm not—"

"Well, *I* know that," Elyza said tolerantly. "You needn't look so sick. And you needn't worry. I managed not to marry Sir Edward, and I can manage just as well not to marry you."

Mr. Crawfurd, who had suddenly gone scarlet—a colour that did not at all agree with his purple bruise—out of a feeling that he had forever forfeited by his churlish behaviour the right to be considered a knight *sans peur et sans reproche,* stammered that he hadn't meant—he didn't mean—

"Of course you don't," said Elyza cordially. "It is only that you don't care to marry anyone. I know just what you mean, because that is the way I feel, too. I mean, I don't care to marry anyone, either. I'm going to be an old maid and perhaps raise dogs."

Mr. Crawfurd, looking at her rather doubtfully, said he didn't think she'd care for that.

Elyza looked as if she didn't think so, either, but said nothing, and at this point the movement of the dance separated them.

221

During the interval that elapsed before they came together again, Mr. Crawfurd, although punctiliously performing the proper steps, found himself doing a great deal of powerful, if rather incoherent, thinking. The sight of the suddenly stricken look upon Elyza's face as he had suggested that she might not care to go through life as an unmarried female, his secret admiration of the resourcefulness that had allowed her to put an end to his duel with Sir Edward, coupled with a general feeling that she was really an extraordinarily good fellow, if one could so express oneself about a young lady, all at once fused together into a rather exalted feeling that if he, Nicholas Crawfurd, were to step into the breach and offer his hand to her, it might really not be such a bad thing all around. She was, he decided, as he and Elyza came together again and he critically examined her piquant face with its quite disproportionately enormous, black-fringed dark eyes, a deuced pretty girl, and game as a pebble as well, and if one had to marry and settle down in life some day, as his mother was forever reminding him it would be his duty, as the heir, to do, one might really do a great deal worse for oneself.

The upshot of all this hurried meditation was that, at the conclusion of the set, he remarked in a very *dégagé* way that it was a deuced hot night and what about seeing what Mrs. Lymburn had provided for them to drink? He had already observed that the refreshment buffet had been set up quite at the edge of the lighted portion of the grove, where one might easily wander off into the sort of secluded, romantic spot suitable for the making of a declaration, and with Machiavellian cunning but the purest of motives he now led Elyza in this direction.

Having provided her with a glass of lemonade and himself with a bumper of champagne, which he rather felt he needed under the circumstances, he was encouraged to invite her, with a man-of-the-world air, to take a turn with him in the moonlight. As this seemed to be an idea that had already occurred to a number of the other guests, who were unobtrusively disappearing—by some peculiar coincidence, always in pairs—from the lighted areas, Elyza promptly agreed, and in a remarkably short time found herself, to her utter astonishment, backed against a tree with Mr. Crawfurd on one knee before her, giving voice to the inanities peculiar to a young man launching into his first offer of marriage.

"Nicholas Crawfurd!" she said severely, when she had recovered from her surprise sufficiently to be able to speak. "What in the world has come over you? Are you foxed?"

Mr. Crawfurd, looking up at her indignantly, said scornfully, "What—on one glass of champagne? What do you take me for? Now, see here, Elyza—" Considering that the conversation had now taken such a turn that it seemed somewhat inappropriate to continue it upon one knee, he rose and went on warmly, "You needn't try to bam me into thinking you want to be an old maid, and I don't know why, if you're going to marry someone, you shouldn't marry me as soon as Edward Mottram. He's a

223

deuced dull sort of fellow, I can tell you; wouldn't suit you at all."

"Yes, I *know* that," Elyza said helplessly. "But I don't wish to marry him, either, you see. Oh, Nick, *do* be sensible—" She broke off suddenly as what sounded like a feminine scream, immediately stifled, came from very near them, just on the other side of a small thicket. "What was that?" she enquired.

Mr. Crawfurd, impatient at the interruption, said probably someone having a bit of fun.

"No, it wasn't," said Elyza positively. "It didn't sound a bit like that. She sounded quite terrified, whoever she is. Come on!"

And with an entire disregard for Mr. Crawfurd's loverlike feelings she picked up her skirts and ran quickly around the thicket, followed by her reluctant suitor.

But the sight that met his eyes as he rounded the bushes was sufficient to galvanise him into a state of excitement quite equalling Elyza's. A closed carriage was drawn up here, where a woodland ride penetrated the grove, and as Elyza and Mr. Crawfurd came up a struggling female form was being forced inside it by a tall man in impeccable evening dress, who then swiftly entered the coach himself. The door was shut; a figure upon the box immediately gave the horses the office to start, and in the space of seconds, before Elyza and Mr. Crawfurd, transfixed with amazement, could move or speak, the carriage was rolling off rapidly down the ride and had disappeared into the darkness.

Elyza was the first to recover herself.

224

"That was Corinna!" she said excitedly. "It was! I recognised her frock! *And* it was Lord Belfort who forced her into that carriage Oh, Nick! Do you suppose he is *abducting* her?"

Mr. Crawfurd's first instinct was to pooh-pooh the idea, which to his mind smacked more of the romantic villainies one's grandparents were wont to bore one with in their reminiscences of their salad days well back in the interminable reign of the present king than of the realities of the prosaic nineteenth century. But an uneasy conviction that Elyza had been speaking the truth held him silent. Certainly Corinna—if it had indeed been Corinna, as Elyza appeared quite certain it was—had not gone willingly into the carriage, and he knew Lord Belfort's reputation as a wholly ruthless man, capable of going to almost any lengths to get what he wanted. And that he had long wanted Corinna Mayfield was common knowledge in the *ton*. Mr. Crawfurd had an uneasy feeling that he ought to do something, but what there was to do, beyond alarming Lady Mayfield with a perhaps totally apocryphal tale of her daughter's abduction, he could not see.

Elyza, however, was made of sterner, and certainly more adventurous, stuff.

"We must go after them!" she decided at once. "I am sure it is his plan to make Corinna marry him by taking her away with him like this at night, so that she must either be ruined or consent to have him!" Her eyes, Mr. Crawfurd noted uneasily, had begun to glow with what seemed to him a wholly unnecessary fervour, for he had all the well-bred young Englishman's dislike of involving himself un-asked in other people's affairs. "We *must* save her!" she declared.

Mr. Crawfurd said feebly that perhaps Miss May-field would not wish to be saved.

"Girls are queer cattle—well, you know that your-self!" he said, suddenly realising that he was talking to one of them. "It's quite likely she intended to have Belfort all along—only pretended to give him the cold shoulder to drive him into some romantic foolery like this—"

Elyza interrupted him indignantly. "Nicholas Crawfurd!" she said. "You call yourself a friend of Mr. Redmayne's and you can say a thing like *that!* You know he is desperately in love with Corinna and she with him! If you let Lord Belfort take her off now, you will have ruined Mr. Redmayne's life!" She looked about her determinedly. "We must go after them at once—do you understand?" she said. "Where have the carriages been left? Oh, I know! It is quite close here." And she uttered once more the unwelcome words, "Come on!"

Mr. Crawfurd followed her, protesting all the way. "But I have not brought a carriage; I came with Cleve!" he said. "And we have no notion where they have gone! If it is really your idea that he has ab-ducted Miss Mayfield, we had far better go and in-form her mother—"

Elyza rounded on him scornfully. "Why? To frighten her into a fit of the vapours?" she de-manded. "That is the only thing that would come of it, and by the time she recovered sufficiently to *do* anything, it might be too late!" She had by this time the satisfaction of seeing before her the open field upon which were drawn up, in waiting ranks, the carriages in which the company had driven out to the grove. "And if *you* don't know where Lord Belfort is taking Corinna," she continued, pursuing her way with determination towards Redmayne's whitewinged curricle, which she had immediately picked out from the throng of other less striking equipages, "*I* do! I heard him say only the other day that he had had his yacht brought to Newhaven; of course he intends to carry her abroad! But he shall not succeed, if I can prevent it!"

Mr. Crawfurd, observing her purposefully approaching Redmayne's groom, who was lounging against the curricle in conversation with a stout coachman in splendid livery, said in some alarm, "But, see here, Elyza! I simply *can't* take Cleve's curricle—"

"Why can't you?" said Elyza. "*He* would certainly wish you to do so, I am sure! After all, it is Corinna we are hoping to save!"

And to Mr. Crawfurd's agonised discomfort she addressed the groom, informing him succinctly that she and Mr. Crawfurd required the curricle for a short time on a matter of the upmost importance.

"And I think it would be a good idea," she said, as he stood staring at her, "if you would go to find Mr. Redmayne at once and tell him that if he can borrow another vehicle he should come after us as soon as possible. Tell him we are taking the road to Newhaven and that Miss Mayfield is in danger." She turned impatiently to Mr. Crawfurd. *"Do* come and help me up so we can be off quickly!" she said. "I daresay it is not a matter of so much as ten miles to Newhaven, and if we do not start at once we may be too late!"

Mr. Crawfurd, exchanging a glance with the bewildered groom that ignored social position and represented merely the appeal of one harassed member of the male sex to another in the face of female tyranny, obediently came round and helped her into the curricle, and then jumped up himself and took the reins.

"What a pity Mr. Redmayne wasn't driving his greys tonight!" Elyza said, looking with dissatisfaction at the splendid bays harnessed to the curricle, which statement at last gave Mr. Crawfurd something to be thankful for. As generous as Redmayne had always been to him, he could not believe that he would take kindly to his going off with his prized greys without so much as a by-your-leave, and it was with a sense of gratitude to Fate for at least sparing him this added trial that he gave the bays the office to start and guided them across the field to the road.

So masterfully had Elyza taken the lead in the affair that it was not until the road had been reached that it occurred to him that his driving off alone with her to Newhaven at this hour — no matter for how laudable a purpose — would place her in almost as compromising a position *vis-à-vis* him as was Corinna *vis-à-vis* Lord Belfort. One glance at her intent, determined profile, however, was sufficient to convince him that trying to bring her to appreciate this fact would be a waste of time and energy; and at any rate, he reflected, beginning to take a more philosophical view of the matter, he already planned to marry her, so no real harm would be done, after all.

So he gave the bays their head and, in the intoxication of driving full tilt along moonlit roads behind what he characterised as a team of prime 'uns, sixteen-mile-a-hour tits if he had ever handled any, soon lost his gloomy doubts in the exhilaration of the chase.

Chapter Seventeen

Meanwhile, Redmayne's groom, having watched the curricle disappear from view, exchanged a few pithy words on the subject of the unaccountable vagaries of the Quality with the stout coachman and then set off in search of his master.

He had some little difficulty in finding him, for Redmayne was not dancing, nor did he appear to be sampling the refreshments that the Lymburns had liberally provided for their guests. It was not, in fact, until the waltz that had been in progress had ended that the groom came up with him as he was enquiring of Mr. Everet, with an expression of some exasperation upon his face, whether he had seen Miss Leigh.

The groom, feeling his uncertainty as to the wisdom of accosting his master during a social function considerably abated by the knowledge that he knew the answer to this question, touched his hat and said hoarsely, "Guv'nor!"

Redmayne swung round. "Well?" he asked, rather impatiently.

"I know where she is," the groom said hastily, feeling it

suddenly necessary to justify his presence before his master's unsympathetic gaze.

"Where *she* is? Where who is?" enquired Redmayne sharply. "What's the matter with you, Stubbs? Have you been drinking?"

"Me, sir? No, sir!" said Stubbs indignantly. "You can't say you ever seen me with the malt above the water when I was on duty." He went on rather sulkily, "It's that Miss Leigh—"

"Miss Leigh?" Redmayne pounced upon the words. "What about Miss Leigh? Do you say you know where she is? Speak up, man!"

"Well, sir, haven't I been a-tryin' to tell you?" said Stubbs, with some indignation upon his own part. "She's gone off to Newhaven in your curricle with Mr. Crawfurd—"

He got no further. "To Newhaven! With Crawfurd?" Redmayne cut in, incredulously. "What sort of cock-and-bull story are you telling me?"

"Tain't no cock-and-bull story, neither!" the groom said stubbornly. "Ain't I seed 'em with my own eyes? Took the curricle right from under my nose, they did, the two of 'em, and, 'You go and find Mr. Redmayne,' she says to me, 'and tell him we're off to Newhaven and he should come after us. And tell him,' she says, 'that Miss Mayfield is in danger—' "

"*What!*" The exclamation came from Mr. Everet, who had been following the interchange up to this point with an appearance of bored amusement, suitable to a disciple of the great Mr. Brummell, upon his face. The boredom now abruptly disappeared; he took a step forward and addressed the groom urgently. "Miss Mayfield—she said Miss Mayfield was in danger? You're certain of that?"

"As certain-sure as that I'm a-standin' here on my own two feet, sir," Stubbs declared promptly, gratified to see that he had at last produced a sensation. " 'You tell him,' she says, 'that Miss Mayfield is in danger,' and then she and Mr. Crawfurd drives off in *your* curricle, sir," he said disapprovingly to Redmayne, as if washing his hands of the whole affair, "which if you'll say fair you'll say it warn't *my* place to stop them, and if Mr. Nicholas don't overturn it before ever he gets to Newhaven you may call me—"

"Redmayne!" Mr. Everet interrupted this self-justifying speech in a vibrating voice. "I am going after them! At once!"

And he began to stride off, only to find that he was being accompanied by Redmayne.

"I'll come with you," said Redmayne, in what seemed a noticeably exasperated tone. "Damn it, if that little monkey has been up to her tricks again—!"

Mr. Everet looked astonished. "That little monkey? Miss Mayfield?" he said.

"No! Elyza! Miss Leigh! She has been getting herself into one scrape after another, and now this! Haring off to Newhaven with young Crawfurd in the middle of the night!"

Mr. Everet said in a somewhat reproachful tone that, if Miss Leigh and Crawfurd had reason to believe that Miss Mayfield was in danger and had gone to her assistance, he must applaud their action, no matter how unconventional it might appear to the eyes of the world.

"Yes, that is all very well," Redmayne said, still, it appeared, so violently exercised over Miss Leigh's part in the affair that Mr. Everet, who had never seen his rather

232

inscrutable calm shattered before, was moved to look at him in slight surprise. "But ten to one she has got it all wrong and Miss Mayfield is in perfect health and safety — and even if she has not got it wrong, it is *not* her business to look after Miss Mayfield!"

Mr. Everet again looked at him reproachfully, but as they were by this time nearing the field where the carriages had been left, he neglected to express his opinion of such callousness in regard to Miss Mayfield's well-being and concentrated his attention instead upon finding his curricle.

This was soon done, and he was about to mount to the driver's seat when, with a sudden change of mind, he handed the reins to Redmayne.

"Deuce take it, it goes against the grain with me to admit it, but *you* are the better whip," he said, "and this is a case where minutes may tell the tale." He added darkly, as he jumped up into the curricle beside Redmayne, "She was dancing with Belfort. If he has contrived to do her any harm —"

Redmayne said, in a voice of controlled patience, that it was more than likely that it was Miss Leigh who had contrived to land both herself and Miss Mayfield in a bumblebath, and then added, in a tone of such sudden ferocity that it made Mr. Everet stare, that he would break every bone in Nick Crawfurd's body if his totty-headed act of driving her to Newhaven led to any harm to her.

So the two gentlemen, each nourishing thoughts of black vengeance, pursued their breakneck journey through the tranquil, moonlit landscape, thundering on to the peril of any stray vehicle in their way, brushing wheels with a down-the-road-looking young man in a smart phaeton, who was unwise enough not to give them room to pass, and causing the more nervous passengers in a lumbering stagecoach to inveigh against young Bloods who, when a trifle up in the world, drove in such a way as to endanger the lives of respectable citizens. Mr. Everet, if he had not been so preoccupied with his anxiety over Miss Mayfield, would have found the experience educational as well as exciting, and, even as it was, took the time to form a mental resolve to ask Redmayne to impart to him upon the next feasible occasion his trick of featheredging a corner at full speed without overturning his vehicle.

But this and all other considerations were driven from his mind when, as they were approaching Newhaven, they suddenly came upon a scene of utter confusion in the road before them. Two vehicles, it appeared — Redmayne's white-winged curricle and an elegant closed carriage — were entangled in a maze of struggling horses and crashing wood, and masculine oaths and feminine shrieks rent the air in concert with shrill equine neighs.

As Redmayne and Mr. Everet sprang down from their curricle, they saw Corinna suddenly tumble from the closed carriage, followed closely by Lord Belfort; at the same time Mr. Crawfurd, leaving Redmayne's curricle to Elyza, leapt down and, approaching Lord Belfort, attempted to grapple with him. This obliged Lord Belfort to abandon his efforts to restrain Miss Mayfield, but not for long; as a celebrated amateur of the Fancy and habitué of Gentleman Jackson's Bond Street Boxing Saloon, he was able to meet Mr. Crawfurd's impetuous onslaught with aplomb, and in the space of only a few moments Mr. Crawfurd, for the second time in the space of less than four-and-twenty hours, was stretched at full length upon the ground.

Lord Belfort turned again to Corinna, who had fled, shrieking, to Elyza and the curricle, and was in imminent danger of being trampled under the hooves of the frightened horses. From this danger she was rescued by Mr. Everet, who, rushing to her side, pulled her out of the way of harm and then, clasping her in his arms, enquired in impassioned accents if she was hurt.

Meanwhile, Redmayne had approached Lord Belfort, and a brief but spirited encounter then took place, which would have gladdened the heart of any gentleman of sporting proclivities, had any such been present and in proper case to enjoy it. Lord Belfort, it is true, made some effort to postpone it by beginning a very hurried explanation as to the reason for his presence in a closed carriage with an obviously reluctant Miss Mayfield at this hour on the road to Newhaven; but Redmayne, who was obviously in no mood to listen patiently to anyone, invited him grimly to come on, with what, to Elyza, were now entirely predictable results. Even as she herself battled to curb the frightened team Mr. Crawfurd had entrusted to her, she set up a cheer of triumph as she saw Lord Belfort join Mr. Crawfurd on the ground.

Redmayne, having completed this task, strode over and, swinging himself up into the madly careening curricle, jerked the reins from her hands and gave himself up to the problem of bringing the bays under control. When he had leisure to speak, he turned a face of such furious exasperation upon her that Elyza involuntarily quailed before it.

"Of all," he gritted, from between clenched teeth, "the bird-witted little idiots — !"

Elyza coloured up, but her chin lifted defiantly.

"I am *not* an idiot!" she said. "I have saved Corinna from being run off with by Lord Belfort—or at least Nick and I have—and I should think that *you,* of all men, would be grateful to me!" She looked at Miss Mayfield, who was drooping, still clasped in Mr. Everet's protecting arms, beside the curricle, and suddenly her face paled. "Oh!" she said faintly. "He is—he is kissing her! And she—s-seems to like it!"

"I hope she may!" said Redmayne, in the same furious voice. "And I hope you may, too, for that is exactly what is going to happen to you!"

And to her exceeding astonishment she suddenly found an arm flung about her in a rough embrace, and her lips crushed beneath Redmayne's. The moonlit night, all at once turning into a magical fairyland where a gala display of the most extraordinary fireworks imaginable was being presented, swung and glittered around her, while she, now one with the very centre of the universe, tightened her own arms about his neck, in complete disregard of his momentarily somewhat inadequate control of his team.

"But—but you are in love with Corinna!" she stammered as he at length perforce released her to prevent his horses from trampling to death the equally preoccupied pair beside the curricle.

"The devil fly away with Corinna!" said Redmayne unchivalrously. "If you mean I was gudgeon enough to fancy myself in love with a girl I'd seen only once in my life, and to travel halfway around the world to find she existed only in my own imagination, I shall have to plead guilty! Also to having been fool enough to try to impress her and the world with a social consequence I don't possess! But I have not," he went on, looking at

Elyza severely, "been so clothheaded as to run off to Newhaven with her in the middle of the night, with the result that I should have felt obliged in honour to offer her marriage!"

Elyza, who was still feeling quite dazed from the experience of the past few moments, contemplated these words for a short time without replying.

"If you mean by that," she said at last, trying to speak reasonably, "that Nick will feel obliged to offer to marry me because we went off together after Corinna, then that is all right, because he already has."

"He has!" Redmayne looked staggered. "But why the devil — ?"

"I think he was sorry for me," said Elyza candidly, "because Sir Edward does not wish to marry me any longer." Suddenly recollecting the disagreeable situation in which they had left Mr. Crawfurd, she peered anxiously over the side of the curricle. "Oh!" she said. "And that reminds me — had we not better go and pick him up? Oh, he is getting up himself!"

And indeed Mr. Crawfurd, staggering to his feet at that moment, was to be seen looking down in some bewilderment at the recumbent form of Lord Belfort, also beginning to show signs of life.

"By Jupiter!" exclaimed Mr. Crawfurd, an expression of incredulous satisfaction dawning happily upon his battered countenance. "Did *I* do that?"

"No — silly!" said Elyza, unable to repress a gurgle of laughter. "Mr. Redmayne did!"

Mr. Crawfurd, bewilderment once more seizing him, took in Redmayne's presence in the curricle beside Elyza; his astonished gaze then travelled to Mr. Everet, who was still tenderly supporting what appeared to be the half-fainting but entirely blissful figure of Miss Mayfield.

"I say!" exclaimed Mr. Crawfurd, looking apprehensively at Redmayne. "Do you see—?"

"Yes, I see!" said Redmayne, with some asperity, and reddening slightly, which, as colours are notoriously difficult to see by moonlight, fortunately went unobserved. He went on rather hastily, "If you are in a case to take these reins, Nick, I shall retrieve Everet's curricle so that he may drive you and Miss Mayfield back to town. I trust," he added, looking his own vehicle over as Mr. Crawfurd obediently scrambled up beside him, "you haven't damaged mine sufficiently that it isn't fit to go!"

"Well, I don't think you should say it in that tone," Elyza remarked defensively, "because it was really very clever of Nick! He managed to draw in front of Lord Belfort's carriage, you see, and swing the curricle across the road so that it—I mean the carriage—couldn't go any farther, and it is not *his* fault that Lord Belfort's coachman was not quick enough to stop his carriage in time." She pointed to Lord Belfort, who had just succeeded in getting to his feet and was pursuing a hasty but wavering course towards his own vehicle. "Look!" she said. "He is getting away! Hadn't we better stop him?"

Redmayne, who was pursuing his own course towards Mr. Everet's curricle, which his chestnuts had luckily decided not to run away with, being, like all their kind, much inclined to stop and do exactly what they saw other horses doing rather than go off on their own, said over his shoulder, "Why?"

"Well," argued Elyza, "he *was* trying to abduct Corinna!"

"Then Corinna may have him up before a magistrate if she chooses," said Redmayne. "But I doubt very much that she will care to. "

"No, my God!" said Mr. Crawfurd, impressed by this logic. "Raise the deuce of a dust to make the business public! Much better to let him go off abroad, which I daresay is what he will do now. Can't hope to go about as usual any longer, with all of us holding a what-you-may-call it-sword of Damocles over his head," he concluded, looking very self-satisfied with his own scholarship. "He—this fellow Damocles," he explained kindly to Elyza, "was a sort of old Greek who had to eat his dinner with a sword suspended by a single hair over his head."

"Well, *I* think," said Elyza uncompromisingly, "that if he did what Lord Belfort tried to do, it would have served him exactly right if it had fallen on him and injured him dreadfully. If *I* were a man—"

Happily for Lord Belfort, at that moment expeditiously entering his carriage and directing his henchman to drive off at a gallop, she had no time to urge her male companions to further action, for just then Mr. Everet and Miss Mayfield approached the curricle.

"May I express my eternal gratitude to you, Miss Leigh, and to you, Crawfurd," said Mr. Everet fervently, "for your prompt action upon Miss Mayfield's behalf? I shudder to think what might have happened if you had not taken the matter into your hands!"

"Well, it was all Elyza's idea, really," Mr. Crawfurd said modestly, while Elyza, feeling like Flora Macdonald or some equally intrepid heroine of history, blushed and preened herself.

"Yes—and just like her!" Redmayne's voice said bluntly, as he came up leading Mr. Everet's team and curricle. "Rash, generous to a fault, and extremely prone to land herself in the briars!" Elyza, her bubble of romantic play-acting pricked, looked at him indignantly, but Redmayne went on to Mr. Everet without heeding her. "Here is your curricle, Jack. Fortunately your cattle didn't bolt. I hope you and Miss Mayfield won't be too crowded by being obliged to take Crawfurd up with you, but at all events he may serve you as a chaperon."

Mr. Everet, his glowing eyes fixed upon Corinna, said in the quite besotted voice of a man who has just attained his heart's desire in female form that a chaperon might no longer be considered necessary in this case, as Miss Mayfield had just promised to be his wife.

"Very sorry to cut you out, old boy," he said, with what was obviously total insincerity, for anyone looking less sorry about anything at that instant it would have been difficult to imagine, "but she says it was always me she cared for, though she may have been carried away for a brief moment to believe she might be forming an attachment for you."

"Oh, yes!" murmured Miss Mayfield, blushing and hiding her face against Mr. Everet's shoulder. "It was always you, Jack! I knew only too surely, when I saw your attentions to Elyza—"

"Angel!" said Mr. Everet. "As if I could ever for a moment have cared for anyone but you!" Withdrawing his attention with difficulty from Miss Mayfield, he went on after a moment, to Redmayne, "So I daresay it might be better if *you* took Crawfurd up with you. I mean to say— Miss Leigh's reputation and all that—"

"Thank you, but I shouldn't dream of depriving you," Redmayne said politely. "You see, Miss Leigh and I are also about to become betrothed, and I am afraid I should find Nick confoundedly in the way when I came to make my declaration."

Elyza's startled eyes flew involuntarily to his face, and Mr. Everet blinked.

"*About* to become betrothed!" he exclaimed. "But how can you be certain, if you haven't yet put it to the touch—?" He looked at Elyza. "Oh, I see!" he said, the radiance in her eyes suddenly enlightening even his at present rather addled wits. "*He* is the man you said you were—"

"Yes!" said Elyza, blushing and speaking rather hastily. "But there is no need to say anything of that now. Good night, Corinna. Good night, Mr. Everet. I hope you will tell Lady Mayfield that she is not to trouble herself about me any further tonight, for of course Mr. Redmayne will take me home."

The thought of Lady Mayfield, who had by this time undoubtedly succumbed to strong hysterics owing to the unaccountable disappearance from the pic-nic not only of her daughter, but also of the young lady for whom she had agreed to make herself responsible for the evening, was sufficient to spur the departure of Mr. Everet and Miss Mayfield. Mr. Crawfurd scrambled down from Redmayne's curricle and up into Mr. Everet's; the party *à trois* drove off at a rapid pace, and the party *á deux* was left seated in a stationary curricle upon an empty moonlit road, with nothing stirring about them but a soft ripple of breeze in distant trees.

It was Redmayne who first broke the silence. "What," he asked abruptly, "did Everet mean when he asked you if I was the man you—?"

"The man I told him once I was in love with," Elyza

said in a very small voice. "And it is quite true — only, please, if you really are still in love with Corinna and are only asking me because you are d-disappointed — "

"Does this," enquired Redmayne, "look as if I am disappointed?" — and to the entire disapproval of his team, who were accustomed to receiving his full attention while he held the reins, he repeated his performance of a short while back in regard to kissing his fellow passenger. The team, discovering that erratic backing and halfhearted attempts at rearing up between the shafts had no effect whatever in recalling him to a sense of duty, gave it up and stood waiting with admirable docility for their two passengers to complete their all-absorbing conversation, which seemed to consist for a time merely of murmured words of pure folly.

At last, appearing to grow somewhat more rational, they began to speak in a more coherent manner.

"But when" — that was Elyza's voice, still filled with incredulous wonder — "*when* did you stop being in love with Corinna and begin to be in love with me?"

"I can tell you the very time and place," said Redmayne promptly. "It was on the Steyne, at the start of my race with Everet, when you stepped forward and pulled that yellow riband from your hat. It was," he said, with a sudden flight into poetic expression quite foreign to his usual manner, "as if the scales had dropped from my eyes."

"Oh!" said Elyza, still a little doubtfully. "But you didn't say — I mean you didn't *do* — I mean the next time I saw you, at the Royal Pavilion, you didn't *seem* — "

"My darling Elyza," said Redmayne, "I know I did not. The truth of the matter is that I had been knocked so a-cock by the notion that I didn't really care tuppence for Corinna that I wasn't quite certain at the time of my own complete sanity. It comes as the devil of a shock, you see, to realise you've let a milk-and-water miss with a pretty face charm you out of your senses, and that you've been building your life for two years around a girl who never existed except in your own imagination. And then to find at the same time that you've been overlooking the one girl in the world you *could* really care for and wish to spend the rest of your life with—! Well, good God, look at the difference between you! You may have been the maddest little fool in the three kingdoms to go after Corinna as you did, but do you imagine for a moment that she would ever have mustered up the courage to do the same for you, if the circumstances had been reversed?"

"Yes, but I didn't do it for *her;* I did it for *you,* because I thought it would ruin your life if she married Lord Belfort," Elyza said, blushing, which confession struck her companion as indicative of such singularly beautiful nobility of character that he found it necessary to kiss her again, thus causing the off wheeler to lose all patience and make a strenuous effort to kick the floor-boards out of the curricle.

"Here!" said Redmayne, transferring his attention from Elyza to his reins. "What are you up to, you devil?" As he brought the team under firm control once more, he said to Elyza, "I daresay we had best go on. Your Mrs. Winlock may not be the kind of female to fall into a fit of the vapours, like Lady Mayfield, at the thought of having mislaid you, but it won't do to have her getting the wind up too, and making any more of a stir about your disappearance than Lady Mayfield has probably done. I've already had to speak very strongly to Miss

Piercebridge, you know, to keep her from spreading about the tale of your discreditable adventures on the Bath Road."

"Oh!" said Elyza guilty. "Miss Piercebridge! I had quite forgotten her! Did you speak to her? And did you give her a thousand pounds?"

"Yes to the first; no to the second," Redmayne said, giving his team the office to start. "You absurd infant, don't you know that the last way in the world to rid yourself of a person with ambitions to become a blackmailer is to give him money? I arranged an interview with Miss Piercebridge this morning as soon as Graham and I had dropped you off in the Marine Parade, and I don't think you will be troubled any further with her threats to reveal that you and Mr. Smith are one and the same person."

"But what did you *say* to her?" Elyza asked, impressed.

"Well, for one thing, that I was going to marry you as soon as l could find a quiet moment alone with you to ask you." He glanced down at her, his impassive blue eyes softening as they rested upon her slight figure. "Do you think me an unconscionable coxcomb for being so sure of you?" he asked. "But it seemed to me I couldn't be mistaken after you had braved all the world to give me that yellow riband!"

For answer, Elyza merely rubbed her cheek violently against his shoulder. He put one arm about her, and she leaned her head against the Bath superfine of his coat, remaining silent for so long as the horses wended their way back to Brighton through the magical moonlit night that her lover, pardonably curious, was at last moved to enquire, "What are you thinking of now?"

"Only how happy I am," said Elyza, without stirring or lifting her head. "And that it *must* be true, and not a dream, because there is a horrid hard button cutting my cheek — No, don't!" she said, as he moved apologetically. "If I am *quite* comfortable I shall be sure it is all a dream, and that I shall go home and Mrs. Winlock will tell me that I must marry Sir Edward, or Nick, or someone else I don't care to marry at all!"

"Well, she won't have the chance to tell you that any more," said Redmayne decisively. "We'll give her our news tonight, and I'll write at once to your father. Is he likely to raise any objection, do you think?"

Elyza, with the besotted assurance of any newly engaged young lady that her betrothed is so magnificently above criticism that no one in his right mind could possibly find him anything other than perfect, scornfully said of course not. But they were to have the opportunity of hearing Sir Robert's own views on the subject at a far earlier date than either of them at that moment suspected.

Chapter Eighteen

Though the hour was quite advanced when Redmayne at last brought his curricle to a halt before Elyza's residence in the Marine Parade, the house was ablaze with lights and Mrs. Winlock's carriage was seen to be drawn up in waiting before the door. Redmayne, entrusting his team to the groom in attendance upon Mrs. Winlock's vehicle, sprang from the curricle and was engaged in helping Elyza down when the front door opened and out stepped a very large gentleman in a magnificent caped driving coat.

"Papa!" cried Elyza, staring in utter amazement.

The large gentleman stopped and stared, too. "Is that you, Elyza?" he said after a moment, in a rather belligerent tone for a father who had not laid eyes upon his offspring for a period of several months. "Well, well, it's about time! What have you been up to—eh? Had Emily Mayfield here a short while back. Silly woman. Always was. Seemed to think you'd gone off to Newhaven or something of the sort with a young fellow named Crawfurd. Servants' gossip. Told her she oughtn't to listen to it, but Mrs. Winlock took it into her head I'd better go off and see, though it's a deuced uncomfortable thing to be doing at this time of night, especially after you've been travelling all day."

During this somewhat uncordial monologue he had dutifully embraced and kissed his daughter and now led the way back into the house, where he was helped out of the magnificent driving coat by Satterlee and relieved of his high-crowned beaver and gloves. He then stood revealed as a corpulent gentleman of middle age and imposing appearance, dressed in the very height of elegance from his starched cravat to his gleaming boots. Mrs. Winlock, who had run downstairs from the drawing room at the sound of the commotion below, took in the sight of a slightly dishevelled Elyza in company with Redmayne, compressed her lips momentarily in complete disapproval, and then pinned a bright smile upon them and came rapidly across the hall to place her hand lightly upon her ward's arm.

"Why, Elyza, you naughty child, what *have* you been thinking of, to put such a fright into us!" she said. "And Sir Robert coming in so unexpectedly to find us in such a flurry! But all's well that ends well, I daresay, and here you are safe and sound, after all!" Her eyes for the first time flicked over Redmayne's quietly waiting figure. "How kind of you to bring her home, Mr. Redmayne!" she said, with rather icy civility. "And now I daresay you will excuse us; it has been such a long time since Miss Leigh has seen her father, you know!"

Redmayne, ignoring her patent wish for his immediate departure, said politely that he regretted the intrusion, but that as he had something rather particular to say to Sir Robert, it might be as well if he remained for a short time.

"Eh! What's that? Something to say to me?" said Sir Robert. He put up his quizzing glass. "You're Crawfurd, eh? I don't think we've met."

"No, sir," said Redmayne. "We haven't. But I'm not Crawfurd. My name is Redmayne."

"Not Crawfurd, eh?" Sir Robert looked at Mrs. Winlock with an air of some satisfaction. "Told you so, m'dear," he remarked. "Hen-witted female, Emily Mayfield. Never got the straight of anything in her life. Well, if you have something to say to me, young man, we'd best go upstairs. No sense in standing about here in the hall."

Mrs. Winlock, smiling her most charming smile at Sir Robert, said of course he must come upstairs at once and make himself quite comfortable.

"I cannot tell you how vexing I find it, dear Sir Robert," she went on, as she led the way up the stairs and into the drawing room, "that you should discover us in such a pother, for you must know that Elyza and I have been going on charmingly here up to this time. Brighton is so very gay this summer—"

"Gay every summer, ever since Prinny took it into his head to make it fashionable," Sir Robert grunted, depositing his corpulent form in a winged armchair. "Can't say it's a place I'd choose to take a young girl myself—set of shocking loose-screws about, every sort of riot and rumpus being raised—but I daresay you know best. Told you I'd leave it all in your hands, and if we come out all right and tight, with Elyza going off properly in the end, I'll have you to thank. Be the first to admit it."

Mrs. Winlock, who was quite aware that she had nothing at all to boast of to Sir Robert at the moment on the subject of finding an eligible husband for Elyza, made haste to turn the subject, remarking to Redmayne that if he really had something of importance to say to Sir Robert — "though for my part," she said, with a tinkling laugh, "I cannot conceive what it may be, at this hour of the night!" — perhaps he had best say it at once, as it was growing late and she was sure Sir Robert was fatigued.

"I'm sorry, sir," said Redmayne equably, addressing Sir Robert. "I shan't take up much of your time at present, though I hope I may have a longer conversation with you at some early future date. But I thought it best to let you know at once, in the event any gossip about what has occurred this evening should reach your ears, that I have asked Miss Leigh to be my wife and she has done me the honour to say that she will. Of course I am aware that an immediate marriage must depend upon her obtaining your consent —"

He got no further, for at this point he was interrupted by both Sir Robert and Mrs. Winlock.

"Want to marry her, eh?" said Sir Robert, looking undecided as to whether to give vent to his relief that he was so easily going to be freed from the responsibility of a daughter whom he scarcely knew or to his indignation at Redmayne's unceremonious introduction of the matter.

And at the same moment Mrs. Winlock exclaimed in incredulous amazement, "Marry Mr. Redmayne! Elyza, you sly thing! And all the while I believed it was Cor—"

A thought suddenly seemed to strike her; she bit off the words and stopped speaking, her eyes narrowing slightly as she regarded Redmayne. Sir Robert, finding himself with a clear field, decided it would be more seemly to let indignation hold sway, and remarked in an aggrieved tone to Mrs. Winlock, "Well, well, no one ever tells me anything! The last letter I had from you, ma'am — at Meknes, it was; dull sort of place; can't think why the Sultan cares to live there — you gave me to understand you were arranging to marry her off to young Mottram. One reason for hastening my return. Don't want that woman in my family on any terms — Augusta Mottram, that is. Poisonous sort of female — almost caught me with her languishings and her vapours thirty years ago. Got her father, old Mindess, after me to make me marry her because of some crotchet she'd taken about our having been stranded alone for a couple of hours at an inn when my phaeton lost a wheel. Well, he caught cold at that, I can tell you; no man has ever contrived to put the change on *me!*"

And Sir Robert, apparently having momentarily forgotten the subject of the present proposed marriage in his rehearsal of his lucky escape from a past one, glared triumphantly around the room.

Mrs. Winlock said, with sycophantic eagerness, "No, no, I should think not indeed, Sir Robert! And I quite understand your feeling about the Mottrams! I grieve to say that Augusta Mottram *did* take me in for a time, but I — though not, alas! gifted with *your* perspicacity, dear sir — soon found her out for what she really is! And as for Edward Mottram, I may tell you that he is in no way a suitable husband for our sweet Elyza. Such a very dull young man — to say nothing of the estate's being sadly encumbered! Now Mr. Redmayne, on the other hand, is quite able to provide a position in the world for Elyza such as befits her station as your daughter. He has only recently returned from India, but I understand that the

Prince, who has heard excellent reports of his valuable services there from Sir Oswald Coxeter, has already been gracious enough to entertain him upon several occasions at the Royal Pavilion —"

Had the drawing-room ceiling chosen that moment to descend upon the heads of the four persons seated beneath it, Elyza's astonishment could not have been greater. Mrs. Winlock praising Redmayne, Mrs. Winlock coming down upon her side in an attempt to persuade Sir Robert to allow her to marry him! This was a wonder she had never thought to see. She looked at Redmayne, and the almost imperceptible expression of amusement in his blue eyes as they rested upon Mrs. Winlock suddenly brought enlightenment to her. But of course! she thought. Mrs. Winlock had been employed to find a suitable husband for her, and, having failed to do so, she was now attempting to make capital out of the situation by convincing Sir Robert that the young man who had providentially appeared upon the scene as a suitor for his daughter was an entirely eligible husband for her.

Sir Robert, who at heart was quite as anxious as Mrs. Winlock to see his daughter settled in lawful matrimony, looked appraisingly at the young man before him.

"Redmayne, eh?" he said, still a trifle crossly. "Don't know the name. Or no — wait a bit! Wiltshire family?"

"No, sir. Yorkshire," said Redmayne. A slight flush reddened his bronzed face. "My father was a clergyman of respectable family but very straitened means," he said steadily, "and my mother's family were all yeoman farmers, though there was a distant connexion with the Kerslakes. I was sent to India in the employ of the East India Company when I vas very young, and until his

251

death six months ago was associated there with Mr. Angus Macquoid. He left his fortune to me when he died."

"Macquoid? The Nabob?" Sir Robert looked interested and, in spite of himself, impressed. "Good Lord! But he was as rich as Golden Ball, I've heard! Left it all to you, eh?"

"Yes, sir."

"And you want to marry my little Elyza!" said Sir Robert. "Well, well, I daresay you know *her* history, so it'd be the pot calling the kettle black if tried to say you ain't good enough for her. I married beneath me, the world will tell you, but there was never a happier pair than my Bess and I, though I lost her all too soon."

Sir Robert, who rarely thought of his Bess now but had convinced himself for the moment that he was suffering from an incurable wound of the heart, here looked as melancholy as a very well-fed and splendidly dressed gentleman could, and Mrs. Winlock instantly looked sympathetic.

"Dear Sir Robert!" she said. "How cruel our memories of the past can be! I too have suffered a loss, you know!" Which she had indeed, some twenty years before, but as the late Mr. Winlock had been a good deal older than she was and of a parsimonious disposition, which had led to frequent deadly quarrels between him and his spouse, any memories she cherished of him were of a rather astringent nature. "And how very wise you are," she went on, bringing the conversation back neatly to the matter at hand, "to place so little importance upon rank, dear sir! I am sure it is of far more moment to Elyza's future happiness that she and Mr. Redmayne share a mutual regard! Not," she added, pursing up her lips in an attempt to look prim, "that I in the least approve of the modern practice of allowing a gentleman to approach a young lady with a proposal of marriage before he has received the permission of her guardians! But I daresay," she went on, with a gracious glance at Elyza and Redmayne, "that a great deal must be forgiven on the grounds of a youthful warmth of feeling—"

She was interrupted by Elyza, who had jumped up from her chair and now for the first time in her life approached her father without trepidation.

"Papa," she said earnestly, "do you really mean that I may marry Mr. Redmayne? Because I wish to do so quite dreadfully, you know!"

"And I," said Redmayne, rising as well and coming over to take Elyza's hand in his, "wish it even more, sir! May I send my solicitors to confer with yours tomorrow? Whatever you may wish for Elyza in the matter of settlements, I shall be very happy to agree to!"

Sir Robert, who wished at the moment only for his bed after a long and fatiguing day, tried to look as if he were considering the matter, failed, and said, "Well, well, well—we shall see about it! All Macquoid's fortune, eh? I can see you needn't play the nip-cheese over settlements! But now, sir, if you will excuse me—I've had the deuce of a long journey today, you see! Talk it all over tomorrow, eh?" He hoisted himself out of his chair and kissed Elyza's cheek. "Good night, m'dear. You've always been a good girl; said just that to Emily Mayfield when she came here maundering about your running off with that fellow Crawfurd. 'Girl's never caused me a moment's anxiety in my life,' I said to her. 'Not likely she'd begin now.'" He gave two fingers to Mrs. Winlock as he bowed good night to her in turn. "Looks as if you'd done a bang-up job of work, Mrs. W.," he said approvingly. "Getting her off in her first Season—well, they told me you were the one who could do the trick, if anyone could."

"Oh, Sir Robert!" said Mrs. Winlock, quite overcome, but not so overcome that she did not go on to say, with modestly downcast eyes, "And may I hope, then, that if you should chace to hear of some other motherless girl who is in need of the experienced guidance of an older woman in taking her first steps in the world, you will recommend that *I* be called in once more, dear Sir Robert?"

"To be sure I shall," said Sir Robert gallantly, whereupon Mrs. Winlock, raising her still brilliant eyes to his, said, "Oh, I *am* so grateful to you, Sir Robert. And now I shall just show you upstairs to your bedchamber myself, so that I shall be certain that everything is *quite* as you like it."

She walked out of the room with him, leaving Elyza pink with indignant astonishment.

"Well!" she said. "Did you ever hear anything to equal that! Quite as if she had contrived the whole thing herself, when she was forever telling me not to be so cordial to you, and that I had ruined myself by letting you wear my riband in your race!"

"But she *did* contrive it, in a way," Redmayne pointed out, looking down at her with a smile. "If she hadn't shown herself such a brimstone to you, and pushed you to the point of running away from London, I should never have met *Mr. Smith* on the Bath Road and ten to one we should have had only the merest nodding acquaintance now, instead of being—as I take it we are, by your father's words—all but formally betrothed. Which reminds me," he added, as he drew her into his arms,

254

"that — much as this marriage has been talked of — I have never actually made you the offer in form, Miss Leigh. May I now — ?"

"Mr. Crawfurd," announced Satterlee, entering the room with a long-suffering expression upon his face indicative of his opinion of young gentlemen who paid calls at this unseemly hour of the night, as well as of other young gentlemen who were to be found embracing young ladies in his employer's drawing room. *But this,* the expression seemed to say, *is what one might expect of Brighton!*

"Oh, I say, Elyza!" exclaimed Mr. Crawfurd, popping in, as it were, under Satterlee's guard. "I'm frightfully sorry, but I *had* to come round and see if you got home all right! There is Lady Mayfield having the vapours all over her drawing room, what with Corinna wanting to be engaged to Jack Everet and my coming back to town without you, and asking me how I could have let you go off with a hardened seducer — Well, I'm sorry, Cleve," he said apologetically, "but you know what women are when they fly into a pucker!"

"Well, you may go back and tell her that not only am I not seducing Elyza, I am proposing marriage to her," said Redmayne impatiently. "Or, rather, I was, until you barged in! Co away, Nick! Don't you see you're not wanted?"

Mr. Crawfurd, somewhat above himself with all the excitement of the evening, said, "Right you are, old boy!" and nodded, taking in the situation with a sapient eye. "No wish to intrude, naturally! Happy to report to Lady Mayfield that all's right and tight! May I be the first to felicitate you?"

"No!" said Redmayne emphatically. *"Go away!"*

Mr. Crawfurd, never one to fail to take a hint, smiled understandingly and withdrew. Mrs. Winlock's footsteps were heard coming down the stairs.

"And now," said Redmayne to Elyza hastily, "before that dragon returns, *will* you—?"

"Oh, yes, *yes!*" said Elyza, with equal haste.

Mrs. Winlock, coming into the room to behold her ward locked in a fervent embrace, smiled a smile of brilliant self-congratulation as she noiselessly withdrew to await a more appropriate moment to make her entrance upon the scene.